Praise for *THE*

"A subplot involving terro
but the virus itself and th
could appear in the real world is quite enough to keep you turning pages to see who will live, who will die, and how the invader will be vanquished."
—*Publishers Weekly*

"*The Gemini Virus* rocks its genre, setting a new standard for public fear. Wil took a familiar theme—a deadly pandemic—and crafted it into a tense and very exciting story. I've been a sci-fi fan all my life, and this is, by far, one of the best doomsday books I've ever read. A taut thriller that grabbed me from page one."
—Robbie Dupree,
Grammy-nominated singer and songwriter

"A chilling and horrific outbreak story. If you're a fan of *Outbreak, The Hot Zone,* and *Contagion* (the movie), you'll love *The Gemini Virus*."
—*No More Grumpy Bookseller*

"Disturbingly plausible . . . thought provoking and frightening."
—*Bookloons*

"If you are a fan of medical thrillers, or you like movies like *Contagion* and *Outbreak,* I definitely recommend this."
—*Book Twirps Book Reviews*

"One of those books where you look up and realize you've read fifty pages without noticing that any time has gone by."
—*How Mysterious!*

"Has everything you could want in a disaster story, including a fast pace. It's an edge-of-your-seat read that will have you grimacing, sighing, crying—and reaching for your disinfectant."
—*LitStack*

THE GEMINI VIRUS

Wil Mara

TOR®

A TOM DOHERTY ASSOCIATES BOOK
NEW YORK

THE GEMINI VIRUS

A Tor Book
Published by Tom Doherty Associates, LLC
175 Fifth Avenue
New York, NY 10010

www.tor-forge.com

Tor® is a registered trademark of Tom Doherty Associates, LLC.

ISBN 978-0-7653-6393-0

Tor books may be purchased for educational, business, or promotional use. For information on bulk purchases, please contact Macmillan Corporate and Premium Sales Department at 1-800-221-7945, extension 5442, or write specialmarkets@macmillan.com.

First Edition: October 2012
First Mass Market Edition: September 2013

Printed in the United States of America

0 9 8 7 6 5 4 3 2 1

For Tracey. Always, for Tracey.

ACKNOWLEDGMENTS

I want to extend my deepest gratitude to the many terrific people who gave of their time and considerable talents to assure that this book hit all the proper high notes. First and foremost, to my wife and children, without whom my world would possess neither light nor beauty. To Melissa, for her boundless patience, riotous good humor, and perfect editorial touch. To Tom, for his immovable faith. To Miriam, for her masterful juggling of the details. To Matt, for some great relief pitching. To Marty, Elinor, and Robert, for their priceless "tech support." To Jane and Patti, for their early comments and suggestions. To Edward "Doc" Block, for being forthright enough to make me see that the first few titles really were awful ("Virus Mutatus?! Uh, no—that sucks."). To Robbie, for one helluva good quote. To Scott and Andy, because I gotta slip them in there somewhere. To Janet and Mark, and also to Tony, with genuine appreciation. And, of course, to my continuing readership.

THE GEMINI VIRUS

PROLOGUE

A New Illness in Three Parts

Monday, September 24
Ramsey, New Jersey

DAY 1

Bob Easton prided himself on his health; always had. It made him feel just a little bit superior to everyone else, especially the smokers, the drinkers, the dopers, and the guys who ate eggs and bacon for breakfast, pork roll for lunch, and spare ribs for dinner. They were all fools. The human body was a temple, and you didn't desecrate the temple.

He watched his diet to the point where he drove his wife, Bernice, out of her mind. He inspected everything before he put it in his mouth, brooded over "Nutrition Facts" charts, and could quote *Men's Health* articles from memory. He also exercised—a brisk jog every morning at precisely five thirty, followed by a short calisthenics regimen in the makeshift gym in their basement. His friends either made fun of him or were openly jealous. Nevertheless, he vowed to keep it up until he was no longer able, which he prayed wouldn't occur until he was in the Centenarians Club. That was his goal—three digits. And his physician, Dr. Petralia, thought he had a decent chance of making it. "You never get sick," Petralia said during the last checkup. (Easton had two per year, religiously.) "And it's not easy to die if you don't get sick, right?" Sitting on the cold exam table in his blue paper smock, Easton smiled and nodded. *That's right—no sickness, no death. And I don't get sick . . . ever.*

Except he was sick now. He was very sick.

The biggest mystery was how it happened in the first place. He had personal policies designed to protect against illness. One was to avoid others who weren't feeling well. If he heard someone coughing at the plant, he'd send them home. (As a floor manager with seniority, he could do this.) If someone blew their nose more than once in a restaurant, he'd leave. He also avoided schools and day care centers; they were bacterial playgrounds. This led to several fights with his oldest daughter, Kelly. She lived nearby and couldn't always pick up her two sons, who were in first and third grade respectively. Yet she knew not to contact her father even in an emergency. He wouldn't go near a public restroom. If he had no choice, he'd stand a foot back from the urinal and wouldn't flush. (If he had to take a crap, he'd wait until he got home, no matter how dangerous it was to his intestines.) He also used a paper towel on the doorknob when he went out. Nothing, in his opinion, was more vile than a public-restroom doorknob. He had a recurring nightmare about being forced to lick one.

So how did this happen?

The fever came first, stirring him from a deep sleep. He stumbled out of bed, dizzy and disoriented, and collided with the bathroom door because he didn't realize it was closed. This awoke Bernice, who asked if everything was all right. He grumbled something unintelligible, and she drifted away again. When he flicked on the light switch, the glare exploded with such intensity that the pain in his head ballooned until it felt like his skull was cracking open.

He dug through the medicine cabinet because he believed there was a thermometer in there somewhere. He couldn't locate it and thought about asking Bernice for help. Then he decided to forgo the inevitable sarcasm that would surely follow. He continued searching through the standing army of outdated prescription bottles, over-the-counter medications, travel-size containers, skin creams, and body lotions, and finally found it inside a repurposed Tupperware container that was also home to an old comb (with loose strands of hair still in it, he noticed), a pair of scissors, and several dental tools of questionable origin. He retrieved some cotton balls and a bottle of isopropyl alcohol and then sanitized the thermometer beyond reason.

After setting the tip under the wet flesh of his

tongue, he pressed the back of his hand against his forehead. He knew this was no way to gauge a fever, but he did it anyway. The heat was something close to nuclear. *I'm on fire!* He felt around in different places. *I'm cooking inside my skin. . . .* He inspected himself in the mirror and saw a face that was deeply flushed, the cheeks bright red. It was like looking at someone else.

The thermometer beeped and Easton looked. Then he wish he hadn't.

102.5°F.

He took it a second time, and it went up to 102.7 degrees F. Some crazy voice in the back of his mind said, *When you get to a hundred and three, sell!*

I'll call Petralia at nine and get in there first thing. Meanwhile . . .

He sorted through the over-the-counter meds, found nothing for fevers that hadn't expired, and settled on a washcloth soaked in cool water. Then he eased back into bed, where Bernice was snoring away like a sailor. His heart pounded in the stillness, and he began feeling the aches for the first time—neck, elbows, fingers, and knees. *Like an old man on a park bench,* he thought, *throwing bread crumbs to the birds.* He slept fitfully for two hours, was barely able to move when he awoke, and stayed there in his flannel pajamas feeling grossed out by the heat and sweat of his own body. *My* sick *body,* he thought with a mixture of depression and irritation.

Bernice initially responded, as he expected, with dumbfounded astonishment. She stood at the foot of the bed studying him, apparently in search of some sign of deception. Then, utilizing the gifted insight that he always found infuriating, she said, "You don't look so good."

"I appreciate the penetrating diagnosis."

"Should I call your doctor?"

"I'll do it. Please get me the phone."

It was going on seven thirty at this point; too early for Petralia to be in the office. Still, Easton got the answering service to make the first available appointment. His heart sank when he was told by the operator that "Doctor P" was away on vacation in Greece and wouldn't be back for another two weeks. She asked if he would like to make an appointment with Dr. Fisher instead. Easton considered it briefly, then declined. Ol' Doctor P had been his man for the last twelve years and knew his body better than anyone. He wasn't about to start fresh with some kid whose diploma still had wet ink on it.

Bernice, in the baby blue nightgown that Easton thought of as part of the *Golden Girls* Collection, shuffled to the doorway and stopped. Her eyes were nearly bulging with timid astonishment; she could not remember the last time her husband had been unwell.

"What time is your appointment?"

"He's not there today."

"He's not there?"

"He's on vacation."

"Oh . . ."

Easton sat hunched over on the bed's edge, hands

bunched together as if in prayer. Around the edges of his closely shorn silver hair, tiny beads of sweat had formed.

"I've, uh . . . I've got to go to ShopRite and get something."

"Isn't there anything in the cabinet?"

"No, I didn't see anything for fevers that was still good."

We haven't had anything for fevers since the kids were here, Bernice thought. That seemed like an eternity.

"Do you want me to drive you?"

He could sense the concern in her voice, and it softened him. He gave her a sideways glance and smiled. "No, but thanks. I'll be okay." He finished with a quick wink, which he knew she always loved. She smiled back.

In truth he felt worse than before, and if anyone else were offering the lift, he would've taken it without hesitation. But no one, in his opinion, was a lousier driver than his wife; he'd just as soon go on roller skates. No, this was something he had to do himself.

When he took the first step out of bed, the room spun. He leaned against the dresser for support. Perfume bottles clattered against one another; two brushes tumbled to the carpet. When Bernice stepped in to help, he held his hands up and assured her he was fine. A small voice told him he was, in fact, quite a long way from fine. Nevertheless, he struggled into jeans and a sweatshirt.

He couldn't remember the last time he'd bought over-the-counter medication, and he was overwhelmed by the array of choices. Sudafed, Robitussin, Mucinex, Vicks . . . antihistamine cough and cold suppressant, nondrowsy nasal decongestant, multisymptom expectorant . . . coated caplets, liquigels . . . day and night, extended release . . . original flavor, orange, cherry . . .

"You gotta be kidding me," he muttered before coughing into the crook of his arm. It was wet now, phlegmy. He settled on something with the words FEVER REDUCER and COLD AND FLU. That sounded reasonably close.

"Oooh, you look awful, Bob," the woman at the register said as she inspected him over her half-moon glasses. Her name was Doris Whittenhauer, and she was the Gal Who Knew Everyone.

"Thanks, Doris. I feel awful, too."

"Are you sure this is the right stuff for what you have?" She waved the box in the air.

"Do you *know* what I have?"

"No."

"Okay, then."

He coughed again, so violently this time that several heads turned.

Whittenhauer leaned back with a grimace. "Seriously, I think you should call your—"

"I already did. He's on vacation."

"So go to whoever's covering for him."

"I just might," he replied, and now he meant it. Yes, Fisher was just a kid, but Easton could swear his condition had diminished even in the brief span since he first walked in. *Something's not right. . . .*

The woman standing behind him was Katie Milligan, a plain and wholly unattractive thirty-four-year-old who'd held the same clerical position in the town's public works department since her first summer following high school. She opened her tiny purse and took out a tissue as soon as she realized Easton was the same man who'd been hacking his lungs out when they were in the medicine aisle together. She covered her nose and mouth and took a step back when Easton sneezed mightily and caught only part of it in his hands. His eyes were red and watery, his skin pale. She agreed with the cashier that he needed to see someone, but she didn't inject this into the conversation. As a general rule, she did not enter conversations unnecessarily. She lived alone with a tankful of tropical fish and a hundred old books, and that was just fine with her.

She watched in horror as Easton, finished with his transaction, wiped his nose on the sleeve of his lumberjack's coat. It left a shimmering string of snot in its wake, which he seemed not to notice.

As he passed through the automatic doors, he looked down at his change. This was a lifelong habit. *Count your change, always*. The medicine rang up at $6.53 (which he thought was a rip-off), and he'd paid with a ten. So he should have $3.47 left.

He was fingering through the coins when the punch came. Not a real one, for there was nobody within twenty feet of him. But it felt real enough—like the boxer's fist in the center of his gut. The money tumbled from his hand, the bills fluttering down and the coins bouncing everywhere. He wrenched out a terrible sound and staggered to the nearest car to steady himself. His mind swirled; his breathing became heavy.

When the second punch arrived, he fell to the ground in a heap. With his hands pressed against his stomach and his dignity stripped away, he rolled around on the blacktop groaning. Several people came rushing over, asking if he was okay. He wanted to say *Do I look okay?* but couldn't summon the breath. The third and fourth shots weren't so bad, but they furthered the humiliation by causing him to urinate in his pants. A small crowd had gathered now, and several were on their cell phones calling for an ambulance.

A message flashed through Bob Easton's brain: *This isn't a cold. This is something else.*

DAY 3

If the management at Bally's Hotel and Casino had a way of checking, they likely would've been puzzled by the fact that each of its 345 guest rooms had its thermostat set between 70 and 78 degrees F—except for the one on the seventeenth floor that was occupied by Ms. Doris Whittenhauer, supermarket checkout clerk from Ramsey, New Jersey. By 4:30 A.M., with the air conditioner blowing at maximum for the third straight hour, the temperature had fallen to 62 degrees F. The heavy gold curtains had been pulled shut, eclipsing a magnificent view of the Atlantic Ocean. Thus, the only illumination came from two night-lights Doris brought along—one in the bedroom and one in the bathroom. She always took night-lights with her when she went on her regular trips to Atlantic City.

She sat motionless and naked in the tub, which was filled to the edge with water chilled by the ice cubes she'd requested from room service. Two champagne buckets stood dripping in their tripods outside the doorway. The woman who answered the phone when Doris called the second time said, "Didn't we just send one?" Doris didn't reply; she just hung up. When the knock came at the door, she said to leave it out there, she'd get it in a minute. Then her trembling hands reached out and grabbed it—hands that barely looked human anymore.

It began Tuesday morning, about twenty-four hours after the encounter with Easton. At the age of fifty-two, Doris knew her body well enough—the sudden drop in strength meant an illness was coming on. (She always imagined a pressure gauge with its needle moving slowly to the left.) But the trip to AC was already set in stone. She'd received a postcard from Jennifer, her personal casino hostess, more than a month ago. It said a comp room was ready whenever she wanted it. She started going down there with her ex, Alan, back in '96 when they were still trying to keep the marriage afloat. As it turned out, he had not one but two girlfriends tucked away in the area—the first at Caesars and the second at the Taj. The final straw for Doris was when the Taj bimbo showed up at Bally's one evening and demanded to know who she was. Alan managed to talk his way out of it, and Doris let him. It was over anyway.

In spite of the soap opera, she made some friends at Bally's and, truth be known, liked coming down from time to time. It was a quick and inexpensive way to escape the routine and recharge the batteries. Alan did the right thing after the divorce and disappeared, moving to Texas to live with a brother. She never heard from him again, which was great. As the years passed, Doris went from a Gold Club member to Platinum, and then Diamond. That meant free rooms, food, and booze, as well as the end of having to wait on line for anything. The staff treated her like the Queen of Sheba, quite a respite from the grind at the supermarket.

She hadn't been down in almost three months. She wasn't a big fan of the shore between Memorial and Labor Day. The casinos were elbow to elbow with every obnoxious out-of-towner. The best time to go, she had learned, was in May or September—warm enough to stroll the boardwalk and breathe the sea air, but still far outside the nightmare of tourist season.

Jennifer booked her a deluxe suite this time—wide-screen plasma TV, a smaller one set into the bathroom mirror, art deco accents, everything granite and walnut. . . . Gaudy, but she liked it. She also had over four hundred dollars in comp money. Her plan was to spend two days courtesy of the house, playing the slots and maybe a little blackjack, getting a twenty-four-ounce porterhouse at the Reserve (her favorite), and, hopefully, seeing the girls—Susie from Manahawkin, Alexandra from Margate, and Lynn from Smithville. She didn't have their phone numbers or email addresses, didn't even know their last names. But they were part of the fabric of her Atlantic City world, and she found comfort in their company.

She realized an illness was on the way as she was setting the last of her things into her suitcase. She immediately connected it with Easton and cursed him out loud. *Probably the damn flu,* she thought. *So much for the guy who never gets sick.* Well, flu or not, she was going down there. She'd been looking forward to it and badly needed the break—three twelve-hour shifts in the last week alone, plus her boss, the twenty-eight-year-old manager of the store who had been there for only half a year but had the unbeatable qualification of being the owner's son-in-law, had been an even bigger jerk lately than he usually was. The idea of sitting home with an ice pack on her head watching reruns of *M*A*S*H* was out of the question. Besides, she hated having plans ruined at the last minute. She'd have to be in the hospital on her way to emergency surgery before she let go of this trip.

She locked the door of her apartment just after eight thirty that morning, stuffy and light-headed. The drive would take about two and a half hours, the great bulk of which would be spent on the Garden State Parkway. She brought along two different meds from the bathroom cabinet, plus a box of tissues for the passenger seat of her faithful '06 Toyota Corolla. She listened to Elvis and Everly Brothers CDs on the first half of the journey, singing along in her soft, passable alto. When the fever, chills, and sweating started, however, she got on the cell phone with her sister, Rita, in western Pennsylvania and cursed every breath that kept Bob Easton alive. She had no way of knowing he was already dead.

By the time she pulled into the valet area, the aches had set in. They weren't so bad in her knees or neck, but the one in her lower back was torturous. She received a jolt every time she moved, like a poke from an electric prod. When she finally got out of the car, she had to muster all her strength to keep from crying out. She was more than happy to let someone else carry her suitcase to her room this time—it was worth every penny of the two-buck tip.

She tried unsuccessfully to unpack, took two Sudafed tablets, then went down to the casino floor. She found one of her favorite video poker machines—Ultimate 4 of a Kind Bonus Poker—and sat down reverently before it. She lit a cigarette, inserted her comp card, and asked a waitress for a gin and tonic. A few of those, she figured, and the cold would disappear. She didn't see Susie or Alex or Lynn, but one of them would show up eventually. She made the maximum bet on her first spin, won double in return, and immediately felt better. She was in business.

The coughing and sneezing started about a half hour later. The cough wasn't unusual; most of the people in the aisle had a nasty hack from years of smoking and boozing. But the sneezing made her stand out. By late afternoon they were coming every few minutes. One rose so quickly that she sprayed the machine glass with it. She still had some tissues from the car, but they didn't last long. The waitress brought a pile of napkins, then another. Everyone within earshot identified her as the sick lady who should've stayed home. She received two scoldings for being so inconsiderate, as if Atlantic City were a bastion of class and civility.

Six o'clock was supposed to be dinnertime: her much-anticipated visit to the Reserve. But she didn't feel up to it now—all she wanted to do was take more Sudafed and lie down. The pain in her back had grown roots, forcing her to take baby steps to the elevator. Alexandra was sitting at a blackjack table, but Doris pretended not to see her.

She ordered room service—hamburger and fries—but ate very little. She forced down a few bites because she figured her body needed some kind of nutrition. Then she lay on the bed and closed her eyes. The curtains were open, the last shreds of daylight fading fast. The clock on the nightstand read 7:32, and she was soon asleep.

She was jarred awake three hours later by a rumbling in her stomach, followed by a hot rising in her throat. She rolled quickly and vomited over the edge. It came out in two gushes, and the wet slapping sound made her guts tighten. Residual particles felt like cigarette embers on her tongue. She tried spitting them out, then raked them off with her fingernails.

She fell back on the pillows and collected her thoughts. *I'm in Atlantic City, at Bally's . . . Room 1733. . . . I've been looking forward to this trip for weeks.* She saw her cell phone on the small circular table by the window and wondered if she should call her sister. *Maybe . . .* She put a hand to her forehead—it was filmy with perspiration and burning hot.

The odor from the vomit began drifting up. She covered her nose and turned away. Her breathing was heavy now, heart pounding. *I need to take more Sudafed.*

As she got to her feet, the first cramp struck her lower abdomen like the head of a sledgehammer. She yelped and went down, her knees on the floor while her upper body slumped across the second bed. Another blow followed, more vicious than the first, and she spilled onto the floor. Tears began flowing as she pressed hard against her stomach to dampen the pain. She curled into a fetal position and rolled onto her back. A guttural scream came to the surface with such force and clarity that it surprised her. Then a series of stuttering moans as the pain finally began to fade.

She turned over and got onto all fours. Sweat collected in the center of her forehead and fell away in large drops, making *pat* sounds when they hit the carpet. She got to her feet and went to the bathroom, where the Sudafed box stood on the vanity.

She ripped out another pill and sloppily filled a glass with water, knocking it back with an alcoholic's greediness.

Even in the dim glow of the night-light, the image in the mirror halted her. Her face was bright red and slightly swollen; it almost looked like someone else. The glass fell from her hand and clattered on the marble, miraculously remaining unbroken, as she covered her mouth and began sobbing.

She fled back to the bedroom and called her sister on the cell phone. The conversation was brief and hysterical. Doris, whose memory was mythic among her friends and family, reported every detail. Rita listened patiently, then told her to stay calm; she was getting dressed and driving out to get her. Meanwhile, Rita suggested, she should try to get some more sleep. Doris followed this advice after pulling the curtains shut, covering the vomit with a white towel, and turning on the air conditioner—the latter because she was suddenly feeling unusually warm. Then she stripped down to her bra and panties, crawled into the second bed, and cried until she slipped away.

She woke again at exactly 4:22. It was the itching that did it this time, first on her arms and legs, then her cheeks. It worsened as her senses defrosted—became maddening, really. She scratched the back of her left calf with the big toenail of her right foot. Then along her right forearm with her left hand. And then the right hand went to her right cheek. It became a bizarre, almost comical symphony of choreographed movements. Soon it was everywhere—behind her neck, along her sides, and around her still-sore abdomen. While each scratch temporarily reduced the itch, it also increased the heat under her skin, like she was triggering little fires everywhere. When she realized how far the temperature had dropped in the room, she threw the covers off. She generally disliked the cold, but now she was grateful for it.

The odor filled her nostrils again, which was puzzling. *How could it still be that bad?* When she realized her fingers were wet and sticky, the answer to the mystery zoomed into her head like a missile—

Oh no . . .

She groped for the light and looked down. What she saw was so surreal it made her light-headed. They weren't just blisters rising from her body; they were tiny *balloons*. Many were deflated, broken by her fingernails, and leaking a wheat-colored pus with wispy streams of scarlet.

Oh my God.

She got to her feet, trembling uncontrollably, and went into the bathroom. She was about to turn on the overhead light, then decided against it. The night-light would be enough. *I don't want to see it that well.* As a fresh round of tears began rolling down her cheeks, she stepped in front of the mirror.

Then she screamed again. And again. And again . . .

The blister-balloons were everywhere—stomach, arms, thighs, neck, and particularly her face. Her eyes had become sheltered slits. The nostrils were two large dots. And the mouth was reduced to a tiny orifice barely able to open and close within the tight confines of the swollen, bubbled surface. Each time she stretched the skin to let out another howl, more swellings exploded, the viscous fluid jumping out in grisly squirts.

Feeling her sanity slipping away, she filled the basin with cold water and soaked a washcloth. Then she pressed it against her cheeks. Her skin was boiling now and itching relentlessly. Since the washcloth did provide some relief, she turned and began filling the bathtub. She was concerned, however, that it wouldn't stay cold, so she went back into the bedroom and called room service. When the first champagne bucket arrived, she dumped out all the ice, stripped naked, and stepped in.

There was no way she could have prepared for the shock—like thousands of needles being fired into her body in a matter of seconds. Her teeth began chattering, and her lips made the slow transition from pink to purple. Numbness settled into every muscle and tendon. She was unable to slow her breathing but did manage to move her limbs in slow, waving motions. At least the itching and burning began to quiet down.

The ice jingled along the sides with an almost musical cheerfulness. After it melted, she got out and called for the second bucket. She took no notice of the slurring in her voice, nor did she find it strange that she called the woman who answered the phone "Colleen"—an old elementary school friend.

The frigid water didn't seem so bad this time, she thought. Cool and brisk. Maybe she could do this every once in a while at home. She'd tell the other girls at the supermarket about it, too. Maybe they'd like to join her; that'd be fun.

Three hours later the itching-burning returned with a vengeance. Shortly thereafter, the elderly man in the room next to hers was awakened by what he thought was the sound of shattering glass. A call was placed to the front desk, and a manager was sent up. He knocked on Whittenhauer's door, first politely, then less so. He used his magnetic master key—a plastic plate that resembled a credit card—and stepped cautiously inside. A veteran of Operation Desert Storm who had killed at least a dozen enemy soldiers, he knew something was up as soon as the smell hit him.

He found her ravaged body curled in the bathroom in a puddle of blood that was still spreading. The jagged piece of mirror she'd used to take her own life was jutting out the side of her neck.

Eleven more Bally's customers would discover they had become infected the next morning. The morning after that, thirty-six.

DAY 5

"She hasn't come out of there in about a week, I'd guess," the super told the two officers. "Something like that." He was a mousy little man with wild gray hair and sandpaper cheeks, well past his prime and thoroughly defeated by life. His corduroys were worn smooth at the knees, and there were flecks of dandruff along the shoulder straps of his vest. "That's what Mr. Fent said," he went on, motioning toward Fent's door down the hallway.

He'd been the super in Katie Milligan's building for over twenty years, and he found her to be a very strange woman—never smiling, never saying hello, scurrying in and out of her tiny corner apartment and quickly locking the door. In the six years since she arrived, he'd been inside just once: to replace a pressure valve on one of the radiators. Milligan kept the place neat to the subatomic level, which was nice enough. But she followed him around the whole time, watched his every move. No friendly chitchat, no offer for a glass of ice water—just those paranoid sapphire eyes pressing down upon him.

"When did Mr. Fent call you?" the older officer asked. The super already thought of him as *the Bully*. Big gut, thick mustache, broken blood vessels around his nose from years of drinking and God knew what else.

"This morning."

Officer Jim Dugan, aka the Bully, looked at his watch. "It's twelve twenty now. What took you so long to contact us?"

He stuttered for a moment; guys like Dugan always stifled him. "I tried calling *her* first, and when I didn't get any answer, I called the landlord."

"That would be Mr. Arnold?"

"Yes."

"Where's he?"

"In Florida."

"Why?"

"He lives down there all year, he and Mrs. Arnold. They never come up, ever."

Dugan nodded to his partner, the young man the super had classified as *the Kid,* and said, "You should be writing this down."

In truth, Dugan, as senior officer present, should be doing it. But Bill Teague had learned not to argue with the full-tilt bastard they'd assigned to be his lord and master during his rookie year. He took out his notepad and miniature-golf pencil and began scribbling.

"And what did Mr. Arnold say to do?" Dugan asked, continuing the interrogation.

"Call you."

"Is it unusual for Ms. Milligan to stay in her apartment for long periods?" Dugan knew who she was since, technically, they were both town employees. He'd seen her around, thought she was a whackjob.

"Not really."

"Then why the call from her neighbor?"

The super looked to Teague first, then back to Dugan. "The smell," he said, lowering his voice.

"The smell?"

"Mr. Fent said it was coming through the baseboard vents. I went in and checked, and he was right—it was terrible. Like rotting food."

Dugan turned to the door. It would've been customary—not to mention polite—to start with a gentle, ordinary knock. But he'd apparently missed this lesson in law-enforcement etiquette and went straight to hammering with his fist.

"Ms. Milligan? This is the Ramsey police. Could you please come out here for a moment?"

No answer.

"Ms. Milligan?"

More banging. Then he rang the bell.

Still no answer.

"You've got the key, right?"

"I do, but—"

"No 'but,' just open the door."

The little man paused only briefly—Mr. Arnold had told him not to let the police in without calling him first—but it was enough to cause Dugan's thermometer to rise. The redness first appeared high on his chest, then spread rapidly up his neck and kept going until his face took on the color of a boiled ham. Teague had seen the progression many times and braced himself.

"Open this damn thing or I'll cite you for obstruction."

The jangling key chain was out in a flash. "Okay."

As the door drifted back, Dugan's first thought was that the weather stripping around it was superb because the difference in air quality inside and outside the apartment was unbelievable. *It reeks in there.*

And Dugan had a feeling he knew why. "Stay back," he told his new friend.

"But Mr. Arnold said I should—"

"Absolutely not. You stay out here. Bill, let's go."

He ordered Teague to close the door behind them—the super stood in the hallway with a helpless look as he disappeared from view. Dugan was sure he'd call the landlord on his cell phone within seconds, the little worm.

They were in a short hallway and surrounded by darkness even though it was early afternoon.

"Look for a switch," Dugan said. Teague found one by the door and flicked it. Then he gasped.

Dugan didn't doubt for a minute that the numerous smears on the cream-colored walls and the hardwood flooring were blood—mostly. Between his early days in Paterson and what he hoped would be his final years here in Ramsey, he'd been to enough homicide scenes to identify a bloodstain a mile away.

But there was something else—a crusty, golden yellow substance that was reminiscent of earwax. It was mixed with the blood as if blended in some kind of macabre cocktail. *Shaken, not stirred,* he thought crazily.

"What's this yellowy stuff?" Teague asked, leaning down to get a closer look.

"I have no idea," Dugan replied. "But don't touch it. We'll have Frawley's guys come and collect samples."

Teague did as he was told. On a mildly rebellious impulse, however, he moved in close enough to sniff a particularly crusty area. In that instant, he realized the mystery substance was the source of the ungodly smell (and that there must be plenty more of it around). In that same instant—although there was no way he could've known it—he had issued his own death warrant.

They went from the hallway to a small dining room. Dim rectangles of light glowed around a pair of blackout shades. Teague drew them up, revealing more of the blood-crust smears. They looked as though they'd been randomly applied with a paintbrush.

Then another peculiarity—in the china cabinet, everything from the Audubon plates Milligan had painstakingly collected over the last twenty years to the priceless Hummel figurines her beloved grandmother left to her had been shattered. Equally strange was that the glass on the cabinet doors was intact. It was as if each item had been removed and smashed, and then the pieces put back inside. There wasn't even any debris on the walnut table or the Persian rug.

"What the hell . . . they were replaced in their original spots?!" Teague said, almost whispering.

Dugan only nodded in response, then started into the adjoining living room. After the first step, however, he stopped—the carpeting under his foot made a wet, squishy sound.

"Oh man," he said, reaching for his flashlight.

It wasn't blood, it was water—water and what appeared to be thousands of little white flecks. Getting to his knees, Dugan saw that the flecks were actually tiny stones. They were about the same size as the copper BBs he used to shoot squirrels and birds outside his bedroom window as a kid.

"Jim, c'mere. . . ."

Teague also fired up his flashlight, and the beam found a fish tank in the darkness, lying on its side. The spilled-out contents included a heavier shoal of tiny stones, plus a bubble filter, a can of flake food, and a ceramic model of Cinderella's Disney castle. The latter had obviously served as a home to Milligan's finned friends.

But where are they? Teague wondered. *Why aren't there any dead fish on the floor?*

His curiosity was satiated a moment later when Dugan found the light switch. They were standing at one end of a long room that looked as though it'd been attacked by a gang of drunken apes. Every piece of the sofa set had been overturned, the three framed paintings (all real, by the look of them) were slashed with large *X*'s, and the small-but-functional fireplace was stuffed to the top with antique books; the kind that most people like to smell rather than read. But it was the fish—and what happened to them—that made Teague's stomach roll. He was an animal lover at heart.

There was a large corkboard attached to the wall by the kitchen doorway, and they had been pinned to it with plastic toothpicks. They were arranged in neat rows, four columns of five for a total of twenty. Each one had a yellow Post-it Note underneath, with identifications in Milligan's enraged scribble—

Cardinal Tetra
Paracheirodon axelrodi

Tiger Barb
Puntius tetrazona

Common Angelfish
Pterophyllum scalare

Dugan moved in close and inspected the collection. "What the hell is this all about?"

Teague hung back and diverted his eyes to other parts of the room. There were more smears everywhere, plus the oddly unsettling sight of a pizza—whole, not even one slice missing—facedown on the carpet in front of the coffee table. It looked as though it had been stamped down, as if Milligan (or whoever) tried to drive it through the floor. The empty box was still on the table, and Teague recognized the name on the lid—Kinchley's, right here in town. Best pizza he ever had, although he wasn't sure if he'd be able to take another bite without thinking of Katie Milligan.

"The smell is getting worse," Teague said. What he meant was *We're getting closer to . . . whatever*. Two other sentiments in his voice included *I think I'm about to see my first dead body* and *I'm not sure if I'm ready for this*.

"I know," Dugan replied without the slightest note of empathy. "Something's not quite—Oh *God*!"

He had ventured into the kitchen, and now, only seconds after he fired the overhead light, he stumbled backward and almost fell through the open doorway.

"Oh my God! OH MY GOD!"

Teague never heard him scared before. Now the fear in his voice was as clear as the peal of a church bell.

He rushed over to help steady him. Then, over Dugan's shoulder, he saw it. . . .

"Is that—?"

"Yeah."

"Oh Lord . . ."

Through the clear glass of the blender, which was sitting on the counter and still plugged in, was the unmistakable form of a human foot. It had been hacked off just above the ankle, and the two jagged bones of the narrow tibia and wider fibula were preventing the lid from sitting flush. A huge puddle of dried blood—with very little of the yellow mystery sauce this time—was spread out on the floor, and a serrated bread knife lay nearby. Bloody tracks—one a normal footprint, the other a dark dribble-trail occasionally broken by roughly circular punctuation—led away from site, past the two of them, then curled left in a hairpin turn down a second hallway they had yet to explore.

They moved in no particular hurry toward the blender. The dismembered foot was unquestionably that of a woman, and neither had any doubt it was once the property of Katie Milligan. It was beginning to turn black from the bloodless rot, making it look as though it'd been hanging in a smokehouse. The most remarkable feature, however, was the blistering—it was so widespread that there were no clear areas. Most of the bubbles had been broken open, as evidenced by the deep scratch-lines. But a few remained. It made Teague think of a wicked case of sumac poisoning he'd had as a child. Ten times worse than ivy, with an itch that drove him insane for three solid weeks. *This looks like it was ten times worse than* that, he thought. At the base of the blender jar, about an inch of the golden mystery sauce had accumulated and congealed.

Dugan, mesmerized by all of it, reached up and pulled his tie loose. Sweat was pouring down his face and neck, and his breathing was becoming audible.

"What now?" Teague said softly.

Dugan's first attempt at a reply was squelched by whatever had built up in his throat. He cleared it, then said in a feeble croak, "Let's check the rest of the place."

"Sure," Teague said. It came out just slightly sarcastic. *Gee, can we?* Under normal circumstances, he would've suffered the Wrath of Dugan for that indiscretion. But his boss didn't even seem to notice.

They followed the blood trail to the second hallway. There were two doors—one at the far end, the other immediately to the right. The latter was half open. After taking a deep breath, Dugan pushed it all the way back and hit the light switch. Milligan's bathroom was, literally, a bloody mess. Towels lay piled on the floor, stained in scarlet and amber. The bowl hadn't been flushed in a while and badly needed to be. Both men couldn't help but give the contents a cursory glance. Neither was certain what he saw, nor did he wish to be. There was also a puzzling stack of ice-cube trays on the toilet tank.

The tub was filled within an inch of the rim, and drifting placidly on the surface of the blood-clouded water was what appeared to be sizable sections of scratched-off (or peeled-off) skin. They drifted with the silent grace of lily pads, which somehow made them all the more grotesque.

Dugan lingered, and Teague realized it wasn't because he was in any kind of trance this time—he just didn't want to go into the last room. The feeling was mutual, quite frankly, but they couldn't leave until they did. And there was no greater truth in the universe than the fact that Bill Teague wanted to get the hell out of this apartment.

"One more to go," Teague said, "and then we're done."

"Yeah," Dugan replied. "Okay."

As they went down the hallway together, side by side like groom and bride, they realized two things. First, the room at the other end was, without a doubt, the primary source of the smell in the apartment. It seemed to be seeping right through the door and growing exponentially. And second, there were *machines* of some kind running inside—they could hear several different mechanized hums and rhythms, as if Milligan were secretly managing a small production facility.

They paused when they got there, both wishing they were anywhere else on earth while their hearts boomed like war drums. Dugan took something from his back pocket—a small, cylindrical container that looked like lip balm. Largely unknown to the general public, it was indispensable to medical examiners worldwide—a quick stroke under each nostril made you all but impervious to the wretched stench of decaying flesh.

He applied it quickly, then handed it to Teague. "You'll want this."

"Thanks." Teague's fingers were shaking. When he was finished, he replaced the cap and handed it back.

"Good?"

"I hope so."

"Okay." Dugan licked his lips. "Here goes."

He surprised Teague by grabbing the knob and pushing the door back in one quick motion. Teague realized he was working from the Band-Aid theory—yank it off fast and maybe it won't hurt as much.

Even in the blackness, they could see her, or at least what was left. She had hanged herself from the ceiling fan while it was running—and, gruesomely, still was. The overworked motor groaned unevenly as the paddles turned at a lazy, diminished speed. The darkness obscured all fine details, but the spare light from the hallway revealed the silhouette of Milligan's body, clad in a long nightgown, each time it cycled by.

"Holy hell . . . ," Dugan said hoarsely.

"Turn it off," Teague told him, the slightest touch of hysteria in his voice. "Turn it off!"

"What?"

"The fan! Turn off the *fan*!"

"Oh . . ."

He reached in and felt for the switch. There was a round fader knob just inside the doorway, but he pulled back with a girlish squeal when he realized it was encrusted with some kind of dried substance.

He swore copiously as he wiped his fingers on his shirt. Then he reached into his front pocket and retrieved a handkerchief. Covering his hand as if preparing to do a magic trick, he tried again.

He meant only to turn the knob until it clicked and shut the fan off. In his heavily distracted state, however, he inadvertently depressed it, powering the fan's three-globed lights. Now every detail was in plain view.

A part of them didn't want to look—but of course they did. Teague was paralyzed while the circuitry in his brain sparked and sputtered in an attempt to comprehend the sight before him. Dugan's reaction wasn't quite so succinct—his face went from the flustered ham-pink to a deathly pale. His eyes widened like those of a surprised child. Then he opened his mouth to speak, but instead he fell to his knees and vomited explosively. He tried to stem the flow with his hand, but the force was such that it merely squirted between his fingers.

Milligan's skin—visible only on her face, arms, and the tip of the remaining foot that peeked out below the hemline of her gown—had swollen to such a degree that she looked like an overinflated toy. The arms were almost comical in their Popeye-esque exaggeration, the foot like a child's "monster foot" bedtime slipper. And her bloated face seemed as though one poke with a needle would blow it to pieces.

The balloonlike blistering was ubiquitous, many of the larger examples lying as flat and flaccid as downed parachutes. Others dangled from her body like little price tags. The calico coloring ranged from black to purple to lavender. Neither Dugan nor Teague had any way of knowing the lavender was the result of Milligan's blood vessels literally melting under her skin, a late-stage symptom of the disease that was already taking up residence through their own systems.

As the initial shock wore away, they began noting other details. First, the room was *freezing*—at some point Milligan put an air conditioner in each of the two windows and cranked them up. Then there was the puzzling "crimson ring"—a spattery line of dark red coloring that ran, unbroken, in a roughly circular pattern around the room. Teague figured it out first and nearly lost his own lunch as a result—bodily fluids of one kind or another flying off Milligan's rotating corpse for God only knew how long. But the most horrific feature, by far, was Milligan's neck—wrapped in a woolen scarf and tied in a knot that had grown increasingly tighter, it now shared roughly the same circumference as an ordinary garden hose. This, the two men realized, was the reason Milligan's head hung down at such a sharp angle. A few more hours and it would've detached and zoomed off somewhere.

Dugan got to his feet, wiping his mouth with the back of his sleeve. He took one more look at everything, then could look no more. He reached in and closed the door, then said, "Let's get the hell out of here."

ONE

"Okay, this is one I'm sure you'll like," Beck said confidently, advancing through the songs via the button on the steering wheel. "This was one of my favorites when I was a kid."

"Back in the late Pliocene?" his passenger asked.

"I was born in the early Holocene. Now, listen."

As Beck cruised north on Connecticut's I-91 with the rented convertible's top down, his ID badge flipped and bounced against his chest. It read MICHAEL BECK, EPIDEMIOLOGIST, and right under that, CENTERS FOR DISEASE CONTROL, ATLANTA GA.

The song began quietly, a simple drumbeat accompanied by silvery high notes in a playful intro. Then a call-and-answer segment featuring bass, sitar, and piano. Finally, Robbie Dupree's eternally soulful voice delivering the first line.

"It's called 'Steal Away.' It was a huge hit when I was a kid; the DJs loved it. It gets airplay even now and is included in movie soundtracks once in awhile. Not so bad, right?"

He glanced over in time to see her roll her eyes,

which made him smile. *She's heard me prattle on about this before—"The Lost Age of Melody," I call it, back when songwriters ruled the music business and hits had hooks you couldn't get out of your head.*

"Yeah, it's great. I'm totally blown out of my seat."

"Oh, come on. It's not that bad." He sang along with the chorus in a voice that was good enough for private use but would surely earn the wrath of the *American Idol* judges. "And this guy's new album is terrific. I've played it a few times for you."

"Well, it's certainly better than that other stuff you like . . . what do you call it? Exotica?"

"Like lying on the beach in Hawaii with a mai tai in your hand. Pure bliss. Martin Denny, Les Baxter, Arthur Lyman . . ."

"Yawn."

"Lyman was the best."

"But it's all so *lightweight,*" she said.

"That's what's great about it. The music you listen to . . . my God, it makes you want to grab a machine gun and start thinning out the neighborhood."

She turned to him with a smirk. "That's what's great about it."

"Ahh, right."

She went back to her trademark I'm-so-damn-bored posture—chin in hand, lips tight, and the tiniest trace of resentment in the eyes. He smiled again and decided to let her be. Maybe the song would seep through her defenses, act as a kind of antidote. Music had the power to bring warmth and joy and relief to a troubled soul, he knew, and Cara Porter was certainly burdened with a troubled soul. One look at her gave that away—the goth makeup and jewelry, the perpetual scowl, the hunched shoulders. Beck had taken a huge chance on her. When she ended up on his doorstep with a freshly minted master's degree in one hand and a résumé in the other, he thought someone down the line had made a mistake. Then he caught a sense of the real person behind the armor and thought he detected much more. In time, he came to realize he had been correct. When she was working, an alternative persona—the one, Beck thought, represented the true individual—emerged. The professional Cara Porter was inspired, intuitive, and boundlessly compassionate. Their exchanges were more substantial and mature. And her sensitivity, usually kept so carefully guarded, was remarkable. From human patients to laboratory animals, she treated all living things with uncommon kindness and respect. *This one,* Beck often thought, *has the seeds of greatness. Now, if we can just get them growing. . . .* He came to think of her as a surrogate daughter, although he never told her this for reasons of his own.

"I'm not saying everything you listen to is bad," he said. "For example, that Guns N' Roses album, *Chinese Democracy,* is pretty good."

"It's excellent."

"I agree. I do play it when you're not around, you know. I'm not a *total* dork."

"Just mostly."

He nodded. "Yes, just mos—"

An iPhone trilled.

"Is that yours or mine?" she asked.

Beck waited until it called out again. The ringtone was the first few bars of "On and On" by Stephen Bishop. "It's a good melody—must be mine."

She shot him a look as he grinned and drew the slender device from his front pocket. He also thumbed down the volume via the button on the steering wheel, and his beloved "lightweight" '70s music disappeared.

"It's the boss," he said, looking at the caller ID. Then he put it on speaker. "Hello, there."

"Michael?"

"Yes?"

"I can barely hear you."

"We're in the rental car right now with the top down. Hang on a second."

He pulled to the shoulder and engaged the roof. It came up like a giant hand in a monster movie. Once it was in place, he set the phone on the dashboard.

"Better?"

"Yes. Listen, where are the two of you?"

"On I-91, heading back from the conference."

He could sense she was stressed even beyond what was customary for her. After working together for eleven years—the first nine when she was drifting up through the CDC's ranks, and the last two after she was elevated to the top role—there wasn't much he didn't know about her. Sheila

Abbott was the type who lived for stress, ate it in handfuls. The kind, it seemed to Beck, who followed the motto, "There's something wrong if there's nothing wrong."

"What's up?"

"I need you in northern New Jersey as quickly as possible."

Beck checked his rearview mirror, then eased onto the road again to search for the first available U-turn.

"Something's happening, I assume?"

"Seven deaths, all in the town of Ramsey. Two of the dead are police officers, so the news media already has it and is running with it."

Beck shivered. Could a problem exist that wasn't made forty times worse because of the media's love for scaring the hell out of everyone?

"Well, that should help keep things under control."

"Tell me about it."

"What do we know so far?"

"The victims were covered with large pustules from head to toe and exhibited symptoms of extreme delirium. It also appears they had extensive subcutaneous bleeding."

"Pustules *and* subcutaneous bleeding?"

"That's right. The first autopsy report says there was dissolution of everything from the mucous membranes to the GI tract, with heavy bleeding into the lungs, out the mouth, everywhere. It was as if the organs melted like ice cream."

"My God."

Beck found an exit ramp and changed sides, heading south now.

Abbott said, "It almost sounds . . . smallpox-esque, doesn't it?"

Beck nodded. "That's what I first thought when you mentioned the pustules, but . . . do we even know if the agent is viral and not bacterial?"

"It's viral. That's been confirmed from samples."

"Okay."

"Aren't the pustules and the subcutaneous bleeding symptoms of two different forms of smallpox?" Porter asked.

"Yes. The pustules are symptomatic of the common form, and the internal bleeding is an indicator of . . . what?"

"The hemorrhagic form. The nasty one."

"Correct. Very good."

Hemorrhagic smallpox was one of the most horrific diseases imaginable. Unlike the more common form of smallpox, the hemorrhagic variety featured minimal manifestations on the outside of the body, such as dark papules. Instead, most of the damage is subcutaneous. Internal bleeding will occur first in the mucous membranes and gastrointestinal tract, but can also affect the spleen, kidneys, liver, bladder, and reproductive organs. Sometimes the whites of the eyes also turn a deep red. Hemorrhagic smallpox mostly affects adults and is nearly always fatal.

"I don't know of any cases where both symptoms occurred together," Beck said, "so my gut tells me this is something different. Sheila, are any other CDC people on the ground?"

"No, but Ben Gillette is waiting for you at Valley Hospital in Ridgewood. They've moved all the bodies there."

Gillette was one of New Jersey's county epidemiologists, and Beck knew him from the University of North Carolina. He was a quality guy, in Beck's estimation, serious and focused and thoroughly professional. One of his favorite memories of their college days was the time he had to pick up Ben from the Chapel Hill police station after he was arrested for stealing street signs. Gillette's girlfriend had dumped him for one of the university's wrestling studs, and he responded with a night of binge drinking and driving around in his '74 Corvette with a pair of Vise-Grips.

"I know you're a long way from your home in Seattle, but I need you to do this. Along with everything else, you need to be my eyes and ears on the ground."

"Not a problem. What about autopsies?"

"They've done some and are doing more now. I'll send the information as I get it."

"Okay. We'll be there shortly."

"Please call and let me know what's happening. New Jersey's governor is crawling out of his skin."

"I would imagine. What's the latest—?"

"Hang on. . . ."

During the ensuing silence, Beck said softly to Porter, "Use the GPS on your iPhone to figure out the route." She nodded and dug the unit out of her black leather bag, which had a small plastic skull dangling from one of the metal loops.

"Michael?"

"Yes?"

"That was Ben. Three more deaths have just been reported, same symptoms, and it looks as though six other people are in various stages of the infection."

"Oh boy."

"This looks like it could be something, so get moving."

"We're moving," Beck said, pressing the gas as he weaved through the early afternoon traffic.

"And keep me updated."

"I will."

TWO

Epidemiology concerns itself with the finding and study of factors that negatively affect the health of a human population. That means epidemiologists are, first and foremost, detectives. They are concerned with the overall effects of an illness on large populations (macro) rather than specific symptoms or individual patients (micro). The results of their investigations then form the basis of a response strategy both in the short and long term—they aid not only the treatment of afflicted persons but also play a critical role in the containment and, hopefully, eradication of the illnesses. An epidemiologist's casework can also lead to the establishment of improved guidelines and protocols in health-care facilities around the world.

Michael Beck was considered one of the best in his field. A brilliant student at UNC Chapel Hill's School of Public Health, he earned his doctorate at the age of twenty-seven and immediately took a field position in the AIDS-ravaged lands of Sub-Saharan Africa. Four years later he moved to the

Ivory Coast to help quell the rampant spread of Lassa fever. In the summer of 1994, he wrote the first of two textbooks, *Modern Epidemiology: Practices and Principles,* which became a graduate-level standard in its first edition. The second book, *Epidemiological Case Studies,* dovetailed the first as a kind of expanded supplement. Affordably priced as a paperback and updated biannually, it cemented Beck's reputation as a leader in the discipline. Healthy sales also assured him a handsome secondary income. In 1998, he returned to the United States at the urging of Sheila Abbott, whom he had met while taking a summer course at Johns Hopkins. She had started with the CDC as a public liaison in '90 and was patiently climbing the administrative ladder.

Beck pulled into one of Valley Hospital's VISITING PHYSICIANS spots less than two hours after receiving Abbott's call. Valley was located in the town of Ridgewood, about eight miles south of Ramsey. It serviced roughly fifty thousand people per year in New Jersey's upscale northern suburbia. The hospital was a sprawling brick-and-glass structure that looked more like a corporate office in an industrial park. Categorized as a not-for-profit organization, it took in about $450 million annually and employed more than three thousand health-care professionals.

As the May sun sank away and twilight settled around them, Beck and Porter got out of the car and headed for the entrance. No sooner had they taken their first steps when they were descended upon by a herd of reporters and cameramen. What struck them as unusual was the fact that everyone in the crowd was wearing a surgical mask. A few had them tied over their nose and mouth, but most left them lying against their shirts.

With the bright lights glaring, the assault began—

"Excuse me, Dr. Beck?"

"Are you Michael Beck of the CDC?"

"Dr. Beck, are you here to investigate the epidemic?"

They ignored Porter, which was fine with her. She couldn't help but feel a little sorry for her boss, though. Beck had become something of a minor celebrity in recent years, crystallizing into the "media face of the CDC" after his involvement in several high-profile cases. With his good looks and easygoing manner, he was a natural for the cameras. He disliked it nevertheless, which Porter found admirable.

Beck shielded his eyes and said, "Yes, I'm Michael Beck. Please, let me through. Please . . ."

They parted but maintained the attack.

"Dr. Beck, is this the result of a terrorist plot?"

"I don't know. I just got here."

"Do you know what the illness is?"

He kept walking; they followed. "I'm sorry, I don't." He was trying to be patient, Porter realized. *I would've told them all to go screw off by now,* she thought. *Parasites . . .*

As he stepped onto the walkway in front of the emergency room, the double doors slid apart and an aging security guard came out. He also had a surgical mask, plus a pair of latex surgical gloves.

"How many have died so far?" One reporter shouted, holding out a small digital voice recorder.

"I don't know yet."

"How many are—?"

"Guys, I just got here." Beck gave a little smile, trying to defuse the tension. "I don't know anything yet. Let me go find out."

"Come on, get back," the guard ordered, pushing a few of them away with his forearm. They responded with a selection of profanity and one halfhearted claim of infringement against the First Amendment.

"Dr. Gillette is inside, waiting to see you," the guard said, his breathing heavy. His name tag read E. HORTON.

He's been dealing with them for a while now, Beck thought. "Thank you."

"Here, put these on before you go in," Horton handed each of them a surgical mask while the reporters continued firing away.

Once inside, they found a selection of people waiting in the emergency room—a pair of young women, one crying while the other held her; a little boy lying across his mother's lap with his right arm in a temporary splint; an elderly man with an oxygen mask over his face, the small metallic tank parked in its two-wheeled carrier by her feet; a few others. Aside from the man with the oxygen, they were all wearing the surgical masks. A sign taped to the wall, hastily made with black Magic Marker on ordinary white paper, said, IF YOU SUSPECT YOU HAVE CONTRACTED THE INFECTION, PLEASE REPORT TO THE RECEPTION NURSE AT ONCE.

A door by the vending machine opened and Gillette came out. Lush black hair with prominent streaks of silver, fashionable glasses, and warm green eyes that still held a faint twinkle of fun and mischief. He wore a long white lab coat with the hospital's logo above the left breast pocket. And even though he had one of the ubiquitous masks, Beck could tell he was smiling.

"Michael, good to see you." He offered his hand.

"You, too, Ben."

"And Cara, how are things?"

"Fine, thanks."

"Is this guy treating you okay?"

"More or less."

Beck realized Gillette was acting casual for the sake of the others in the room. He had known Gillette long enough, however, to spot the truth behind the lie—he was worried.

To maintain the façade, Beck said, "So, I understand you've got some kind of outbreak on your hands."

"Yeah, come on back and I'll go over what we know so far."

Gillette opened the door and led them down a long white corridor. When they pulled down their masks, Beck realized that Gillette looked a little older than he remembered—the lines around his face a bit deeper, the cheeks slightly more haggard. It'd been about two and a half years since he last saw the man, at a Christmas party in Scottsdale, Arizona. But they kept in touch a few times a month via email and the occasional phone call. Beck had been in California dealing with a bird flu scare when Gillette was appointed New Jersey's state epidemiologist, so he sent a gift (a $250 certificate to Red Lobster, where they used to go as a "treat" in their penniless college days) along with an intentionally saccharine Hallmark card. Gillette was still single even though he had all the qualities of a "good catch"—charm, intelligence, money, and decent looks. Beck was all but certain he wasn't homosexual, so the mystery of his bachelorhood always puzzled him.

"I'm sorry about the press on the way in," Gillette said. "We can't get rid of them."

"Don't worry about it."

"The Organ Grinders of Doom."

"A brain-eating virus would starve to death out there," Porter quipped.

"How did they find out so quickly?" Beck asked. "The two police officers?"

"Yes. They have media informants at the station, as you know."

"Any idea how the officers became infected?"

He was in sleuth mode now. Porter had seen the transformation plenty of times. He was data gathering: the first step in the process.

"They were on a call. A woman who hadn't come out of her apartment in a few days. One of her neighbors noticed a nasty smell from the vents. She was a quiet type, kept to herself a lot. But she worked for the town and hadn't been seen in a while." Gillette lowered his voice, as if imparting a secret. "They found her hanging by the ceiling fan in her bedroom, Michael, and it was *still going*. Her body was nearly black and covered with vesicles. When the trauma cleanup crew cut her down, her head came off." He shivered. "I've seen a lot of bad stuff in my time, but this . . . I saw the body down at County. What that woman must have endured."

"And the police *touched* her?" Porter asked.

"They said they didn't. In statements given before their symptoms became severe, they both insisted, independently, that neither one touched her. The younger cop said they didn't even go into the room. If that's true, then we're talking about mighty powerful contagions."

Beck stopped walking. "When did this happen?"

"What, exactly?"

"The officers' deaths. When did they succumb?"

"On Monday, both of them. Yesterday."

"And when did they find the woman?"

"Friday afternoon."

"From exposure to death in *four days*?"

"Yeah."

"My God, Ben . . ."

"I know. This is what I told Sheila. We're not dealing with chicken pox here."

"What else can you tell me?"

"Not much. I've only been here since yesterday, remember. When the first case arrived on Sunday afternoon, the specialist called the NJDHSS, who then called me. As soon as I examined the bodies, I called her. That was this morning. Then she called the two of you. Everyone has followed the procedure to the letter."

"How many deaths so far?" Porter asked.

"Twenty-six."

Beck's eyes fixed on Gillette. "How many?"

"Twenty-six."

"Sheila said ten."

"That was two hours ago."

"There have been sixteen more *in the last two hours*?"

"That's what I've been told."

"All in this town?"

"No—seventeen here, four in Mahwah next door, and five in nearby Upper Saddle River."

"What's the mortality rate?"

"Based on the cases we know now, almost ninety-five percent."

Beck stopped again. "*What?*"

"That's right—just under ninety-five percent of the people who contract this thing die."

"And the others?"

"Beyond salvation. Physically disfigured, brain and organ damage. They're all comatose. Extent of the damage varies, but certainly none of them will return to their former selves. Machine-assisted living."

"Worse than dead."

"Yeah."

They began walking again. "Do you have any live patients right now?" Beck asked.

"We've got two, both brought in last night. We have them isolated, of course, and sedated."

"I need to see them, Ben. Right now."

"Of course." Gillette looked at him sheepishly. "One of them, Michael . . . um."

"What?"

"Well . . . follow me."

The corridor terminated at a steel door with the words INFECTIOUS ISOLATION AREA—KEEP CLOSED in bold letters. Underneath was a variety of hazard symbols. On the other side was a second corridor, dimly lit, eerily quiet, and reeking of disinfectant. Beck and Porter could also hear the increased air pressure. This was by design to contrast the reduced pressure of the isolation rooms. About forty feet down, the walls became large panes of glass—observation windows. The first two rooms had empty beds; the third did not.

The patient was a white male, late twenties to early thirties, dyed blond crew cut, muscular. Around him, a series of machines stood blinking: machines that, Beck knew, would not be removed from the room because they, too, would carry the contagion. Most of the patient's body was covered by a hospital sheet; only his arms, upper torso, and face were exposed—and they had been ravaged. There was a tattoo on his bare biceps, but the image was too distorted by the massive blistering to be recognizable. The fourth finger on his left hand was black and gangrenous. It took Beck a moment to realize this was due to the strangulation from the wedding ring when the tissues began to swell. What was most horrifying, though, was the suffering visible on the man's face. *In spite of the heavy sedation, he's still feeling it.*

"Thomas McKendrick," Gillette said, retrieving the folder from the plastic rack outside the door. "Thirty-two years old. Landscaper, married, one son."

"Does the boy or his mother have it?"

"Not as far as we can tell. We're watching them, though."

"I'd like to go in and examine him."

"Sure."

"Cara, you should see this, too."

"Okay."

Gillette said, "Come and get prepped."

He took them into a narrow, brightly lit room with three large scrub sinks on either side. The widemouthed basins tilted downward, like ice machines in a hotel hallway. On the wall above each was a large mirror, and bottles of sterilizing cleanser stood on the shelves over the faucets.

There was a tall cabinet at the far end of the room. Gillette opened it and took out two boxes. Each was uncolored cardboard with the words PERSONAL PROTECTIVE EQUIPMENT (PPE) KIT on the top. Underneath was, TO BE WORN PRIOR TO ENTERING NEGATIVE AIR SPACE.

Beck and Porter opened the boxes and removed the contents, then discarded the masks and gloves the security guard had given them. Then, following a procedure they could've performed blindfolded, they methodically donned their costumes. The fluid-resistant gown came first, made of a tough polyethylene-coated polypropylene and colored a medium blue. They slipped their arms into the sleeves, then tied the dangling plastic strips behind each other's backs. Next came the shoe covers, with rubber band inserts that grabbed the ankles. The N95 respirators looked like ordinary dust masks, and the narrow strip of aluminum that ran over the bridge of the nose had to be pinched and pressed to facilitate a custom fit. They tested this by placing both hands over the mask and exhaling to feel for air leaks. After that, they covered their hair with "shower cap" bonnets, and their faces with transparent shields fitted onto their heads with rubber straps. Finally, the gloves had to be stretched over the sleeves of the gown to protect the wrists. The entire process took about twenty minutes and was performed with excruciating delicacy; haste usually resulted in unseen rips. Then they went out with Gillette trailing behind.

Beck had been satisfied with the isolation rooms at first glance. Each had two doors with a "neutral zone" in between. Recent studies of AIIRs—airborne infection isolations rooms—around the nation showed that single-door chambers often permitted escape of infected air. Particularly bad were those with doors that didn't close automatically. Beck could see the hydraulic modules at the top and thought someone had done their homework. Also satisfactory was the solid ceiling, which did a much better job of maintaining negative air pressure than a false one. A digital monitor on the wall near the interior door read −3.1 Pa (Pascals), well above the recommended minimum of −2.5 Pa in comparison to the pressure of connected, "ordinary" areas.

"How many air changes per hour, Ben?" His voice was slightly muted by the respirator.

"Ten. This is one of the better hospitals in the state for infectious containment."

State regulation required that at least six complete air changes occurred in an isolation room per hour, twelve if the area was newly constructed. The infected air would go through a high-efficiency particulate filter before being blown outside. HEPA filters were able to remove at least 99.97 percent of airborne particles with a diameter of 0.3 micrometers. They were originally designed for the infamous Manhattan Project to prevent the spread of radioactive material. Now they had contemporary applications that ranged from domestic vacuum cleaners to nuclear plants.

As Beck and Porter entered the neutral zone, they noticed the drop in air pressure—instead of pushing against them, it seemed to be pulling away. This sensation increased further when the first door hissed to a close and electronically unlocked the second. Infectious airborne particles needed positive airflow to move from host to host, but in a negative-flow environment, they were essentially sucked away before they had the opportunity. The positive-pressure atmosphere of connected areas further served to keep the infectious agents trapped within the AIIRs by surrounding it with what was essentially an invisible force field.

Then they caught the odor; even through the respirator, it was awful. A musky blend of fluids, pungent and sour and miserable. It reminded Porter of unwashed laundry and school locker rooms and mold-spotted food in the back of her apartment refrigerator.

For Beck, however, it conjured unwanted memories of a very different species. He tried to fight them off, but that wretched scent pulled him back, over seas and across borders and beyond the safety buffer of time. He began to recall his own words, as clearly as he had written them on the pages. . . .

Sunday, April 12

We all arrived in Yambuku today. Our single-engine plane landed in an open field near the village just as the sun was going down. I was hoping the heat would taper off in the darkness. But it has to be ninety degrees at least, and the humidity hung on us like a wet blanket. No sooner had we unloaded our gear than our pilot, a bone-skinny Kinshasan named Oudry, jumped back into the cockpit with profuse apologies and zoomed off again. Ebola is killing the Congolese by the thousands right now, and this is one of the hottest of the "hot zones."

We stood there in the middle of the jungle with our gear around our feet, and I wondered if I'd made a mistake by asking for this assignment. No—begging for it. I pleaded until Maurice gave in and wrote me the recommendation. Like any good professor, he never wants to let go of his students. He prefers to keep them under his wing, like a protective parent. That's because he's an academic at heart, in love with classrooms and laboratories and libraries, whereas I want to get out there and start doing it instead of eternally studying it. He was disappointed, but I think that came more from fear than anything else. He thinks I'm going to make a mistake and kill myself. But what's the point of all that training, all that education, all those years of hard work, if I can't go out and make a difference? I've tried to tell him this a thousand times, but I don't know if it ever sank in. In the end, he gave me the green light, and that's all that matters now. Here I am, in one of the most neglected parts of the world. Our job is to study the outbreak in this area and see what we can do to get it under control. I'm feeling very confident of our success. I'm eager to show dear Maury what I'm capable of.

We picked up the bags and cases and walked the two hundred yards to the village. It lay at the base of a wooded hill, and the lights from the huts were pretty from a distance.

Monday, April 13

Very few of the adults are over the age of forty. Life expectancy here is around fifty-two, and that's under normal conditions. The village leader is an elder named Guychel. He greeted us yesterday in a distinctly businesslike manner. The strain has drawn deep lines around his eyes, eyes that have seen too much suffering already. He's missing two fingers on his left hand, and he walks with a slight limp. His voice, high and unsteady, speaks broken but understandable English. I already knew he had attended the Université de l'Uélé in Isiro but was unable to finish his degree. He returned to this village to care for ailing relatives who then died. Since the rest of the villagers knew of no one else with a formal education, they asked Guychel to stay.

We put on our protective gear in the morning as he led us to the makeshift hospital: nothing more than a mud-brick hut. Many eyes were upon us now, and, to be completely honest, I got a charge at being regarded like some kind of savior. Relatives loitered about, some of them crying, others so battered by grief, they looked dazed.

The sight that awaited us inside was terrible. Bodies lay on straw mats on the floor, arranged in such a fashion so as to create a racetrack-shaped walkway. Kerosene lamps sat on the little tables, sending up thin lines of black smoke. Some of the patients had their hands and feet tied because they writhed about as madness took them. Others lay still and awaited the mercy of death, their chests barely moving under stained blankets.

I crouched alongside one woman, whom I judged to be in her thirties, and got out my penlight. I inspected her eyes and found the whites had turned a cloudy pink. Another woman, a bit older, had signs of bleeding around the nose and gums, plus a rash on the roof of the mouth. The third patient was a very young boy; maybe five or six. He had a small toy truck clutched in one hand: a Matchbox. I couldn't help but wonder where he got it from. Guychel told me his parents were already dead. His throat was so swollen, he was barely able to breathe. Pus ran from his tonsils in amber streams.

There were seventy-two patients in total. It took the five of us nearly eight hours to draw all the blood samples we needed.

Tuesday, April 14

In another mud-brick hut, slightly smaller than the hospital, we have our laboratory. I think they gave us this building because it's the only one with a sturdy table. We had to separate the sera from the blood cells with a hand-generated centrifuge—a startling difference from the modern machinery back home—label each sample (also by hand), then pack them in dry ice. That also took hours. Oudry is coming in the morning to take them back for shipment to the States.

Two of the patients died in the evening. One was the little boy with the Matchbox truck. They buried him with it, next to his parents. There were no markers in the graves; the locals just knew where they were. They seem to know where everyone is buried.

Friday, April 17

We have now managed to separate the infected villagers from the healthy ones. That's always step one in an outbreak—isolate the sick from healthy to keep the illness from spreading any further. Then, with Guychel's help, I began interviewing people in the latter group to get a sense of where it originated. As far as I could determine, it was brought to this community by a young man named Prince. Prince had been in Badjoki—another Ebola hot spot just northeast of here—visiting a cousin. This is disappointing information, as we already knew about Badjoki. So Yambuku is likely not the location of the virus's origin, but rather just another satellite zone.

There were six more deaths today, and four new patients.

Monday, April 20

There were seventeen more deaths over the weekend, and eleven new cases in spite of vigorous efforts to keep the healthy villagers from the infected ones. Most were parents. How do you tell a mother or father they cannot see their dying child? How do you summon the objectivity to physically force them from doing so? The five of us are not a security team. We cannot stand guard outside the hospital day and night.

Wednesday, April 22

They began burning the bodies this evening. Not only the recently deceased but also those who were already buried. We determined that they all continued to pose health risks, and Guychel supported us, so they went along with it. We helped out as best we could, although we are completely exhausted. Some of the bodies were only buried two or three feet down. I cannot describe the hideous condition of the corpses. The little boy with the toy truck already looked as though he'd been dead for a month. The toy truck tumbled from his folded hands and bounced on the soft earth. My God . . . piles of blackened, lifeless bodies, children being tossed into it by their weeping parents. The stench of rotted, boiling flesh as the smoke rose into the night sky. If I live to be a thousand years old, I will never get the scent of that pyre out of my memory. Now I know what death smells like.

Friday, April 24
K and I hiked up to another village about two miles away this morning after Guychel told us the outbreak had reached there. But we were at the site only about a hour before my cell phone rang. It was M, telling me I had to come back, there was some kind of emergency. He would not, however, give me any details, only that I needed to hurry. K and I are taking a break now, out of breath, but should get back within the next thirty minutes or so. I have never heard M so upset; he isn't the type. I cannot imagine what's going on, but something in my gut tells me it isn't good.

THREE

"Michael?"

Ben's gentle voice pulled him back.

"Hmm?"

Cara was staring at him, too.

He took note of them standing there and, with a mighty effort, shoved it all out of his mind. Pretending he didn't see Ben's ongoing stare of concern, he went to the patient's bedside, his shoe covers shuffling softly on the polished floor.

McKendrick's face was twitching, the pain relentless and determined. Beck's instinct was to reach out, stroke the young man's hair, tell him he would be all right. But the goal here, if the situation was to be regarded with the necessary objectivity, was to save those who could be saved. That meant the patient had to be viewed as a lab specimen: a source of information. Beck could never fully adopt this into his thinking, in spite of the many who had urged him to do so.

He checked McKendrick's vitals—temperature 102.7 degrees F, heart rate 120, blood pressure 144 over 103, respiratory 23. All accelerated, even with the sedatives. There was a nuclear war going on inside this body, and the native forces were losing in a blowout.

He reached down and pressed on one of the larger pustules with his forefinger. It expanded outward for a second, the tissues straining visibly, then exploded. The honey-colored pus eased between the other blisters with a sluggish viscosity.

Porter said, "Do you want me to collect a sample?"

Gillette responded through the intercom—"You're more than welcome to, but I've already collected several from that patient, as well as all the others, and sent them out." He was watching through the observation window.

Beck leaned down to get a closer look at the exposed left arm. Even through the blistering, he could see the gathering darkness beneath the skin—a faint mauve scarlet.

"Do you recognize this?" he asked Porter.

"Subcutaneous bleeding, looks like."

"Ben?"

"Correct."

"And the others had it, too?"

"Yes."

"Organs, everything?"

"Everything. When they did the autopsy on one man in his early sixties, they said his insides looked like a stew that had been cooking too long."

Porter issued a tiny laugh. It would've been easy

to dismiss this as insensitivity, but Beck knew she was merely focusing on the dark humor of it to protect herself. One of her many defense mechanisms.

He studied the ring finger more closely. It looked like the finger of a gorilla. *Even if this man survives, that part of him is already gone,* he thought. It was as if the finger served as a preview for the rest of the body a day from now.

McKendrick's head lolled to one side, and a narrow string of blood ran from the corner of his mouth to the pillow. Taking a penlight from the bedside table, Beck gently examined the oral cavity. The tongue and gums were decorated with weeping sores of various shapes and sizes.

"Ben, has everyone had these ulcers, too?"

"Yes, to a person."

In his bent-over position, Beck noticed the extensive bandaging on McKendrick's right biceps.

"What happened to his other arm?"

"He tried to burn off one of his tattoos."

"You're kidding."

"No, when the EMTs came for him, he was locked in his garage trying to burn off one of his tattoos with kerosene and a cigarette lighter. It's a grinning spider, and he was screaming, 'It's going to eat me!' "

"A bit delusional," Porter suggested.

"I'd say. Severe mental distress."

"So the infection crosses the blood–brain barrier," Beck said.

"It appears so."

"God . . ."

He gingerly pulled the sheet down to McKendrick's abdomen. Porter didn't laugh this time, but instead let out a small gasp. The torso was covered with the same fluid-filled vesicles as the arms. It was like an uneven sheet of Bubble Wrap.

"That, too, is surprising," Beck said.

"What's that, Michael?"

"When Sheila and I were talking in the car, we both commented on how it sounded as though you could argue a case for smallpox. But then there were other symptoms—" He pointed to the chest area. "—like this that were inconsistent. Cara, see what I talking about?"

"Smallpox vesicles are usually concentrated on the arms, legs, and face."

"Whereas these—"

"—are spread evenly across the patient's entire body."

"Right." He set the blanket back carefully.

"They're burning all the sheets after changing them, too."

"Good idea," Beck said. "Where's the other patient?"

"In the next room here." Gillette pointed down the corridor.

"I'd like to see her now."

"Sure. But prepare yourself."

He let Porter return to the neutral zone first, where she removed her PPE following standard procedure. Facial shield, bonnet, and shoe covers were placed in a burn bag. Then the gown, grasped at the shoulders and pulled forward so the contaminated outside layer was kept away from the body. The gloves came off at the same time, trapped inside the gown. Bare hands were washed in a small sink with microbial soap. The respirator was removed by pulling the rubber strap forward from the back. Finally, hands were washed again.

They returned to the scrub room and put on a fresh set of PPEs—including Gillette. Then they went to the second AIIR.

Beck immediately sensed something different. If the specter of Death were merely lingering in the last one, it had taken up residence here. In the corridor, the microblinds had been fully shut. Inside the neutral zone, Beck saw that the lights in the room were so low, they were nearly off. *Funerary,* he thought. *It has the feel of a funeral.* It was still and silent, save for the soft electronic beeping of the equipment. And, in spite of the microblinds, the patient was kept behind a curtain that someone had pulled all the way to the wall.

Beck glanced back at Porter, who stood behind Gillette with unabashed fear in her eyes.

"Are you okay?"

She only nodded, her gaze fixed on the curtain.

"Okay."

He was not a man given to melodrama, unlike some he had encountered through the years. They used patients like exhibits in a freak show, through which they could impress and intrigue their audience. Beck despised them with the heat of a supernova, and he countered their toxic effect on the medical profession by performing his duties as nontheatrically as possible.

With that in mind, he brought the curtain back casually. As the patient came into view, however, his heart began pounding. From the corner of his eye he saw Ben lower his head and cross himself. Cara, her defenses stripped completely away now, said unevenly, "Oh my God . . ."

It was a woman in her late twenties to mid-thirties. Beck drew this conclusion mostly from her dark hair, which lay long and thick on the pillow. It had no visible streaks of gray or silver, nor did it bear the odd shades of artificial coloring. It was likely the only part of her anatomy still in its original form.

The face had been so radically altered that it was impossible to envision what she once looked like. The pustules ranged from marble-sized to a few that were as big as golf balls. One hung from her cheek with a sickening heaviness. Her eyes and mouth were partially open, as if she was awake but no longer possessed the ability to react. Her skin was an uneven dark purple now that the subsurface bleeding had reached an advanced state.

Beck checked her vital signs. "What's keeping her alive?"

"I have no idea," Gillette said, "but it won't be much longer."

The bedsheet, Beck noted, was different from

McKendrick's in that it covered her body all the way to the chin. It also had dozens of pale-colored moisture spots, the result of constant vesicle bursts. He had no doubt the nursing staff changed the bedding at the required intervals—they simply couldn't keep up with the rate at which her body was deteriorating.

"Why is it bloody right there?" Beck asked, pointing to a spot alongside the woman's midsection. It looked about where her hand would be lying. He also noticed similar spotting on the opposite side.

Without waiting for an answer, he leaned down and carefully lifted the bedsheet. Nothing could have prepared him for what he saw next.

First, there were piles of sloughed skin everywhere, blistered and crusted and sticky. They were literally sliding off her body like meat from the bones of a slow-cooked roast, then accumulating in small heaps.

The blood, Beck discovered, was running from a stomach wound that had been stitched shut and was covered by several layers of gauze.

"What happened?"

"A large kitchen knife," Gillette said.

Beck turned back to him, incredulous. "She was *stabbed*?"

Gillette swallowed visibly. "She did it to herself, Michael."

Beck's eyes widened slightly. Porter was frozen.

"She had—" His voice became wobbly. "—she was seven months pregnant."

These words hung in the air for eternity. No one

breathed or even moved. The electronic beeps ticked off the seconds as time temporarily lost all meaning.

Gillette cleared his throat. "Her husband said he awoke in the middle of the night to the sound of her screaming. She was trying to cut the baby out in order to save it from the infection."

A tear ran down Porter's face and stained her respirator.

Gillette took a deep breath. "She killed the child when she stabbed it."

Porter, her eyes red-rimmed and swollen, studied Beck carefully. They had been in similar situations, and his reaction never ceased to fascinate her—not only was he not crying; he barely appeared affected at all. If anything, he seemed *angry*. Although she couldn't see it under his respirator, she knew his jaw had tightened, his lips pressed together. And his eyes took on a blank, distant stare that was a little frightening. He had never once raised his voice to her, never even became mildly irritated—yet there was some type of rage dwelling inside him. She was sure of this. In spite of the kindness and generosity, in spite of his gentle manner and boundless patience, there was a dark side to the man. *Hatred,* she always thought. *He hates human illness more than anyone I've ever seen.* And she thought she caught a glimpse of it at times like this. What she had not been able to determine, however, was how it got there in the first place.

Gillette's cell phone twittered. He reached up and pressed the button on his Bluetooth earpiece, which neither Beck nor Porter had noticed because it was covered by the bonnet. The conversation didn't last long.

"Fourteen more deaths," he said, "including one in Avenel."

"Where's that?" Beck asked.

"About thirty-five miles from here."

For the first time since Cara Porter had known him, Beck swore out loud.

"This thing could grow, Ben." He kept his voice low even though there was no one else around. "This could be the one. It has all the traits."

"I know."

"It could take millions. And developing a vaccine could take years."

Gillette nodded gravely.

"I know."

FOUR

Dennis Jensen leaned against the doorway between the kitchen and the living room of his small Cape Cod. He had the cordless phone pressed to his ear and his blue Arrow shirt pulled out of his cotton trousers. His tie and jacket for work were hung over one of the chairs at the small table where he and his family had just finished breakfast. He would not be using them today, however, as he had already called out sick. It was just after eight thirty, and a beautiful blue day was beginning to form outside. Neither he nor his wife, Andrea, took much notice of this—every shade and blind in the house was shut, as they had been for days.

"Yeah, okay. Sure, sure. I appreciate it, Elaine. Love you, too. I'll let you know what's happening. Bye."

He thumbed the OFF button and turned to Andi, who was standing in the living room with her arms wrapped tight around herself. She had also called out sick and was wearing sweats and a T-shirt.

"What did she say?"

"There are about a hundred and thirty deaths now for sure," he said. Andi shook her head. "And more cases are coming in all the time. Every hospital has full staffs working around the clock, and they're still asking for help from other places. But everyone's scared. No one wants to touch the infected patients. You can hardly blame them. Three doctors and eight nurses have died already."

They turned back to the TV, which was on the New Jersey Network. NJN had been broadcasting the story with increasing frequency, and yesterday it was asked by the governor to provide information around the clock: *the Death Network.*

"And they don't have any idea what it is yet, right?"

"No. But they're pretty sure it's not smallpox, anyway."

"Well, that's good news, I suppose."

"Elaine said the Centers for Disease Control is leading the investigation. The World Health Organization is working with them, too."

"Terrorists?" Andi asked. "Al-Qaeda? Another Bin Laden?"

Dennis shrugged. "She said she hadn't heard anything about that, either."

"Do they know goddamn *anything*?"

Andi rarely used profanity; one of her duties in the marriage, it seemed, was to make sure *he* didn't. This was a sign she was nearing a meltdown.

"Not much, it seems."

Dennis moved alongside her and watched the next report: another five deaths in Long Branch, a shore town about an hour south of them. One of the victims was a twelve-year-old boy who had just made his first honor roll. Andi started sobbing. When the little boy's school picture flashed on the screen, Dennis lost it, too.

They first heard about the outbreak three days earlier. While driving to his job as an insurance-claims analyst, Dennis heard something on the radio about the sudden death of two police officers in Ramsey after they found a body hanging in an apartment. The report was mercilessly graphic, talking of giant, weeping pustules and hunks of blackened skin. One of the officers shot himself with an unregistered rifle he kept in a drop-ceiling in his basement. It sounded gross enough to make Dennis want to set down his iced coffee for a moment, but he picked it up again when the broadcaster moved on to stock futures and baseball scores. He dismissed it by the time he pulled into the parking lot—just another scratchy note in the endless dissonance of media symphonics.

He mentioned it casually that evening as he and his family were unwrapping their Wendy's. Andi hadn't heard anything about it. She was an HR director at an injection-mold facility and was usually on the move from the moment she walked through the door. She was also more inclined to listen to music during her fifteen-minute commute than the news. She shuddered at the thought of bodies covered in huge, oozing blisters while their organs dissolved; "gross" had never been her thing.

She was going to make a comment when she became distracted by their seven-year-old daughter, Chelsea, who needed help opening a packet of barbecue sauce. Chelsea preferred it over honey mustard when she had chicken nuggets, which made her father proud. Their other child, Billy, was five and hadn't yet been introduced to the manifold delights of barbecue-flavored anything. The conversation then shifted to Billy's daily adventures at kindergarten, and the story was forgotten.

It reentered their lives the next day when Andi heard two of her coworkers talking about it in the kitchenette. The infection was now in Mahwah, a small town set between Ramsey and the New York border. Someone was found unconscious in a supermarket stockroom, covered with running pustules. It was one of the night-shift employees, a kid recently graduated from high school and working for minimum wage until he figured out what he wanted to do with his life. Andi felt a chill blow through her when one of the people in the conversation said with a laugh, "At least he won't have to worry about his future anymore." She knew the guy who said it, privately thought of him as a jerk. So did everyone else in the company. Big surprise.

She mentioned this latest development to Dennis during their lunchtime call. The phone on her desk rang everyday at noon without fail. He would be sitting in their Toyota Camry in the parking lot eating a brown-bag lunch, his cell phone unfolded on the dashboard with the speaker on. He was listening to a Yankees game and hadn't heard about it. He turned the sound down and asked her to repeat the information. She could tell by his tone that the idea of the infection spreading into another town was beginning to concern him, and it sure as hell concerned her. Although neither of them came out and said it, this was one of those instances where you assumed *someone* was working on the problem, and surely it would be solved eventually. Andi couldn't help but think of the infection as some kind of living, breathing entity moving greedily from town to town. This idea struck her the previous night during dinner, too—the infection was a *creature,* and its plan was to spread itself far and wide with the objective of killing as many people as possible.

"When it lands here, that's when we move out," Dennis said with a nervous laugh. After eight years of marriage, she knew him well enough—this was a worry that would fester. It had seeped into whatever level held the highest priorities in his thinking. He would try to be casual about it, try not to burden her with his anxiety or let the kids get a sense of it. This was one of the qualities she loved about him—his determination to maintain as pleasant a life for his family as possible. But it definitely would fester.

Andi had an acquaintance in Mahwah, a woman she had worked with at her previous job. She planned to give her a call to see what was going on; maybe some of the details would be helpful. But then she got caught up in other things and forgot. Between work, getting the kids to school, helping them with their homework at night, and getting them bathed and ready for bed, it simply drifted off her radar screen.

The nightmare crystallized into reality when two cases showed up in town. *Their* town. On the other side, yes, but still . . . This was where they'd bought a home, where their kids went to school and played in the local parks. They knew people, had made friends, and had always felt safe. Things like this didn't happen here.

The victims were Al and Helen Griffin, an elderly couple living in the condo complex next to the supermarket where the Jensens sometimes did their food shopping. They'd been there the week before, in fact, because Andi liked the produce. They drove right past those condos, too—and now they were on television. Not images from halfway around the world, of starving children in Haiti or military skirmishes in Palestine. It was surreal to watch a news report that was being broadcast a few streets away. A crowd had gathered around the attractive female reporter on the scene for NJN. Dennis and Andi recognized a few people, one of whom was an old man who usually hung around the Salvation Army thrift store. He was kind of a roving vagrant who made everyone uneasy.

According to the report—further confirmed by the local freebie newspaper—the elderly couple caught the virus while visiting family in nearby

Glen Rock. Three days later, they were both dead. A UPS delivery man saw the wife through the decorative glass partition by the front door, lying in the hallway. A barbecue fork had been thrust deep into her lower back. The husband was found spread-eagle on their bed, six empty prescription bottles on the nightstand beside him.

The morning after the report, Dennis made a point of driving past the condos. He wasn't sure why. He wasn't the type to slow down at a crash site in the hope of seeing a little blood or a hand dangling from beneath a tarp. He supposed he just had to know the situation was real, that Andi's "creature" had truly made the decision to visit, of all places, their quiet little town of Carlton Lakes.

It was real enough. Yellow police tape had been draped across the condo entrance, and two squad cars were parked in the street. An NBC news van with a satellite dish on the roof was down a little farther, the reporter and his two-man crew having bagels and coffee. A family of four—*just like us,* Dennis thought with a shudder—was exiting one of the other condos with suitcases in hand. The children looked bewildered, the parents terrified.

The Jensens watched helplessly as their beloved community dissolved. Handmade signs appeared in storefront windows indicating that business was suspended. Extracurricular activities like aerobics classes for seniors and dance lessons for youngsters were canceled until further notice. The two Albanian brothers who owned the Sunoco station by the highway took to wearing cotton gloves and masks. They asked that people who were paying in cash kindly drop the money into a plastic bag, which was then zipped shut. Credit cards were sanitized with isopropyl alcohol on cosmetic pads. Traffic thinned out on Martin Boulevard, the town's main artery, and everyone stayed inside on the weekends. No one cut their lawn, and there were no joggers or kids on bicycles. At some houses, mail piled up in the boxes because no one wanted to touch it.

Chelsea's principal sent a note home, assuring parents that the staff was taking all necessary precautions to keep the infection out of the school. He included a sheet from the New Jersey Department of Health that gave tips on how to minimize risk of exposure, and another from the CDC on what they knew about the infection so far. Some parents had already pulled their children out anyway; attendance was down about 15 percent. Dennis and Andi debated whether they should do likewise. They felt strongly that education was crucial in a child's life. Learning the value of routine was also important. Chelsea seemed to be a natural, always going with the flow. They were hesitant to interrupt that.

Then one of the other students in the school caught it. A fourth-grader: Peter Something-or-other. They'd heard the name before but couldn't recall it. The family was fairly well known around town, had lived in Carlton through several generations. Because Peter had it, his parents got it. And then some of the others in his class began showing early signs.

That's when Dennis and Andi decided to pull Chelsea out. They tried calling the school several times to leave a message on the absentee hotline the following morning, but the line was always busy. In the end the school did the right thing anyway and closed down pending further notice. There was more information on the website, and a prerecorded call was made to every home. There were no more letters, though, because no one wanted to touch a piece of paper that came from inside that building.

The Jensens prayed hard that Chelsea hadn't caught it, promising God absolutely anything. They were both Christian, and Andi still went to church fairly regularly. Dennis's attendance had dwindled to holidays and family occasions such as weddings and christenings. He still believed in a supreme being, but he felt organized religion had become too much of a business to be trusted. Now he was fearful that he would be punished for his position. *If so, punish me and not her,* he pleaded.

They packed Chelsea and Billy into their minivan and sped two hours south to see Dennis's sister, Elaine. She was a nurse at Point Pleasant Hospital and knew exactly what to do and whom to see. The doctor was a friend of hers, a large and jovial Russian man in his mid-fifties. Wearing rubber gloves and a cotton mask, he took a vial of blood from a fat vein in the crook of Chelsea's right arm and promised to get back to them as soon as possible. On the way home, Chelsea asked if she was sick, which caused Andi to start crying. Dennis said no, it was just a checkup, and they wanted to see her aunt.

The night that followed was the worst of their lives. They held each other and cried until there were no tears left. They drifted in and out of sleep and felt even worse in the morning. They both took off work and played with Chelsea and Billy in their "messy room" upstairs—a controlled disaster zone where the kids were allowed to do as they pleased. The cordless phone was kept nearby. It rang once around ten thirty and turned out to be a window-treatment salesman. Andi, unable to maintain her usually civil demeanor under the circumstances, went into Billy's bedroom and tore the guy a new one. It rang again a half hour later—it was Elaine calling to tell them that Chelsea was fine. Andi wiped tears away and laughed as she thanked her. Dennis sat on the floor with his legs crossed and pulled Chelsea into his lap, then wrapped his arms around her and gently rocked back and forth as she read her favorite book to him. It was one of the most joyous moments of their lives.

But that was yesterday.

"We can work from home until the whole thing blows over," Andi said from the driver's seat of the van a few hours later. It was late afternoon, and the bright blue day had evolved into one of the sunniest and prettiest of the season. "I can do most of my stuff on the laptop. You can, too, right?"

Dennis nodded as they cruised through the center of town. "I guess so."

"Okay, then it's a plan."

She now seemed to be harboring a peculiar kind of optimism, Dennis decided—a Pollyanna belief that the outbreak would evaporate in the not-too-distant future, as if simply regarding it in an offhanded manner were the key. He wished he could share the sentiment, but something held him back: a "certain uncertainty," as he sometimes called it. He subscribed to the common adage that preparing for the worst was always best. *Something bigger is going on. We're not seeing the whole picture, and we may not for some time. This is far from over.* He noticed that many of the stores were shuttered, their shades drawn and the signs in the windows turned around to read CLOSED. There was no one on the sidewalks, which was unnerving in itself—he had never seen this thoroughfare devoid of pedestrians before. Certainly there was life out there, somewhere. But what kind of life was it when every moment was colored by fear? When you were too afraid to perform an act as simple as stepping outside and taking a deep breath?

". . . brought the list along?"

"Hmm? What?"

"Did you bring the list along?"

"Oh, yeah." He took it from the pocket of his shirt and unfolded it. "Got it right here."

"Is there anything else you can think of?"

He scanned it—*bananas, cereal, milk, whole wheat bread* . . . All the normal stuff. That appeared to be the operative word at the moment—*normal.* He thought, *That's what she's trying to get back to—some sense of normalcy. She thinks if we act like everything's okay, then everything* will *be okay.* They had been together too long for him not to know what was going on in her head. *The moment Chelsea received a clean bill of health, Andi saw an opportunity to re-center ourselves. That's what we're doing right now—taking the path back to our center.*

"Do you have ice pops on the list?" Chelsea asked from the backseat. She had the headphones on, and Dennis was surprised she could overhear their conversation. Billy was reading a Richard Scarry book and paying no attention to them.

"Sure do," Andi said.

"Cool."

They bumped over the railroad tracks, followed the curve by the butcher shop, and made a right into the parking lot. The strip mall that spread out like a sleeping monster at the other end was less than three years old. It featured a Baskin-Robbins, a Subway, a women's gym, an Italian restaurant, a dollar store, and a one-hour dry cleaners that Dennis had scratched off his list after they lost two buttons on the first shirt he brought them. The anchor was a massive A&P supermarket.

There were only six other vehicles in sight, all near the front door in a tight group. The lot's full capacity was 420, and on any given Sunday it would be full. Dennis had even driven by in the dead of night and seen more cars than this; those that belonged to the stock boys, the inventory clerks, and the custodians who made up the graveyard shift.

He turned to Andi, who was staring with her mouth slightly open. *She's scared,* he thought. But she wouldn't give in to it. She started forward again without a word, cutting a diagonal path across the empty spine-rows and pulling into a spot away from the group. Dennis was struck by the notion that she may have done this as an act of passive rebellion, as if parking next to one of the other cars was in some way an admission of defeat.

"Okay, let's go!" she said, cheerful as ever. The kids unstrapped themselves and jumped out.

What Dennis and Andi noticed first when they stepped inside—and it turbocharged the fear that was now rising steadily in both of them—was the stillness. No squeaking of dry carriage wheels, no neighbors gossiping, no sale announcements over the PA system. Not even any Muzak. The silence was rigid and endless, as if they were on the moon. Dennis listened hard for any signs of human life, but there was nothing.

"Where is everybody?" Chelsea asked, her little voice producing a faint echo. She was holding her mother's hand and hadn't yet noticed it was becoming warm and sweaty. "Mom? Where is—?"

"I don't know, sweetheart."

"I guess this is a slow shopping day," Dennis said, hoping it would serve the dual purpose of amusing his wife and distracting his daughter. "It *is* a weekday, after all. But that's good, though—no lines, right? So let's get to it." He went back into the foyer and noisily separated a cart from the others.

The produce section came first, and the odor was nearly unbearable. Fruits and vegetables lay rotting in their cases as tiny flies buzzed about. Some had fallen to the floor and broken apart, leaving colorful stains in their wake. Still in defiance mode, Andi began casually sorting through the piles. She found two passable honeydew melons, a half-dozen apples, a bag of Red Bliss potatoes, and a prepackaged head of iceberg lettuce. Under normal circumstances, she would've passed over the iceberg without a second glance, but what little Romaine was left was rusted and, in the more advanced cases, goopy.

None of the familiar figures were behind the meat counter in their white butcher's coats. Andi was about to slap the bell anyway when she peered inside the refrigerated case. Instead of taut, robust cuts of meat resting proudly on black platter-plates wreathed in garnish, there were shriveled hunks of decaying flesh splotched with fuzz. A constellation of mold spots had begun forming on the interior of the case as well. Dennis felt his stomach roll.

Chelsea, who had put a curious hand against the glass, said flatly, "That stuff doesn't look good anymore."

"No," her mother replied, "I don't think so, either. They really need to restock."

"Gross," Chelsea added. Billy, conversely, was staring with the kind of rapt fascination for the grotesque that is the exclusive property of small boys.

"It really is. Let's go."

Aisles one through eight featured only dry goods, but the shelves were nearly empty in some places and half-stocked most everywhere else. In a store where neatness was normally given top priority, it was disturbing to see items standing crooked, set in the wrong place, or lying on the floor. Chelsea remarked that someone really needed to come and do cleanup. Billy began kicking a small can of peas down aisle four and giggling like a madman until Dennis told him to stop.

They discovered human life in aisle nine; the frozen foods. There, at the far end, stood the man they knew to be the store manager. He was a respectable, responsible type, tall and well built, with dark hair combed neatly around the sides but long gone on top. He wore his usual black pants, white shirt, and conservative tie. Next to the tie, Dennis and Andi knew, would be a nameplate that read BILL with his title underneath in smaller letters. He also wore a cotton surgical mask and rubber examination gloves. Both were clearly visible in the distance. *Is it time for us to have those, too?* Dennis wondered as a chill flashed through him. *Excuse me, Bill, but what aisle would they be in?* Bill was also holding a clipboard and had propped open one of the freezer doors with the aid of a small cart.

The Jensens stopped as a group. As they did, Bill turned and saw them. An awkward moment followed. *He's surprised to see us*, Dennis realized.

He wasn't expecting anyone. Then, even more unsettling: *That's because no one's been here in a while.*

Dennis smiled and gave a little wave. Bill returned it from his end, then went back to work. The Jensen herd began moving again, and Andi picked out some french fries, waffles, and ravioli.

When they got close enough, Dennis said to Bill, "Busy today."

That, at least, earned a laugh. "Yeah, packed."

"It really is."

"Can I help you find anything?"

Now Dennis wanted to laugh. *How about the road back to sanity? Can you help us find that?*

"No, thank you," Andi replied. "We know where everything is."

"Okay, well, if you have any questions—" He spread his arms and smiled while shaking his head. "I'll be here."

"Thanks."

No sooner had they left Bill behind than they spotted a second employee—a young girl standing behind one of the cash registers. Her face and hands were also protected by surgical gear. She couldn't have been more than twenty-one or -two and was nervously alternating her attention between her fingernails and her surroundings. *Who lets their kid work in a supermarket during an epidemic?* Dennis wondered with a preemptive loathing for her idiot parents. He tried to rationalize it. *Maybe they don't know. Maybe she's a single mom who got kicked out of her conservative parents' home and came here to start fresh, or something along those lines*. Whatever her story, she looked petrified, and Dennis felt for her. *And for what? Minimum wage?*

Then a thought came that stopped him cold—

We're here, too.

At last the madness of it all seeped through the membrane of denial he had allowed to form.

"I think it's time to go."

Andi, who was presently scratching another item off the shopping list, said absently, "Huh?"

"Come on, let's get out of here."

"What? But we—"

"Andi . . . ?"

She looked up at him, then followed his eyes to register girl. She had never seen anyone so frightened in her life. In that instant, she understood—or at least began to.

"Yeah, okay."

FIVE

That evening, the phone rang twice in the Jensen household. The first call was from Elaine, checking in. The other was from a woman Andi knew in town who wanted to make sure they were okay—and to give updates.

Andi reached for Dennis's hand and squeezed it, then said that Lisa and Ritchie Bennett were dead. She and Dennis first met the Bennetts through mutual acquaintances, and had been to their house a few times. Casual get-togethers, with wine and finger food and modern jazz playing quietly. Ritchie was small, bald, and muscular, with a goatee and a gravelly voice. He had more energy than a roadrunner and a delightfully childish sense of humor. Lisa, tall and thin with silky black hair, was his female equivalent, in direct violation of the "opposites attract" rule. She had a sharp, vivacious wit and seemed unable to go more than five minutes without laughing about something. The last time Dennis and Andi were at their house, about a month ago, they found Ritchie wearing a maroon fez he'd bought on eBay. There was no reason for the purchase other than giddy impulse. They found this endearing.

The idea of the Bennetts lying dead somewhere, their bodies disfigured beyond recognition, made Dennis feel weak all over. He couldn't shut out the image of their blackened, distorted faces. People he knew, people he liked. He had thought several times that the basis for a lasting friendship was there. It wasn't easy to make new friends as you got older, he and Andi were discovering. Adults were often jaded, cynical, used up . . . untrustworthy, petty . . . childish, wildly egotistical. . . . The Bennetts didn't seem to have any of these flaws. They were refreshingly unaffected. The Jensens found this marvelous and decided yes, they'd like to get to know them better. It was something they'd been looking forward to.

Andi, sitting on the living room couch with her legs crossed, was doing more listening than talking now. Tears were streaming down her cheeks, and Dennis brought the box of tissues from the bathroom. He knew she was being loaded up with information, and he wasn't sure he wanted to hear all of it when she was done. *Give me the highlights but leave out the details, please,* he wanted to say. But a valorous part of him felt that if she had to suffer through it, he should, too.

Chelsea came in to show them a drawing she'd made of their house, complete with a bright yellow sun and corkscrew smoke rising from the chimney. She asked why Mommy was crying, and Dennis told her it was because one of her friends was sick. Andi reached out for Chelsea and hugged her with her free arm. After kissing her on the head, she said in a whisper, "Mommy's on the phone right now. Go back and make me another beautiful drawing, and I'll be done in a minute." Chelsea nodded and went back out.

This is a poker tournament, Dennis thought as he stood in the middle of the room, watching his wife. *It's a poker tournament and we're getting into the later stages now, where players start dropping out left and right.* So far they were still in it. They had taken no serious hits—just the scare with Chelsea. That was analogous to going into a hand well behind and drawing the card you desperately needed. Luck stepped in and saved them . . . but how often could you depend on luck? Every moment they remained in Carlton, they were gambling against greater odds. The outbreak was playing the role of the house, and the Jensens were the degenerate customer—and the customer rarely came out ahead when all was said and done. Only fools didn't know that.

Andi finished the call and rattled off the victims list. There were twelve in total, all threads of varying color in the fabric of their lives—the woman at the library who called when a requested book or DVD came in, the young girl at the bank who always gave Chelsea a red lollipop, the semiretired couple who owned the Laundromat. . . .

She covered her face and wept. Dennis stood watching her for a long moment. He suddenly felt detached from it all. He was tired of the crying, tired of the emotional beating they'd been taking. They had allowed themselves to become too complacent about this, too passive. Sitting here for days, literally, waiting for someone to act, for something to be done. *Isn't that the whole problem with this country now?* he thought. *Everyone sitting around waiting for someone else to take care of things?* Who was going to solve this problem? The government? Being born in the '60s, Dennis had never known a time when the government wasn't an object of scorn and ridicule. Lyndon Johnson was president on the day he entered the world. Johnson, then Nixon, then Ford, then Carter . . . Now he lived in an age when people *expected* the government to fix everything for them. The irony was impossible to miss—it had become part of the American ethos to regard civic leaders as corrupt, ineffective, and hopelessly stupid, yet expect those same leaders to act as saviors. How many people were willing to put their very lives in the government's hands?

"We need to get out of here, sweetheart," Dennis said, distantly surprised by how calm he sounded.

Andi looked up, eyes bloodshot, cheeks flushed. "What?"

"We need to go. Someplace far from here."

Andi's eyes shifted away from his in an expression of uncertainty; then she nodded. "Yeah . . . I suppose."

"So let's get moving."

"Where to?"

"The cabin. It's isolated, so it's perfect." He began toward the carpeted staircase that led to the second floor, but she stood and gently took his arm.

"Honey, wait . . . are you sure?"

"I don't want to do it, but what's the reward for sticking around? For taking that risk?"

"Well . . ." She couldn't gather her thoughts here. Something to do with this being their home for so long—and not just the house but the town, too. The whole *community*. She loved it here, and she knew he did, too. It was *their* town. The playgrounds, the schools, the supermarkets, the restaurants. They had blended into the culture, been fully accepted. It was familiar and comfortable. And now, in a time of crisis, they were going to abandon it?

"No one's having any success stopping this," Dennis said. "I don't think we should sit around waiting for it to knock on our door and turn us into a statistic. Lisa and Ritchie, those kids at school, and plenty of others . . . who's next?" He shook his head. "Elaine said they still don't know what it is and they can't contain it. We can't just sit here."

"Yeah," she said, almost whispering. "I know."

He stepped forward and hugged her. "I realize our whole life is here, but . . . we won't *have* lives much longer if we stay."

"I agree."

"The moment they get a rein on this thing—"

"—we'll come right back?"

He smiled. "You better believe it."

"Okay, sounds like a plan."

"We'll leave tonight."

"Under the cover of darkness?"

He sighed heavily. "Like the cowards we are."

"Great."

"Let's go get the suitcases from the crawl space."

He went up the stairs, but she lingered a moment, surveying the living room—the couch and love seat where they all sat for Family Movie Night every Friday . . . the end tables with framed family photos . . . the bubble clock Dennis had bought her for their fifth anniversary, the weights spinning soundlessly. The blinds were drawn, shutting out the world. Fear was waiting out there, drifting by the doors and windows for a chance to get in. Their little pocket of safety was slowly collapsing. It was so quiet right now, so still and calm and perfect. And only a set of walls separated them from a nightmare.

Of course it was ridiculous to stay, ridiculous to put the kids at risk for any reason. But she wasn't so sure that they could simply trot back in here after the outbreak had been contained. (*If* it was ever contained, a mean little voice in her mind suggested.) That felt a little too hopeful. For whatever reason, she couldn't shake the feeling that, regardless of the outcome, their lives would never be the same. That was what lay at the core of her sadness—something so beautiful, so wonderful, and for which they had worked so long and hard, was being brought to ruin. And a part of her was letting it happen. Somehow, her willingness to leave right now was contributing to the crime.

Andi took one more look at their meticulously

crafted little world. Then, taking a deep breath and summoning all the willpower she had, she let go of it in her mind.

They waited until Chelsea and Billy were asleep, then rushed around the house like lunatics, grabbing whatever might be needed. Usually when they went on a trip, they made a list of stuff to bring—the STB list, as they called it. Andi kept it on the family computer and refined it before, during, and after every excursion. She printed a copy that night, then realized it was mostly useless due to the peculiar nature of the situation. *Should've made a list called "Stuff to Bring When You're Escaping Your Town During a Massive Viral Outbreak."* Food, for example, wasn't on there, except for car snacks for the kids. When they traveled, they ate out. It was doubtful they'd be visiting too many restaurants this time around.

So the list was tossed aside, and they went from room to room collecting anything that seemed like a necessity. Since food was obviously in that category, Dennis went into the garage and took down the two big ice chests they kept in the loft. Then he transferred the contents of the refrigerator and covered it with ice cubes and cold packs. There was a fridge in the cabin, and even though it was unplugged, the electricity was always on. It wouldn't take long to get it going. Two boxes of snacks—Cheez-Its for Chelsea, Teddy Grahams for Billy—were taken from the kitchen cabinet, along with a few apples and oranges for the ride. Dry foods—including canned soups, vegetables, fruits, and beans, as well as two boxes of brown rice—were loaded into cardboard boxes along with toiletries—Advil, Robitussin, Tums, Children's Tylenol, toothpaste, brushes, floss, and so on. When it came to shampoo and conditioner, Dennis paused to consider which he should bring—the full bottles or the trial sizes. It was the first time he gave full thought to the possibility they might be gone awhile, that this thing could grow beyond all imaginable proportions, and they might be stuck in the cabin for quite some time. With reluctant pessimism, he grabbed the big bottles from their place on the ceramic shower shelf.

Next was a case of canned food and a leash for Scooter, their nine-year-old golden retriever, along with his two ceramic bowls. Gathering clothes for the kids posed a particularly delicate challenge. Some were piled up in the basement laundry room in a wicker basket waiting to be folded. The rest required an excruciating visit to their bedroom as they slept, which included tiptoeing across the carpet and opening dresser drawers like a cat burglar. All clothes and sneakers and shoes were jammed hodgepodge into suitcases. Schoolbooks went into school backpacks. Toys were stuffed into garbage bags because that was all they had left after a while. If they needed anything else, Hall's General Store was two miles away. Dennis prayed it would be open in spite of the outbreak. If it wasn't, they might be in trouble.

As soon as a box, case, cooler, or bag was full, he took it outside and loaded it into the back of the minivan: a two-year-old stone gray Toyota Sienna that never let them down. On the sixth trip, carrying a shoulder bag full of toiletries and a suitcase bulging with kids' clothes, he heard sirens in the distance. There were two, one about a half tone from the other. Over the line of darkened houses, there was a faint orange glow in the night—a fire. *This town is burning,* he thought, more metaphorically than literally. *It's falling apart. Everything is coming unraveled.* At that moment, he realized the hatchback to the van needed to be kept down. If anyone passed by and saw that it was up, they'd know he and his family were leaving . . . and that could lead to problems. Same with the light on the side stoop that illuminated the driveway—it needed to be turned off. He lowered the hatchback until it quietly clicked shut, then headed back inside. As he got to the screen door, he heard the unmistakable sound of a window being smashed. It was chillingly close; one block away at the most. There was a hedge in their backyard, and several houses ran in a diagonal line beyond it. It might have been one of those, he thought, and his heart began booming.

He asked Andi how the kids were doing; then they both went upstairs to check anyway. One of the two windows in their room faced the back. They peered through the blinds and saw red and blue lights flashing down Grover Avenue, one of Carlton's main thoroughfares. Dennis checked to make sure the window was locked.

By two in the morning, they were about ready to go. Dennis made the third-to-last trip (he was counting) to the van and shut the hatchback yet again. Now there were fire engines racing somewhere, sirens howling and horns blaring. It reminded him of the night of Christmas Eve, when he and his family stood on Main Street and watched Santa Claus go by. That seemed like a million years ago—another lifetime. He felt strangely detached from everything now, emotionally unplugged. He was jolted from this by a series of distant screams: a set of three, all of the same pitch and duration. It was a young woman, perhaps a teenager, and the terror was unmistakable.

He detected movement nearby. A figure appeared on the sidewalk, and Dennis stopped. It was an older man, slightly heavy around the middle, in dark cotton trousers and a button-down shirt pulled free at the front. The shirt was sopping wet, as if he'd been pelted with tiny snowballs. He lumbered along awkwardly, favoring one leg, and his face was an elephantine mass of pustulate swellings and eruptions. Regardless of the disfigurement, Dennis recognized him at once, and a roiling horror came alive in his belly—Jack McLaughlin, the crossing guard he and Chelsea saw every morning on the way to school. Dennis didn't know that much about him: only the bits and pieces he'd overheard in other people's conversations. He was a retired AT&T employee, lived somewhere in town. His wife had died some years ago, and had three kids and a few grandchildren. He had to be in his mid to late seventies now, and he had bothersome knees. Yet he was there bright and early every morning, sitting in his old Buick at the corner until the first wave arrived. Then he'd get out with his handheld STOP sign, ready to admonish any motorist who didn't give the right of way to America's next generation. He had a prodigious memory, too, remembering the name of every child and parent. He retained little details, like which child had just lost a tooth or got a new backpack or came home with a handful of Mylar balloons because they'd just won the Student of the Week Award. Everyone loved Jack.

Dazed and confused, he altered course when he saw Dennis. Whether or not he actually recognized him was unclear. He tried speaking, but this produced only a series of garbled, hitching grunts and hisses, like someone with sleep apnea trying to recapture enough oxygen to continue breathing.

Dennis locked the van wirelessly and leaped onto the stoop, disappearing into the house and locking that door, too.

Andi, hearing the slam, came hurrying into the room. "What's wro—?"

"You know Jack, the school crossing guard?"

"Yeah?"

"He's outside."

"What, right now?"

"Yeah, and he's got the infection. It's all over his face." Dennis made circular motions around his own for emphasis.

"Oh no . . ."

She went into the living room, Dennis trailing close behind. Kneeling on the love seat, they peered through the hanging blinds that covered the bay window. Then they screamed together.

Jack had climbed the steps to the front porch and was no more than ten feet away—a relatively thin pane of glass was all that separated them. Then he began slapping the screen door and yelling like an angry drunk. Andi deciphered commands such as *"Open up!"* and *"Let me in!"* through the wet, phlegmy clog in his throat. He was also coloring his speech with a healthy dose of profanity.

When Jack realized the screen door was unlocked, he yanked it back and started hammering on the other one. It had two locks, which were always engaged. But they weren't made for this kind of abuse. If Jack started ramming with his shoulder, it would be only a matter of time before he was in their living room.

Andi grabbed a chair from the kitchen and tried to wedge it under the doorknob, but it was too small to provide a sharp, tight angle. (*It always worked in the movies,* she thought crazily.) She tossed it back into the kitchen with a curse.

"Jack! Go away!" Dennis shouted. "Go back home!"

Amazingly, this worked . . . for a moment. The pounding ceased, and Dennis could hear sirens outside again. Then Jack launched a new attack, using his whole body.

The door shook with each blow, the top and bottom bending before snapping back. When the wood cracked the first time, Andi screamed like Dennis had never heard her scream before.

He ran into their bedroom, threw open his closet door, and dropped to his knees. There was a row of shoe boxes on the top shelf, and he reached for the last box on the left. The lid slid off and fell away as he brought it down. Inside was a second box of slightly lesser proportions but much better quality—varnished walnut. There was a small keypad set in the top, and Dennis played the five-digit combination. The lid popped up slightly, and he lifted it to reveal a black .357 Magnum. He'd planned to bring it along when they left, the last item to take after everything else was ready. He stuffed it into his back pocket, then turned the box over to shake out the false bottom. Underneath was a fully loaded magazine. He grabbed it and rammed it into the butt of the weapon.

He was back in the living room in less than fifteen seconds. Jack was still pounding away, Andi trying to brace the door from her side.

When she saw the gun, she said, "No, Dennis . . ."

"What choice is there?"

He had always been serious about gun ownership and had taken shooting lessons. Without further pause, he told Andi to step aside, then pointed the weapon high and fired a warning shot. The sound was like ten firecrackers exploding at once. The bullet ripped through the wall, about two inches above the doorframe, as if it had gone through tissue paper.

The silence that followed was puzzling. Did the shot temporarily deafen them, or did Jack get the message and leave? Cautiously, Dennis knelt on the love seat and fingered back the blinds again. Jack was still there, looking up as if watching a bird fly overhead.

"That broke his concentration," Andi whispered.

Dennis nodded. "Yeah. Good." *Maybe he'll forget what he was doing and move off.*

Jack remained there for a time, clearly puzzled. Then he did something Dennis and Andi would never forget—he brought his head down and leveled his gaze until they were staring at each other. *I'm looking Death in the eyes,* Dennis thought, wanting to pull away but oddly unable to.

The sound of their daughter's voice came, as if rehearsed, at the same moment Jack began throwing himself at the door again. She had come down the stairs and was standing on the first landing, just two steps from the living room floor. Even if she couldn't grasp the minutiae of the situation, she understood intuitively that something bad was happening, and that her parents were scared. This, in turn, made her own fear ten times worse.

"Jack, go home! Go on home, Jack!"

Dennis got off the couch and positioned himself about ten feet from the door. He was trying to keep the weapon out of Chelsea's view. *And what happens if he gets in here? Do I shoot him, in front of my daughter? What will* that *do to her mind?*

"I'll get her back upstairs," Andi said.

"Okay."

"Dennis, please don't . . ."

The pounding was getting harder.

"I'll try not to."

Harder . . .

"Jack! Jack, listen to me!" he shouted.

"Let me in, gobbammit. Open ub!"

"Jack, stop!"

The wood in the doorframe was cracking louder now, groaning like the keel of an old ship.

"Jack!"

The sequence of events that followed seemed to unfold in slow motion. The door finally gave way—the side of the frame that held the locks ripped free, bits of splintered wood flying in every direction. Then the gruesome sight of Jack McLaughlin stood in the doorway. Chelsea screamed like a character in a horror movie. Dropping to one knee, Dennis fired a shot into Jack's right shoulder. It spun him around with a bizarre kind of gracefulness as blood exploded in a pink spray. Jack stumbled backwards across the porch in the same surrealistic ballerina fashion, his eyes wide with bewilderment, then fell down the steps and landed in a heap on the lawn. He did not move again.

Dennis kicked the door shut and said, "Okay, time to go."

"Yeah."

"Get Chelsea out to the car, and I'll go get Billy."

Chelsea clung to her mother, crying uncontrollably, as they hurried out of the room. Dennis went up the staircase three steps at a time and found his son still curled in a fetal position. *Luckiest kid in the world,* he thought, tucking the gun into the back of his pants and lifting the child, blankets and all, into his arms.

Billy, thankfully, did not stir as Dennis strapped him into his car seat. Chelsea was gasping for air in the other one, her tears drawing bright track lines down her cheeks.

"I'll be back in a sec," he told his wife.

"I'll start the engine."

"Okay."

He went inside and pulled out every plug he could find: another pre-vacation procedure. Then he went to lock all the doors. When he got to the front, he paused. *Damn . . .* He remembered the screen door had a lock on the tiny handle. He opened the inside door slowly, but drew back when he saw that it was covered with pale, bloody fluids, some running an unhurried race to the bottom. Jack's body was still lying there, little more than a shape in the darkness. *Is he dead?* Dennis wondered. *Could a shot in the shoulder really have killed him?* No chance, he told himself. If anything, the fall did it.

Yes, but you still caused *the fall,* said the voice of his conscience.

He felt a twinge of guilt and pushed it aside. *I'll deal with it later*. Using his foot, he kicked the main door shut. *If someone wants to break in, they'll break in*.

He took one last look around. There were so many memories here, just about all of them good. Andi was right—they loved this house, loved the neighborhood and everyone in it. Would it ever be the same? Was there any chance of them coming back and picking up where they left off? It was doubtful. This was one of those events that altered everything, caused a paradigm shift. *Nothing will ever be the same,* he thought, and within the sadness he also felt anger now.

He shut off the kitchen light and closed the door. As he backed the minivan into the street, he found himself unable to avoid glancing at Jack McLaughlin's body one last time.

It was still lying there.

SIX

DAY 9

The CDC, along with New Jersey's Office of Emergency Management, urged all residents to remain indoors and travel as little as possible. A CDC circular outlined everyday tips to reduce the risk of acquiring the disease, such as frequent hand washing, wearing masks and gloves, and minimizing unprotected contact with your eyes, nose, and mouth.

New Jersey State Police set up checkpoints along major roadways and watched for signs of infected passengers, but since they were not medically trained and had little interest in acquiring the infection themselves, results were varied at best. One middle-aged computer engineer was detained while entering the toll plaza at the George Washington Bridge because he was red-eyed and sneezing. It turned out he was a lifelong sufferer of ragweed allergies, and no one had considered the fact that the pollen count was particularly high that day. Another man in his late twenties, driving an aging Toyota Corolla with multiple primer patches, tested positive not for the illness but for both marijuana and cocaine. Authorities found two more joints and a vial of crack in a guitar case in his trunk.

The suggestion by New Jersey's governor that public water supplies could become tainted triggered a stampede to local supermarkets to purchase bottled water. The CDC added to the fervor by reminding people that water was essential not only for drinking but also cooking and personal hygiene. Examples of price-gouging—in spite of stern warnings from both state and federal agencies—inevitably followed. In one instance, a gas station in Paterson that formerly sold cases of Poland Spring for $4.99 upped its price a few dollars each day. When it reached $22.99, a couple in a black Dodge pickup pulled into the station during the night and tag-teamed the lone attendant on duty—the husband held him at knifepoint while the wife loaded the remaining fourteen cases into the truck bed.

Public schools in northeastern Jersey's six main counties—Bergen, Essex, Hudson, Morris, Passaic, and Union—were ordered closed until further notice. The Department of Health and Senior Services also considered shutting down all restaurants in the area, then decided this was unnecessary since most were closing on their own. Other public places, such as parks and nature trails, were abandoned. Swings and seesaws stood unused, parking lots empty. Shopping malls were desolate, and people began using their sick days until they had to tap into their vacation time . . . then their personal time . . . then time they really didn't have.

In spite of all precautions, the virus continued to find its way around; there was always someone willing to help out. A widow from Riverdale who hadn't missed a Mass at Christ Church since the Reagan administration decided to disregard all official warnings and attend services in spite of feeling feverish, fatigued, and more arthritic than usual. One sip from the chalice during the Eucharist was all it took to infect the eleven parishioners who used it next.

One of those eleven worked the night shift in a convenience store. The following day, just after 1:30 a.m. and while the store was empty, she experienced her first sneeze while making two fresh pots of coffee. Ten minutes later, a truck driver in filthy jeans and a flannel shirt came in. He was hauling a load of unpainted furniture from North Carolina to a warehouse in Maine. He hadn't heard about the outbreak, because he didn't listen to the radio on the road and didn't watch the news in any of the cheap hotels along the way. He hated people as a general rule and tried to have as little to do with society as possible. He poured himself a large cup of the infected coffee, didn't acknowledge the woman when she smiled and handed him his change, and climbed back into his rig. He was the first person to import the disease into the state of Connecticut.

A teenager visiting her boyfriend at college brought it into Pennsylvania.

A father of four who had been recently laid off carried it with him to a job interview in Delaware.

Hundreds of New Jersey commuters took it to work with them in Manhattan.

And so on.

The main chamber of the White House Situation Room could pass for a high-tech conference center in any large American corporation. It is long and narrow, with cream-colored walls, a white drop ceiling, and bright lights, all working in unison to create the illusion of greater space. It is rumored the easy colors and copious illumination were intended to lift the mood of the occupants; the incarnation prior to the 2006–2007 renovation, with its navy carpet and walnut paneling, was often compared to a dungeon. The modernized version also has six recessed flat-panel monitors, adjacent glass-encased booths for making and receiving secure phone calls, and ceiling sensors to block all unauthorized signals in and out. Colloquially known as the Sit Room, it is located in the White House basement beneath the office of the president's chief of staff.

Barack Obama sat at one end of the long table with a pile of briefing memos in front of him. There was also a three-ring binder opened to the first page, upon which he had jotted some notes in his elegant-but-still-legible script, and a half-full bottle of his beloved organic green tea.

Several members of his staff and cabinet were seated around him, but his attention was focused on the woman talking from the large monitor at the far end of the room. CDC director Sheila Abbott was dark-haired and pretty in a way that was somehow mature and girlish at the same time. She wore square-framed glasses and an Italian Cavalli business suit. Her preference for high living was well known to the public, and her detractors—the media included—felt it created an air of vanity and excess. They didn't realize she was not only aware of this perception but cultivated it on purpose. On a personal level, she genuinely enjoyed the finer things and the pride they inspired. But more important, it made people underestimate the devastating intelligence that percolated behind those pretty eyes. She had learned long ago that it was better to be underestimated than overestimated.

"What's the fatality count now, Doctor?" the president asked. He was leaning back in the chair and swiveling gently, but his plain expression gave no doubt as to the solemnity of the occasion.

"As of twenty minutes ago, two hundred ninety-seven confirmed deaths. That includes six teachers and sixty-two children; twenty-one physicians, thirty-four nurses, and sixteen EMTs; forty-nine law-enforcement officers and eleven firefighters. The high rate among law-enforcement and firefighters is due to responding to emergency calls without proper protective equipment. When the outbreak first occurred, of course, they didn't know what they were dealing with. In one instance, all but three police officers were infected on the same force when the virus was brought back to the station after a local call."

"And how many more citizens, of any demographic, have been infected?"

"It is impossible to give an exact count, Mr. President. New cases are being reported every few minutes. At present, I would say between six hundred fifty and seven hundred. And it has a mortality rate of ninety-three percent, with the other seven percent either deeply comatose or with severe brain damage and physical disfigurement."

"My God," mumbled Janet Napolitano, Secretary of Homeland Security.

Abbott nodded. "We've never dealt with anything this potent before."

"Has it spread beyond New Jersey?" the president continued.

"Yes, sir. It is now established in New York and Connecticut, eastern Pennsylvania, and northern Delaware. We've tried to restrict movements of citizens within the epicenter of the outbreak in northern New Jersey, but to keep all people confined to their homes is virtually impossible."

. . . *without a presidential order*, was the unspoken sentiment that lingered in the air. Obama didn't react to it, as he didn't believe Abbott was either baiting or insulting him. She had proven herself to be a dedicated, objective, and focused individual, which was why he appointed her to the top of the CDC in the first place. But he was not yet ready to intercede with the executive order she had been advocating for the last few days.

"What about our continental neighbors to the north and south?"

"No cases reported yet in either Canada or Mexico, and that's probably due to a combination of our efforts to keep the public informed and educated and, strangely enough, the media's efforts to keep the public frightened. Nevertheless, it is my belief that the outbreak will cross an international border sooner or later."

Obama nodded. "Do we have any idea what we're dealing with, Sheila? I'm talking about the causative agent now."

Causative agent . . . The president had taken the time to educate himself on the subject at hand rather than rely purely on the support of his advisers. This habit, born of an insatiable curiosity for all things as well as the belief that well-informed leaders made the best decisions, had earned him a great deal of respect; even the begrudging variety of his most determined opponents.

"Not nearly enough," Abbott said. "Based on the samples we have taken from the victims, we know it is a spherical virus rather than elongate. We also believe it to be reverse transcribing, which means it has an RNA template that the virus feeds into a host cell, forcing that cell's DNA to replicate the virus's characteristics. In essence, this means—"

"The virus hijacks a person's cells in order to create copies of itself," Obama said flatly, "like any other virus."

"Yes, that's correct."

"But you have not yet been able to identify exactly which one this is?"

"No, sir. We are examining samples here in Atlanta, and we've sent more to the National Institute for Medical Research in London. We're hoping to come up with a match or something close to one of the roughly six thousand known viruses worldwide, but so far no luck."

"Do you feel it is a mutant? Maybe something entirely new?"

"At this point, I'm not prepared to make that claim. If it *is* new, that may only mean it's new to us. For all we know, it could have existed in nature for millions of years, and we're only seeing it in humans now. Whether or not it is a true mutation remains to be seen. The probability is very high, though, since viruses mutate all the time. It could be a recombinant between two other, more common strains. It could even be another case of a virus that's common in animals migrating to humans and becoming more virulent as it adapts, as we've seen before in recent years."

"And you're sure this is not smallpox? Not even a previously unknown variant?" This question came from the president's press secretary, Robert Gibbs.

If there was one word the media was getting good mileage out of, it was *smallpox*. It seemed to be set in a larger font every day. The fact that there was no evidence thus far of the virus being a new strain of either *Variola major* or *Variola minor*—the only two contagions responsible for smallpox—didn't seem to matter.

"We are, of course, looking into that. Some

symptoms are similar, but then others are not," she replied. "That said, it's inaccurate, not to mention irresponsible, for news outlets to report that this is a smallpox outbreak. Of course, some are saying the end of the world is upon us. So I don't know how much responsibility we can really expect."

"Could it be a new smallpox variant?

"I don't consider that a very strong possibility."

The president and his people had been harping on the smallpox angle for days, in spite of assurances that the odds of this outbreak being related were slim to none. Abbott couldn't help but wonder if they had some intelligence data leading them to believe some terrorist cell had gotten their hands on samples of the virus and successfully integrated it into a workable, deliverable weapon. Since the World Health Organization declared smallpox globally eradicated in 1980, the government had stuck to the official story that the only remaining samples of *Variola* were sitting in locked freezers in two labs around the world—one at CDC headquarters in Atlanta, the other in the WHO repository in Moscow—and kept for the purpose of benign research. But anyone who took the trouble of investigating further, even via the few reliable sources on the Internet, would know that this was far from the truth. Rumors abounded of loose stocks being taken from the Moscow supply in the handbags and briefcases of defecting scientists. Also, Russia's bioweapons program, supposedly dismantled on several occasions, continued with the development of a particularly virulent strain of the virus in direct violation of the Biological Weapons Convention, of which they were a leading signatory. In April of 1992, then-president Boris Yeltsin confessed to several of these violations and, in a show of good faith, ordered that further research be discontinued. This included a deep slash of funding, which left the weapons labs virtually deserted—and leftover strains of *Variola* and other weapons-grade bioagents ripe for the taking. By the second half of the year, only a handful of guards remained, poorly paid when they were paid at all. Intelligence communities around the world screamed that this provided an open invitation for terrorists, but their cries fell on deaf ears. Abbott could not help but wonder if Obama's staff was worried that the current outbreak was somehow related.

The president turned to Gibbs and said, "Tell the press that there is no evidence of a connection to smallpox at this time, and add Sheila's point that to imply otherwise is irresponsible and dangerous—emphasize dangerous—to the public's interest. People are already panicking everywhere; the press has to stop throwing fuel on the fire."

"That won't stop them from writing about the situation."

"No, but hopefully the salient facts will get through."

"Very good, Mr. President."

Obama turned his attention back to Abbott. "Sheila, where are we with treatment at this point?"

"There are tailor-made drugs for other viruses, called antivirals, that interrupt the virus's replication or release process. Ribavirin, for example, when used with interferon medication, has proven an effective nucleoside analogue. But there's no such drug for this virus because it's new, and it often takes months or even years before we understand a specific virus well enough to design an effective medication. Obviously we are already working on this, and hoping for some luck to fall our way. It does happen from time to time. Remember that AZT, also known as zidovudine or Retrovir, was first introduced in the 1960s as a cancer treatment when it was believed cancer was a viral condition. When it didn't work, it was put on a shelf and forgotten. Then someone decided to try it in the mid-'80s as a combatant against AIDS, and suddenly we had the first HIV 'wonder drug.' "

"Wouldn't it be nice if we could replicate that kind of good fortune," the president said.

"Indeed."

"So how are patients being handled in the meantime?"

"For the time being, we're relying on sedation to keep them comfortable during the early stages of the infection. In the later stages, when they begin to experience dementia, heavier doses are necessary. Sometimes a patient has to be restrained."

"And containment of the outbreak? Steps are being taken, of course."

"Yes. We have over a hundred people in the

field—basically walking around the epicenter—looking for people with early symptoms."

"That's a bit primitive, isn't it?" someone seated in the middle of the table grunted.

"It is, but it works. And we have no better options. If this *were* smallpox, we could at least set up vaccination sites. But this is something new, which means a whole new set of rules and procedures, some of the latter being very 'grassroots' in their approach. Beyond that, we are also posting flyers everywhere—not just at hospitals but in every public place you can imagine—urging people to report any case they happen to see or even suspect. The flyers have an easy-to-remember number for the CDC Emergency Operations Center, for which we've hired two hundred extra people to man the phones. We are working fully in conjunction with health officials in New Jersey, and soon in other states I'm sure, to support their local and state emergency plans. But truly, there's only so much that can be done at this stage. To *completely* contain something that spreads this fast and with this kind of virulency . . . a lot of luck would have to be involved, too. That's just the ugly truth of the matter."

"Speaking of vaccines, is there any progress on creating one?" This came from Kathleen Sebelius, the Secretary of Health and Human Services.

"We now have teams working in three separate locations around the clock. But this is time consuming because it's so hit-and-miss. Since this virus is new, creating a vaccine is like reinventing the wheel. It could take a week, a month, or a year. The reason people still get the flu is because the virus mutates from year to year, making it all but impossible to produce a permanent vaccine. Let's hope this one doesn't have that capacity. Also, we can experiment on animals only, which means whatever we eventually come up with might have no effect on humans—or, like other vaccines that have been hastily formulated, it could end up doing as much damage as the disease itself."

She was thinking of the Fort Dix incident. In February of 1976, a young military recruit at New Jersey's Fort Dix died unexpectedly from an unfamiliar strain of the influenza virus that also had characteristics of a contagion infecting domestic hogs. Then it was discovered that thirteen others were infected. The government, fearing the public could not adapt quickly enough to the new variant, ordered a vaccine be developed and delivered as soon as possible. Just weeks after the population began receiving inoculations, however, more than two dozen recipients were dead while others developed nerve damage, some to the point of permanent paralysis. Further inoculations were canceled, and the government became the target of lawsuits totaling more than a billion dollars. Ironically, no other deaths from the original Fort Dix outbreak occurred, and the illness passed. Nevertheless, many people became gun-shy about vaccines thereafter, never realizing that the great majority worked exactly as intended and were completely safe.

"Okay, Sheila," the president said, "thank you for the update. Keep your people working on this around the clock."

"I will, Mr. President. Thank you."

The screen went blank and most of the attendees filed out of the room. The president, however, remained seated, as did CIA Director Leon Panetta.

"Leon, do you have reason to believe there's a terrorist connection to this?"

Panetta, the affable son of Italian immigrants who would go on to nine terms in the House of Representatives and serve as President Bill Clinton's chief of staff before becoming Obama's "top spy," said, "There is no evidence to suggest it as of yet. Naturally, several groups are claiming responsibility, but none are credible. In the upper levels of terrorist society, no one's saying a word." The president didn't seem eased by his comments. "Do you have a specific concern, sir?"

Obama shook his head. "No, but it's something we have to consider. I'm trying to improve our relations around the world, but it would naïve to think that it could be accomplished everywhere. Syria, Iran, North Korea . . . Hezbollah, Islamic Jihad, Hamas . . . the Taliban, the remaining fragments of Al-Qaeda . . . There are still plenty of people who would like to see America brought to its knees."

"No doubt."

"If this does turn out to be something manufactured rather than natural, I'll have no choice but to respond."

Panetta nodded. "Yes, Mr. President."

"Not what you want to be doing with one hand while holding out an olive branch with the other."

"No, sir."

The president spent another moment in his private thoughts. Then, "Okay, keep the agency's ear to the ground, and the rest of us will keep our fingers crossed."

"Yes, Mr. President."

"And please operate *quietly*. If the press gets wind of any suspicions on our part . . ."

"Of course, Mr. President."

"Thank you."

Ahmed Aaban el Shalizeh stood watching a large CRT television propped on a munitions trunk turned on its side. A small cadre of men lingered around him, but he was the one a random observer would notice first. His robes were tattered and filthy, the leather on his bullet belt dried and rotted. His black turban matched his beard almost perfectly, although the latter was starting to show the first signs of silver. It was his eyes, however, that frosted everyone he met—the left one was as blue as the Pacific, whereas the right was cloudy and lifeless, an orb of dead tissue. Shalizeh had constructed the legend of losing half his vision in the first battle of his career, a firefight in the Malakand region of Pakistan where he was born and raised. The truth was a bit more prosaic—his mother, naturally left-handed, destroyed it through repeated strikes to that side of his head. Shalizeh had cultivated many dramatic stories about himself over the years, to the point where even he had begun to forget where the facts ended and the fiction began.

The makeshift camp was located in a remote desert sector of Iran's southwestern province of Khuzestan. It was originally intended as a hydroelectric plant until construction ceased due to lack of funding. The main building had a slanting, corrugated roof and large bay doors at either end. A twin pair of smaller buildings, made from cinder blocks and with no glass in the windows, stood on either side. Beyond that were about two dozen canvas tents of varying sizes. A gravel road snaked its way to the site, and a pair of aging RVs were parked at the spot where it abruptly terminated. A swift river bordered by scant shrubbery hugged the encampment on the eastern side, and a rope bridge had been built immediately after the current residents arrived. About a hundred yards beyond the adjacent shore lay the foothills of a nameless mountain, and within those foothills was a network of caves that provided suitable cover when necessary. Shalizeh said they could hide in the caves when foreign intelligence agencies flew overhead, either in manned or unmanned planes, to take pictures of them. But they had been here just under one year and so far that hadn't happened yet.

Al Jazeera reported the latest figures from America. On the screen, they showed random images from around the country to underscore the horror—bodies being taken out of a home in shiny black bags, a screaming baby with a hideously swollen face, the unsteady cell phone movie of an infected man jumping from the top of an apartment building. A middle-aged woman in a business suit was crying as someone off camera held out a microphone. Between hitches and sobs, she said that her husband and twelve-year-old son had contracted the illness while she was away on a company trip, and when she got back she found them both dead. It wasn't the illness that had ultimately taken their lives, however, but a bizarre joint suicide in which they pointed shotguns at each other's heads.

Shalizeh turned, grinning. "Wonderful," he said in his native Urdu. "Simply wonderful. This is truly a sign from the heavens." He walked over and draped his arms around two of his men. "Did I not tell you? Did I not foresee it?"

A graduate of Bahria University with a degree in psychology, he was charismatic, intelligent, passionate . . . and thoroughly crazy. He could quote the Koran from memory and was a superb storyteller, dazzling his followers with battlefield tales whose authenticity was doubtable at best. But beneath the intriguing exterior he was a sociopath, plain and simple. He and his men had killed on many occasions—the difference was they believed they were doing it for a cause, whereas he did it largely for pleasure.

"Your faith has not been misplaced," he continued, addressing the entire crowd now. "All is happening as I have predicted, and Lashkar-al-Islam will rise once again. *We will rise again!*" He removed his rifle from his shoulder and fired it into the ceiling. There were hundreds of holes in the corrugated surface from similar outbursts.

The others did likewise, cheering like giddy children. They were twelve miles from the nearest settlement, mostly to discourage escapees. Shalizeh had already tracked down two. It was rumored he shot both in the legs, then buried them up to their necks in the sand. It was this kind of over-the-top lunacy that had slowly diminished his standing in the fundamentalist community. At its peak, Lashkar-al-Islam received weaponry, training, and financial aid from sympathetic factions as diverse as Abu Sayyaf, Islamic Jihad, and the Palestine Liberation Front. But Shalizeh's ultraradical tactics, too gruesome even for "mainstream" terrorists, drove away these supporters one by one until the organization was hanging by a single thread—a thread held by the government of Iran. Then the Iranian people elected a new president, and Shalizeh was not only cut off but targeted as well. He narrowly escaped capture and soon became obsessed with two objectives—revenge against Iran's new reformist administration, and returning Lashkar to its former glory. The opportunity to do both would come, he had said repeatedly.

Now he believed that opportunity had finally arrived.

He walked over to one of his lieutenants, a Syrian named Ashur, and said, "Contact Abdulaziz and send him what he needs." The others braced themselves. The two men had not been getting along lately, mostly on this point.

"My leader, please, this is not a good idea."

"My friend, trust m—"

"I beg of you, do not do this."

"I assure you—"

"Please, don't."

They squabbled for a few more seconds—an eternity to the spectators—until, in one startlingly swift motion, Shalizeh struck Ashur in the chin with the butt of his rifle. Ashur collapsed with a groan, blood leaking from his mouth.

Shalizeh stood over him for a moment, his eyes wild. Then he turned to another of his followers and said, "Are *you* willing to follow my orders?"

The unfortunate soul he had picked, a relatively low-ranking soldier named Kala, nodded quickly. "Then *go*!" Shalizeh barked, and Kala fled.

Ashur got to his feet slowly. Shalizeh took no notice of this, turning back to the television instead. Now they were showing a night clip of several buildings on fire in the Chicago area. The caption read, WIDESPREAD LOOTING IN MAJOR CITIES AS ILLNESS SPREADS.

A smile returned to Shalizeh's lips.

SEVEN

It was one of those dreams where you knew you were in it, knew you couldn't escape it, and—perhaps worst of all—knew what was coming.

Beck was in the rented convertible—the one that should've been returned to Avis after the conference in Connecticut but was now costing the CDC $29.95 per day plus gas and mileage—motoring along northern New Jersey's Route 17. The top was down on another postcard-perfect day, the Appalachians majestic in the distance. Route 17 was a major artery, all the land on either side developed within an inch of its life. Car dealerships, home-improvement centers, anonymous office buildings, health clubs, strip malls. Since this was a dream, most of it was a blur.

Cara wasn't in the passenger seat; she had decided to spend another day at the lab working on vaccines. He wasn't sure where he was going; that information had not been included. He had heard once that dreams were, in fact, complete in their chronologies. But the mind protected the soul by blocking out most of the hurtful segments. If they didn't, many of us would wake with our sanity erased. We'd end up in state institutions, strapped to beds and screaming at the ceiling.

There were a few other vehicles around. He'd been on 17 many times now, and the thickness of traffic had steadily diminished. People went into hiding, or packed their things and moved on. The state had issued warnings not to do so. Roadblocks had been set up, but mostly as a bluff. Unless a federal order was handed down, law-enforcement agencies couldn't actually stop anyone from traveling. Even if they tried, the locals knew every obscure back road. It was said you could go anywhere in New Jersey without touching a highway. Beck had thought it was a myth, but not anymore. It was the most densely populated state in the nation, and with that swollen population came excessive development. Aside from the Pine Barrens in the southern third, the Garden State was now a landscape of concrete and steel. If you wanted to leave and knew your way around, no one was going to stop you.

The stereo was on, spinning one of his beloved '70s CDs. Strangely, though, the song playing was Michael Martin Murphey's "Wildfire." Released in June of 1975, it ostensibly told the story of a lost horse and its owner but was metaphorically a reference to escaping a miserable life for something better. While melodically stunning, certain lyrical passages had always disturbed him. It was one of the few '70s classics that, even now, he could not stand to hear. For this alone he wished he could force himself awake.

An eighteen-wheeler roared past him on the left. The driver blew the horn in several frantic bleats, as if trying to communicate a coherent thought. Beck glanced over and saw that the windows were smoked, giving the rig a sinister appearance. As it rattled past, he saw the letters D.O.A. painted huge on the side of the trailer. A chill blew through him, and his heart began drumming. Then, as the rig dropped its clutch and began barreling away, he tried to scream—*No!*—but only hot air came out. He tried again and again. A distant part of him knew you couldn't muster any vocal force in a dream, any more than you could stop yourself from falling or outrun the swarm of killer bees that was just behind you, their tiny eyes trained on the soft flesh of your neck. But he kept trying.

The rig swerved into the middle lane, in front of him, the horn still blasting. Beck pressed the gas pedal to the floor, and that helped close the distance somewhat. But it wasn't enough . . . wouldn't be enough. . . . He kept on blowing hot air with his useless dream-voice.

The overpass was coming up quickly. It was a pedestrian bridge, with an inward-curved cage along the flanks. He saw the woman running up the steps on the right. When she reached the top she looked to the road, to the rig. As it drew closer, she moved toward the middle. There was a gap in the cage for some reason. She stopped there, and Beck could see she was holding a baby in her arms.

The truck driver stopped working the horn. Then all other sounds ceased—no wheels rattling, no Michael Martin Murphey singing "Wildfire," not even the hoarse whisper of his attempted screams. He had become frozen now and could do nothing but watch. He felt a peculiar pressure on both sides of his head.

The dream went into slow motion. Just before the truck reached the bridge, the woman jumped. Her dress fluttered up behind her, revealing the blackened, vesicle-covered legs. They had been pretty once, the kind of legs that turned heads in bars and on beaches. But that time was long gone.

His vision and perspective somehow zoomed forward, and he saw her and the child clearly for an instant. The face was swollen and disfigured beyond all recognition. Even her loved ones wouldn't be able to identify her anymore. She still wore a diamond-studded watch, which had become nearly buried in the puffed flesh of her wrist. The baby was wrapped in a blanket, stained from the oozing fluids. All Beck could see of the child was its eyes, which were wide and lifeless, and had turned a deep ruby red from the bleeding.

Then she and the child fell from view, normal speed resumed, and all sounds returned. A scream came up effortlessly now, from the deepest parts of him.

He jerked awake in the hotel bed, clutching one of the pillows so tight that his fingers ached. His heart was pounding, his breathing rapid and shallow. He sat up and massaged his forehead, waiting for reality to flood in and chase away the last of the fading images. He noticed the morning sunlight trying to reach in beneath the heavy shades and turned to look at the clock on the nightstand—6:45. He also realized his cell phone was ringing.

The incident had occurred three days earlier, as he was heading to a local diner to get some lunch. Most of the details had been the same—the nice weather, the big rig, the fact that Cara had been absent as she worked with the vaccine team. But there were differences, too—the song that had been playing was "Dancing in the Moonlight" by King Harvest, and the three characters on the side of the truck had been G.O.D., the acronym for Newark trucking company, Guaranteed Overnight Delivery.

Also, the woman wore a black dress, not white.

She disappeared from view, having timed the jump perfectly, and the speeding rig connected with a dull thump. From his vantage point about a hundred feet back, Beck saw the explosion of blood and bone as it cascaded from either side of the cab. It was a sight he would not forget if he lived another thousand years.

The driver jammed on his brakes, smoke rising from around the tires as they cooked on the pavement. Beck stopped behind him and jumped out, literally—right over the door like in the movies. He ran down the driver's side of the rig screaming, *"Don't go near it! Don't touch the blood!"* He realized later, trembling as he drove back to the hotel room with his appetite long gone, that he had used the word *it* because he didn't know what else to say. He couldn't use *her* or *them,* because there wasn't enough left of either victim. The driver, half out of the cab and looking as pale as an autumn moon, obeyed, somehow understanding that Beck was the authority figure here. He climbed down slowly and sidestepped into the highway's left lane just to satiate his morbid curiosity, then went to the cement median and threw up on the other side.

Beck guarded the site until the police arrived. Route 17 remained closed for nearly nine hours as cleanup crews in hazard suits meticulously body-bagged all the remains they could find; then a local maintenance team in protective suits scrubbed the road with hot water and bleach. The woman, as it turned out, was a twenty-two-year-old single mother who had recently been laid off from her job as a receptionist in a small private law firm and was drowning in credit card debt. One of her former coworkers would later give the statement that she had been contemplating suicide anyway. The child's name was Cory.

Beck realized it was the ringing cell phone that had pulled him out of the dream, and he had never been so grateful. He took it from the nightstand and unfolded it.

"Yes?"

"Time to get up, old man."

"Bright-eyed and bushy-tailed, are we?"

"Sure am."

He smiled. "I still can't believe you're a morning person."

"I've been up for a while now. I've already gone down and bought us breakfast. A yummy cinnamon roll for me. And for you, a bland and tasteless bran muffin so you'll crap better."

"Appreciated."

"Get your sorry butt out of bed. I'll be there in ten minutes."

"Right."

She made good on her promise and knocked on the door exactly ten minutes later. They ate quietly at the small circular table while he stared into the screen on his laptop, studying for what seemed like the hundredth time the information he'd collected over the last six days. With the help of a software application that had been written specifically for epidemiological utility, he was able to sort and compare quantitative data in a mind-boggling variety of ways. On the current table, he was trying to detect any patterns on the basis of the victims' ages.

Porter leaned over and gave it a quick glance. "Anything?"

He shook his head. "No, nothing unusual. The virus doesn't seem to discriminate on the basis of age. Not age, race, gender, weight, or even profession."

"Except doctors and nurses," Porter said.

"Yeah."

Beck had a natural genius for detecting trends and patterns within what appeared to be an otherwise meaningless jumble of information. "Finding the underlying order within the chaos," as he said. He was so good at it, in fact, that he had been approached by the CIA while an undergraduate student for possible employment. The ease with which he exercised this talent was even a source of mild guilt for him, particularly when he watched his peers struggle under the same circumstances.

He hit the ALT and TAB buttons simultaneously and toggled to a map. It was a simple line drawing of northern New Jersey, segmented and color-coded by county. Red dots represented known cases of the infection. The greatest concentration, like a large drop of paint with spatter marks around it, was in the Ramsey–Mahwah area. As Beck increased the magnification, the paint drop became more particulate.

"We're certainly in the epicenter, at least in terms of the outbreak. That much is clear. But it doesn't mean this is where it began."

"Someone could've contracted it in China," Porter said, "then taken a plane back here while it was incubating in their body, right?"

"Yes. The origin of the contagion could be anywhere. Happens all the time. This is what's called a common-source epidemic in the sense that the outbreak is attributable to a common noxious influence that's been shared by all persons within a sample group. But that doesn't automatically mean this is the virus's point of origin. I could produce pie charts and bar graphs until my fingers froze, but an epidemic curve isn't going to reveal that. That's where the *real* detective work comes in."

Porter leaned down to get a better look at the data. Beck marveled inwardly at the intensity with which she studied it. There was a time when he would've bet anything the empirical side of epidemiology would've bored her to death. But she always seemed absorbed by it.

"You're using all standard metrics, of course?"

"Of course." He smiled. "You've been doing some homework?"

"I have indeed."

"Tell me what you're looking at. Impress me."

"Well, overall, you've collected many simple counts. Number of men, number of women, number of adults, number of children. Stuff like that."

"Of course. This helps reveal both regularities and irregularities."

"And based on this information here—" She pointed to a small rectangle at the left side of the screen with the number 15,622. "—I believe you're trying to determine an incidence rate."

"Which is—?"

"The occurrence of a disease within a time frame."

"And how do we get that?"

"By dividing the number of known cases that occur within that time frame by the fixed population of an area."

"Bingo."

"The fifteen K is the total population in question."

"Yep, in this case the town of Ramsey. What else?"

"By listing the number of deaths in the same region in relation to *when* they occurred, you can determine what's called prevalence. Once you have enough of that data, you can extrapolate a long-term number. For example, you can come up with a prevalence rate of three-point-five percent within a given population during the course of, say, one year."

"Very, very good."

"And once you have enough data amassed, you can start building statistical pictures of everything from case fatality rates and proportional mortality ratios to cause-specific rates based on age, gender, and other factors."

Beck sat back in his chair, hands clutching the armrests, and beamed. "Bravo, my young apprentice, bravo. I am most pleased."

"Ha."

"And here I didn't think you like the mathematical side of epi."

"I don't," she said quickly, taking a bite of her cinnamon roll and glancing at the latest CNN report on TV. "It's boring as shit. But I also know it's necessary, so I'm going to learn it. Hardly fun, though."

"I disagree. Hunting through stats is like hunting for buried treasure. That's a real thrill."

"Right. All you need now is a bow tie, a pocket protector, and to be stuffed into your own locker." Beck laughed. "So what if the contagion really was produced by a terror organization, like a lot of the media outlets are implying?"

"Sheila and I talked about that yesterday. Until we get confirmation of terrorist involvement—and so far there is *none*—part of my job is to continue focusing on the origin. I can't afford to be as blasé as the media. I have to find out where this thing started. Sometimes that isn't possible, by the by."

"You wrote about that in your book, about the *E. coli* outbreak in 2006. How investigators traced it to that food company in California, and how it was delivered to consumers through bagged spinach. But they never determined how the spinach got contaminated in the first place."

"Right. Sometimes we never figure it out. But it always helps when we do. It helps not just for the current situation, but to obviate future outbreaks as well."

"So you keep digging for clues?"

He nodded once, his attention still focused on the screen. "We keep digging for clues."

Porter marveled at his calm persistence. The Nancy Drew side of epidemiology, as she thought of it, was slow and tedious and sometimes required hours of work that produced little or no reward. He'd been at it almost nonstop since they arrived. More than a hundred interviews of relatives and family members, and nearly another hundred from Ben, who was in constant contact either by phone or email. Some of the interviewees were infected themselves, others so distraught, they were barely able to communicate. Beck was thrown out of one home for being "ghoulish," while the crying mother of a deceased teenager clung to him so hard that her fingernails drew blood from his arm. Of the 1,322 cases they recorded, both in morbidity (illness) and mortality (death), there didn't seem to be any trends or patterns. Six hundred sixty-eight were male, 654 female. Ages ranged from three months to ninety-two years. Some had blue-collar professions, others white, and the rest were either unemployed or retired. Caucasian, African, Asian, European . . . heterosexual, homosexual, asexual . . . Christian, Jewish, Muslim, atheist . . . The virus truly was, as Porter called it, "an equal-opportunity killer." In times like this, she really thought she'd end up with a career in lab work rather than out in the field like Beck. At least the information he was gathering was being fed into the CDC's data bank back in Atlanta: a massive pool of empirical information, augmented almost daily, then shared with health-care professionals around the world.

"So I assume by the tone of your voice that I'll be alone again today?" Beck said, turning off the laptop and shutting the lid. This was a sign he was ready to go. He would tuck it into his bag and be out the door within minutes. Porter actually worried about him, about how hard he was pushing himself. Even though she was in the hotel room a few doors down, she had determined that he was sleeping only about five hours a night, eating on the fly, and taking few breaks.

"Yeah, I'll keep working, trying to come up with an effective antiviral."

"Fieldwork is where it's at."

"Finding an antiviral could stop this thing dead in its tracks. That's important, too, y'know."

"I certainly do, and I'm sure they appreciate the help."

Antiviral drugs were relatively new in the field of health care, the first having been developed in the 1960s to treat social diseases. Methods of development at the time were primitive to say the least, featuring viruses in cell cultures that were bombarded with an array of chemicals until the contagion showed some decrease in virulency. Even if effective drugs could be developed, this approach did not provide information on the how or why. The first significant breakthrough came in the 1980s, when gene sequencing became more common. Once researchers were able to understand a virus's invasive process step by step, it was easier to find "target chemicals" to inhibit it at some point along the way. Over the next twenty years, many antiviral medications were developed, each aimed at a different virus. Some attacked the initial attachment and entry into the healthy host cell, others focused on the genomic replication, and a few hit the virion assembly toward the end of the cycle. The difficulty came with the fact that each virus needed its own custom-made chemical cocktail, and simply stumbling upon the correct recipe could take weeks, months, or years . . . or might never be discovered at all.

"So where to today?"

Beck said, "I'm backtracking the infection of a young man who worked in a video store. He passed away yesterday, but I spoke with him three days ago and he said a woman came in coughing shortly before he developed symptoms. He said she stood out because she was the only one in the store. Kept hacking away and at one point asked for a tissue. Her nose was running so badly that he gave her a paper towel."

"Delightful."

"Yeah. It'll probably lead right back to the circular nightmare we're stuck in, but you never know."

"Good luck."

"Thanks."

He slipped his bag over his shoulder and headed for the door. Just as he got there, he turned back and said, "By the way, here's a delightful detail—the woman in question might be the same one the police found hanging from her ceiling fan. The one whose head came off."

"Neat."

"I thought you'd enjoy that. See you later."

"Bye."

Dennis stood in the kitchen of the cabin two days later, staring through the curtained window over the old porcelain sink with eyes that had been puffed and reddened by exhaustion. He was holding a cup of coffee that was rapidly growing colder, but he was hesitant to take a sip because of unsuccessful attempts to keep his hand from trembling. The Catskill Mountains, under a lazy run of scant clouds in the distance, looked like an image from a postcard.

In times past, Dennis had gazed upon this

dramatic vista and felt a deep gratitude for everything good in his life—his family's health, his not-great-but-decent job, the money he and Andi had meticulously squirreled away. . . . Hell, that he even lived in a place and time where he *could* have health and a decent job and a little spare cash. With over a hundred countries in the world, he could just as easily have been born in some hellhole like North Korea or Cuba. For whatever reason, the view through this window made him think about those kinds of things.

Not today, though. The nightmare images kept running through his mind like some masochistic slide show. He saw them in his sleep, when he was awake, and in the dozy half-minded state that drew a border between the two.

One of the most persistent subsets involved the kindly Jack McLaughlin lying dead on the front lawn. First there was the crumpled heap of his body in the dim glow of the streetlamp. From there Dennis's imagination would have a field day. One time Dennis walked to the body, rolled it over, and found it halfway rotted and boiling with maggots. Another time a laughing Jack was standing at the street corner with his octagonal STOP sign in hand, the blood from the gunshot wound pumping out like red paint. "I made sure they crossed okay," he said in a horrifically garbled voice. Then Billy and Chelsea bounded up wearing their bright school clothes and their backpacks, their smiling faces distorted by the infection.

The other group arose from the road trip the

Jensens took to get here. Normally this was one of the most enjoyable features of their cabin retreat. In the autumn, the sight of the trees radiant with bright foliage took Dennis and Andi's breath away. In the spring, the first signs of life after a long winter's slumber inspired thoughts of rebirth and renewal, putting them in a reflective, taking-stock kind of mood. And Chelsea was delightful with her enthusiastic accounting of each landmark that underscored another milestone in the journey, another layer of their New Jersey "everyday world" falling away as those of their "cabin world" in upstate New York gradually replaced it. There was the busy strip mall visible from the merge that took them from I-287 to I-87, at which point Chelsea would announce in an airline captain's voice that they were now out of New Jersey and ". . . cruising comfortably through the Empire State." Then the rest stop just before the junction with Route 84, marking the midpoint in the trip. "Halfway are we and I gotta go pee!" she would sing every time, sending Billy into a giggling delirium. Finally there was Watkins Steak House, large and looming, situated atop the hillside by the entrance to NY-28—the final leg of the journey. Dennis would say to Andi, "Mmm, steak. Maybe we should stop." Then Chelsea's expected response of, "No, Daddy! I just want to *get* there. . . ." This had become so routine that Dennis looked at her in the rearview mirror just before they reached this point and smiled, and she smiled back because she knew it was coming. Then, of course, they followed their script anyway.

There had been no such playfulness this time, because this wasn't a pleasure trip but an escape. And the layers that were stripped away were not of their pleasant day-to-day life but of a living nightmare. The sight of McLaughlin's body lying on the wet grass had struck a ghastly, discordant note that set the tone for the rest of the journey. And the startling contrast between this excursion and those past was such that it felt as if they had taken a different route altogether. First, they had never gone under the cover of darkness; that in itself smothered any chance for cheerfulness. Then the fact that the strip mall and Watkins Steak House had both been closed. Considering the lateness of the hour, this would've been the case on any calendar day. But the vinyl CLOSED UNTIL FURTHER NOTICE banner that hung across the mall's windows squelched any possibility of dismissing it as routine.

There had been traffic, more so than one would expect at midnight on a weekday, even in the oppressively overpopulated tri-state area. Under normal circumstances and when the weather was warm, Dennis would occasionally wave to other motorists with the unconditional friendliness that surfaces in some people when they're in tourist mode. But such civility didn't seem to be high on anyone's list this time, including his. Like everyone else, he kept the windows up and his eyes on the road. And, he suspected, they all had their doors locked.

Traffic was sluggish early on, all four lanes on I-287 filled to capacity and moving with the difficulty of a snake just out of hibernation. It stretched for miles, all the headlights glittering like a heavy diamond bracelet. What Dennis found particularly unnerving at this point was the quiet—no roaring engines, no music blasting, and, most unusual for this part of the world, no one blowing their horns. Everyone just rolled along in petrified obedience.

The traffic thinned as the journey progressed; at least that aspect had a familiarity to it. By the time Watkins came into view and they eased onto NY-28, around three thirty in the morning, Dennis began to relax a little. *We're just about there,* he thought in the darkness; Chelsea and Billy were now asleep and Andi very nearly so. *We're going to make it.* Soon they were nestled in the protective hills and valleys of the Catskills, cruising along a twisting road lit only by the occasional sodium light.

Then the roadblock appeared.

It had been arranged—unintentionally, no doubt—in sets of two. There were two state police cars parked crookedly with their lights swirling, two sawhorses with reflective orange stripes, and two officers standing ready. There were also two road flares, spitting sparks and billowing smoke like a kamikaze'd battleship.

Damn.

He'd heard something on the radio about roadblocks in some areas, but he didn't think they'd be an issue way out here. It wasn't exactly the Middle of Nowhere, but it wasn't the entrance to the Lincoln Tunnel, either.

Dammit.

One of the officers—a kid of no more than twenty-five, with his cap tilted forward as if to compensate for this—came around to the front of the sawhorse and waved for Dennis first to slow down (one flattened hand slowly bouncing an invisible basketball), then stop (same hand held upright). As he walked toward the van, Dennis noticed the surgical mask draped over his shirt. The cop removed his hat, pulled the mask by its elastic loop over his head, and replaced the hat again, all in one fluid motion. Dennis got the impression he had performed this action quite a few times this night.

He knuckle-tapped Andi's arm. Her eyes fluttered and she murmured something nonsensical, as she always did when prematurely awoken. Then, as the kid came alongside the van, Dennis lowered his window. There was a silver nameplate just above the officer's shirt pocket—A. JETTICK. In a second gesture of seemingly choreographed smoothness, he drew a long flashlight from his belt, clicked it on, and shone it in Dennis's face.

"Hello," Dennis said in an attempt to start things off on a friendly note. "Can I—?"

"Where are you headed?"

Right to business. "To Haroldson's Ridge. I own one of the cabins up there."

"Can I see some identification, please?"

"Sure." He pulled out his wallet and handed over his license. "Do you also want my insurance card and regis—?"

"Just ID, please."

"Okay . . ."

The officer shone the light a few inches from the license, making Dennis wonder if it might melt.

"You are Dennis Jensen?"

"Yes sir."

"Six twenty-two Guidry Avenue?"

"Yes."

"Carlton Lakes, New Jersey?"

"That's right."

The light came up into his face again, then back to the license photo. Then to him, then the photo. Dennis felt the overwhelming urge to sigh loudly in a gesture of protest, but good sense vetoed the idea. He had never been one to antagonize law enforcement, even as a teenager; it never seemed like a particularly smart idea. He did, however, turn briefly toward Andi and roll his eyes.

Then, back to Jettick—"Is there a flood or something, Officer? Is the road out?"

The cop continued studying the license as if he hadn't heard, then said, "No, road's fine."

"Oh, then wh—?"

"You are coming from your home in Carlton Lakes now?"

"Yes, that's correct."

"May I ask why?"

"I'm sorry?"

"Why did you decide to come up here now? And why so late?"

He's probing me, Dennis realized, and felt himself tighten up. He decided in that instant to play it as close to the truth as possible, but reveal no more than necessary.

"We're getting away for a while."

"Is that so?"

"Yes, sir."

The flashlight came up again. This time the beam was directed through the smoked window of the side door. Jettick did display one moment of consideration when he pulled the light off the faces of the two children when he realized they were sleeping. His interest then turned to the copious pile of supplies in the back, which occupied nearly the entire space.

"That's a lot to bring along for just a little getaway, isn't it?"

Dennis shrugged. "We're not planning on staying any longer than we have to."

"Uh-huh." His gaze lingered a moment longer; then he tucked the flashlight under his arm and turned back. The light beam slanted up into space like a beacon. "You're here because of the outbreak, is that it?"

"Yes, that's right."

"You didn't say that before."

"You didn't ask before. Besides, what's the difference *why* we came? None of us are infected."

"I have no way of knowing that. We're not supposed to let anyone through. We've had no cases up here, and we have no intention of getting any."

"I fully appreciate that, but as I said, we're all clean. If you don't believe me, you're welcome to call my sister, Elaine Jensen, who works as a nurse at one of the hospitals along the Jersey Shore. We went to her for a full series of tests a few days ago. We're here because *we* don't want to get infected, either."

Dennis's conviction appeared to rob Jettick of some of his own. He tapped the driver's license on the back of his other hand, his eyes shifting about with uncertainty. In the ensuing quiet, Dennis noticed a symphony of insectine chirps and buzzes that apparently had been playing in the background the whole time.

"I'll return in a moment," Jettick said finally, then walked briskly away.

"Thanks . . ."

"What are we going to do if he won't let us pass?" Andi asked in a whisper.

"I don't know." Dennis said this with an absent shake of the head as he continued watching Jettick. The kid first stopped to talk to his partner; this lasted no more than a few seconds. Then he climbed into the squad car and got on the radio. His face was illuminated by the glow of some device attached to the dashboard, which Dennis eventually realized was a small computer monitor. *Modern technology.*

"We can't go back," Andi said.

"I agree a hundred percent."

"So?"

Dennis ran quickly through a list of options—try to bribe the kid, jam the gas and blast his way through, threaten a lawsuit. . . . None of these ideas sounded like they'd work out too well. He glanced briefly in the rearview mirror and thanked God the kids were still asleep.

When Jettick put down the radio mic and turned to the computer screen, Dennis felt a bolt of shock as a hideous realization struck. *What if he finds out about Jack McLaughlin? What if his body's already been found, and there's an APB out on me?* He didn't even know if law enforcement called them APBs anymore, but they probably had something very similar—and better.

"Uh-oh . . ."

Andi turned. "What?"

"Wh . . . what if he finds out ab—?"

Jettick threw open the door and seemed to spring out of the vehicle.

"Oh shit."

Dennis could swear there was something different about the way the kid was looking at him now. He seemed warier, more alert. Also, while his left hand held Dennis's license, the right was resting on his hip holster. *His weapon. Oh God, he's getting ready to use his weapon.* Dennis's heart began booming, and sweat broke out everywhere. His breathing became rapid and shallow.

"No . . ."

Jettick came up alongside the van, taking position in nearly the identical spot as before.

"I'm sorry, Mr. Jensen, but I can't let you through at this time."

"Huh?" Dennis's hand had gone to his chest, although he didn't remember doing it.

"I cannot get in touch with our dispatcher in order to corroborate your story, or to contact Brick Memorial Hospital about Elaine Jensen."

"You . . ." It took him a moment to register all the implications of what Jettick was saying. *He doesn't know about McLaughlin after all. He has no idea.*

"I'm sorry," Dennis continued hoarsely, followed by a quick clearing of the throat. "You can't get in touch with your dispatcher?"

"No, not at this time."

"Is your radio broken?"

"She's not responding."

"Oh." The relief that had been irrigating Dennis's soul was now transforming into confidence. "Well, how long do you think it'll be before she's back?"

"It shouldn't be too long."

"You don't know for sure?"

"I have no way of knowing where she is."

Hicksville, Dennis suddenly thought nastily. *If a dispatcher suddenly took off in Carlton Lakes without leaving someone to man the radio, Chief Doyle would make sure she never came back.*

"Okay, so why don't you or your partner, or one of the officers, just follow us up to the cabin? It's only a few miles from here. I can show you the deed as soon as we walk in the door. For that matter, the fact that we have the keys to *open* the door should be enough."

"I'm sorry, sir, but I can't do that."

This was the point at which Dennis Jensen began to feel his patience slipping away. He opened his mouth to fire a retort, intent on leveling the kid's smug arrogance in spite of a distant voice telling him he would later regret it. Then he was distracted by a bright flash in the rearview mirror. When he looked up he saw it again—not one, but a pair of lights, small and round, spaced well apart. *Headlights.* They were there for an instant, then gone. The car was swerving crazily as it came up the road behind them.

As he leaned out the window to look back, he heard the screech of rubber on pavement, followed by the hollow bash of metal on metal as the vehicle struck the guardrail. Jettick produced his flashlight like a magician, revealing a red compact: a Honda Civic perhaps. And, in spite of the smoke now leaking from the partially crumbled hood, the car bounced away from the rail and continued to—

—head straight for us.

"Shit!"

The following things happened in the next three seconds: Dennis dropped the automatic gearshift from park to drive, said to Jettick defiantly, "This guy's gonna run into me, so I'm moving!" then jammed the gas pedal and lurched forward, swerving around the sawhorses to the right and coming up alongside the squad car with the swirling lights. Jettick's partner, who looked to be a bit older but had a dullard's expression that suggested he wasn't quite so bright, put a hand up to signal that Dennis should stop, which he did. Then Dennis and Andi turned back to watch what happened next. So rapt was their attention that they were only faintly aware that the sudden, jackrabbit motion had jarred both their children out of sleep.

Jettick lifted his own hand and yelled for the driver to stop. Then his thin figure—nothing more than a dark silhouette against the growing headlights—dove away to avoid being struck. The vehicle made one last maddened, bumper car swerve before slamming into the iron ribbon of guardrail that prevented it from sailing into the darkness and embarking on a sheer drop of at least a hundred feet to certain death. What Dennis saw next would make him think it would've been the more merciful option.

The passenger door swung open, and an indistinct shape dropped out in a heap. In the dark it looked like it could've been a load of laundry the driver had simply pushed out with the flat of his foot. Then the form began to move, and Jettick shone his beloved flashlight on it. There was a woman of nondescript age, wearing jeans and a dusty purple short-sleeved T-shirt. The elephantine arm that was trying unsuccessfully to get her up off the pavement—she looked like she was doing a slow push-up—was mottled with weals and boils. When she turned briefly into the flashlight beam, it revealed the face of a monstrous, Mrs. Potato Head–like creature with a set of quick pen strokes marking off where the eyes, nostrils, and mouth used to be. But what made her appearance truly nightmarish, Dennis would realize later, was that in spite of her malformation, she still managed to convey emotion through facial expression. Dennis had never seen such suffering in another human being.

The woman tried in vain to get moving again, like a bug that had just been slapped but wasn't quite dead yet. Then she rolled over onto her back and lay still. This was when Dennis realized why she had only been using one arm—the other was holding a child against her. It was very small, probably not even a year old, and wrapped in a brightly colored blanket that was now ruined with blood. Its tiny head flopped back like that of a doll, the mouth open, before it ultimately rolled off its mother's chest and disappeared from view. There was little doubt in Dennis's mind the child was already dead.

Wrenching away his terrified but fascinated gaze, he looked into the cab of the vehicle to see who'd been driving. Jettick's flashlight beam did not follow, and Dennis could see only another dark shape. It was a man, that much was distinguishable, slumped to one side with his head against the window. Like the rest of his family, he was no longer exercising the God-given right of independent movement.

The Jettick kid was frozen, his legs spread apart and his right hand still holding the flashlight by his right ear. His other arm hung down and a few inches away from his body, like that of a gunslinger ready to draw. Dennis got the impression he simply didn't know what to do, his gung-ho nature unable to override his youth and lack of experience. In spite of whatever training he might have received, this situation was beyond him.

Although later he would barely remember doing it, and in spite of Andi's voluble protests, Dennis jumped out of the car and yelled, *"Don't go anywhere near them! Don't* touch *them!"* Jettick looked halfway back—a sign that he'd heard—but didn't appear any more enlightened as to what he should do next. Then the mother began moving again. She turned to Jettick, her bloody hair spilling into her face, and tried to speak. What came out was not diction but rather a garble of choked and dissonant sounds. Then she coughed once, her entire body seizing together like tempered coil, and a gush of discolored fluid exited her mouth in a lazy geyser.

That was enough for the kid. He strode lithely to the side of the road and, just getting his hat off and mask down in time, vomited noisily into the shrubbery.

"Oh my God, Dennis . . ."

"Yeah . . ."

Feeling his own constitution rapidly diminishing, he turned to Jettick's partner—who looked deathly pale—and said, "Call for help *now*! Don't try to handle this yourself. And get this road closed, too!"

Unable to take his eyes off the horror-movie scene before him, the cop said, "Uh-huh," and began a delicate walk to the squad car.

Dennis hopped back into the van and pulled the door shut. After one last glance back—Jettick was still on all fours, and the family members were all as still as statues—he said, "We're going to our cabin now. If you want to stop me, you'll have to shoot me. But I'm not keeping my family around here any longer."

Jettick's partner gave an absent nod, but Dennis never saw it. He already had the van in gear and was gaining speed.

He finally gave up on the coffee and set the cup in the basin. Then he rubbed his eyes with the thumb and forefinger of his right hand. He was more tired than he'd ever been in his life. The medicinal value of the scented morning breezes, usually able to cure all spiritual ills, was minimal today.

"Trouble sleeping again?"

He turned. "Huh? Oh, I didn't even hear you come down."

Andi stood there in her flannel pajamas and fuzzy slippers: vivid reminders of home. She had insisted they maintain as much of their normal routine as possible—the kids up at seven, showered and dressed, then a short walk for Scooter, followed by breakfast. Billy had been told they were just "going away for a few days," as it was something a five-year-old would accept without fuss. Chelsea, quite mature for seven, had gone along with the story like a trouper. So far, so good—on that front at least.

Andi came close and wrapped her arms around his waist. "More bad dreams?"

"Yeah."

"The roadblock?"

He laughed softly. "The roadblock. Jack McLaughlin. All manner of wondrous things."

She set her head on his shoulder. "They'll go away, don't worry."

"Yeah."

He marveled again—for perhaps the millionth time in his life—at her inner strength. Their perfect little world had been shattered, yet here she was offering reassurance and comfort. He was better at handling crises when they initially struck, but she was the one who held everything together in the long run. No matter how frazzled she became, no matter how worn or weary, she was, at her core, a rock. He had become dependent on her in this respect. When he had a bad day at work, he knew he could talk to her. When his mother died seven years ago, she was at his side every minute. Nothing ever brought her down. She would bend, but she never broke. He found that amazing.

"Why don't you take Scooter for his walk by yourself this morning?" she suggested. "Maybe see if Mr. Barber is home."

Josiah Barber, nicknamed by Dennis "the Old Man of the Mountain," had one of the other cabins in the area. There were many others, in fact, but only a handful were visible from their upstairs windows. Barber was a former railroad worker who had sold his house in southern New Jersey after his wife died in the late '80s and had lived in his cabin, which he previously used only for weekend hunting trips, ever since. Although he could be crabby and standoffish to some, he had taken a liking to the Jensens and always remembered to keep a civil tongue when Chelsea and Billy were around.

Dennis sighed. "Okay, sure. Why not? . . ."

Scooter was standing behind him, waiting patiently with his ears perked. Dennis knew this without having to look. He and Scooter had become brothers over the years; Dennis loved him as much as he loved Andi and the kids. He was the best pet anyone could ever have—sweet, gentle, playful, always ready to lick your face, tail going like crazy.

He reached over and took the coiled-up collar off the counter. "Okay, big guy, let's go," Dennis told him. He clicked the spring-loaded hook a few times because the sound drove Scooter into a delighted frenzy. He jumped up and down, bouncing off his master with his front paws. Dennis managed a smile.

"See you in a few," he said, kissing Andi on the cheek. She gave him one in return and rubbed his back.

They got outside and began climbing the same trail as yesterday. Narrow, pebbly, and well worn, it cut a winding path through the heart of the surrounding hardwood forest. Some stretches were sharply tilted, others grassy and overgrown. He didn't know how far it went, as he had never taken it to its natural conclusion. For that matter, he wasn't even sure where his family's property ended and the next one began.

Scooter sniffed along like a bloodhound in a murder movie, following the scent of the missing heroine. His senses were still sharp, Dennis could tell. Nine years was a respectable age for a large dog, an age when the basic faculties began diminishing. But not ol' Scoot's. He was as healthy and as happy as a puppy.

The woodland breezes and canine company did Dennis's soul good. The guilt was eating away at him ferociously. It was more than just the shooting of Jack McLaughlin now—much more. Yesterday, Chelsea wanted to call her friend Paige to see how she was doing. Andi told her maybe later, then lied when "later" came by, saying they did try her house but got no answer. The truth was they'd read online that Paige and her parents had been found dead the day before. This led to a conversation that night, after the kids were asleep, where the decision was made not to contact anyone else from the neighborhood. Dennis was the one who finally said it: "We can't. If we do, they'll ask where we are. Then they'll come here, and they could bring the infection with them." They wanted desperately to do something—*anything*—to help. But the risks were enormous. For Chelsea and Billy's sake, they had to remain hidden and follow the latest developments via their laptops. More than eight hundred dead, an estimated seventeen hundred more heading to the same conclusion. Andi commented it was like watching an earthquake from a helicopter. She felt like a coward; Dennis knew what she meant.

The trail leveled off when it reached a sunny cluster of trees. The air was warm and humid here, thick with the scent of pine sap. Scooter began to pull hard against the leash, wanting to go off the trail into a tangle of low-lying shrubs. *Same as yesterday,* Dennis thought with some surprise. He wasn't the type to pull while he was being walked, unlike some dogs. Andi's father had a mutt that damn-near pulled your arm off. Scooter had never been like that.

"Scoot, what's up?" Dennis said, gently trying to draw him back. He didn't want Scooter going anywhere that might earn him a few ticks. That might require a trip to the local vet for Lyme treatment.

But the dog was insistent. Still in his nose-to-the-ground posture, he carved long ruts into the sandy, loamy soil with his front paws while Dennis held him back. *He smells something in there,* Dennis thought, then envisioned another nightmare scenario—Scooter getting bit by some rabid thing. *Wouldn't that be great, him foaming at the mouth like Old Yeller . . . and my having to shoot* him, *too.*

"Scooter, let's *go,*" he said firmly, giving him a tug. He hated doing anything that hurt the animal, but there was no way he was letting him wander into the brush.

Scooter whimpered as he reluctantly abandoned the pursuit, but he kept looking back as they continued down the trail.

EIGHT

Abdulaziz Masood opened the front closet of his Hoboken apartment and took out the cream-colored L.L. Bean barn coat he'd bought last year. It was one of only two coats that hung there, the other a slightly heavier Gore-Tex he'd received in the same online order. Otherwise the closet was as empty as the day he'd moved in, almost three years ago.

He chose L.L. Bean products because he figured they would help him blend in. L.L. Bean was "American wear," as red-white-and-blue as hot dogs and apple pie and corrupt politicians and nearsighted corporate decision makers and a middle class being systematically hammered out of existence. The Bean clothes, the iPod Shuffle, the twice-daily visits to Starbucks, the tiny New Jersey apartment with an across-the-river view of New York City and the criminally high rent . . . *It was so easy to fool these people,* he'd thought a million times. Nearly three years and no one ever came knocking—not the FBI, the CIA, the NSA, or the Department of Homeland

Security. . . . He figured one of them would show up sooner or later, having discovered his association with Lashkar-al-Islam and Ahmed Aaban el Shalizeh. And he was prepared to go down fighting if it came to that. But it never did. He marveled at their stupidity.

He slipped his arms into the coat and adjusted it to sit comfortably on his broad shoulders. He was a very handsome thirty-six, lean and trim and in excellent health. His primary care physician had assured him of the latter during his annual physical. Dr. Bateman was his name. The year before that it was Dr. Clark, and Dr. Evans the year prior. The company where he'd worked kept changing healthcare plans. He didn't really care one way or the other, but he made sure to complain along with his coworkers each time. Complaining was an American thing to do.

He slipped his hands into the large side pockets out of habit, and he found the greeting card. The phrase *Good Luck from All of Us!* stretched across the front in a gentle arc, surrounded by butterflies and flowers and a bright yellow sun. On the inside, over two dozen people had written little comments along with their signatures. Nothing surprising here—*Best wishes!* and *Keep in touch!* and *Really enjoyed working with you!* A guy named Leonard with long hair and wicked acne wrote, *Abduligan the Hooligan—Rock on, man! You're the best!* He worked, at least in theory, on the maintenance staff, but he never seemed to do anything. He'd taken a liking to Masood since day one, something Masood did not want or need. There were a few like that, including a herd of young collegiate types who thought it would be cool to have a genuine Middle Eastern guy for a friend, and a girl named Tabitha who hated her parents so much that she wanted to date him just to get under their skin. She was particularly tough to shake. She had big boobs and a pretty face, and he admitted that he was tempted on a few occasions. But then he'd experience feelings of disappointment and self-disgust. Ultimately he told her he had a fiancée back in Pakistan and was trying to stay faithful. At first this seemed only to motivate her further, but she eventually gave up and set her sights on another target—a black kid in the sales department with nose rings and tattoos swarming around his arms and neck. He'd serve the purpose.

Masood told his boss he'd landed a new job in California. The truth, of course, was a little different. The email arrived last Friday: the one he'd been waiting three years for. It looked like spam, as expected. It had graphics, products, prices, and a fictional company name replete with phone number. He felt an excitement inside like none he'd ever known. *The time has come,* he thought with something close to giddiness.

He ripped the greeting card in half and replaced it in his pocket; he'd throw it in the public trash can by the front door when he got outside. Then he turned and took one last look around the apartment. This was not a gesture of sentimentality, but rather practicality. He scanned for clues to see if there was anything left to do. It still seemed like such a luxuriant place, especially in comparison to the mud-brick house in rural Sukkur, where he'd spent the first sixteen years of his life. Varnished hardwood floors, an icemaker on the door of the refrigerator, Jacuzzi jets built into the sides of the bathtub . . . The apartment had been fully furnished, too. The only possessions of consequence he had acquired were a copy of the Koran and a prayer mat, and he had donated both to a local mosque yesterday morning, leaving them in a box on the back step. He came with nothing, and he would leave only what he had been instructed to leave.

Satisfied, he opened the door and went out. He had a severe coughing jag in the hallway—the third in the past hour—and made no attempt to cover his mouth. It was a warm, phlegmy hack that came from deep down. The infection was taking root.

Good, he thought. *Very good.*

Contracting the virus hadn't been much of a challenge. There was a hospital a few miles away acting as a crisis center. New cases were coming in all the time, and the scene was often chaotic and disorganized. He simply waited by the emergency-room entrance until each victim arrived, then pretended he was a hospital employee rushing to lend assistance. Finally, he began showing the early symptoms—fever, chills, general malaise—late last night. By this morning, he was coughing and sneezing every few minutes. Based on what he'd learned about the illness via television and the Internet, he knew his window of opportunity would be small. He estimated he had about ten to twelve hours before he became incapacitated.

He got on the ferry in Hoboken, a good place to start. In spite of the outbreak, it was still jammed with commuters. *The great American rat race,* he thought as he stood on the lower level, staying inside so the contagions would have a better chance of spreading. *Rat race* was a phrase he'd heard several times. *They live to work, no matter what the risk.* Some of them were wearing surgical masks; others stood by the railing outside, in the fresh air. The rest were apparently comfortable taking their chances. He walked by as many of these types as possible, taking in deep breaths and blowing them out slowly. He had to fight off the coughs and sneezes, but he was getting good at it. He didn't want to draw too much attention to himself.

When the ferry reached the other side, he strolled casually down a very busy West Thirty-ninth Street. He noticed a street vendor, and an idea occurred to him. He bought four large coffees, black and hot, and sat down on a window ledge. Removing the lids one at a time, he took a long sip and then regurgitated it. Then he walked around until he found four homeless men, giving one cup to each. The last man shook his hand and told him he loved him. Masood smiled back.

He ate lunch in the most crowded restaurant he could find—an ESPN Zone—sitting at the bar near the front door so as to infect as many people as possible. The bartender, a bald and muscular man who looked like he attended neo-Nazi rallies in his spare time, eyed him suspiciously. This made Masood nervous. He tried some friendly chitchat, but the guy wasn't interested; he just kept watching. This forced Masood to leave earlier than planned. Before he did, however, he went into the restroom and soaked a cocktail napkin with a copious wad of phlegm and saliva. Then he tossed it onto the counter when the bartender wasn't looking. Maybe Nazi Boy would pick it up.

By midday, everyone was back in their offices, and the sidewalk traffic thinned somewhat. Masood adjusted his strategy by getting on one bus after another. The fever had fully established itself by now, and he was feeling faint and dizzy. At Thirty-third, amid a hail of complaints from the other passengers about his occasional coughs and sneezes, the driver requested that Masood please disembark. He chuckled as he went listlessly down the stairwell, saying harriedly, "Okay, boss, I disembark, I disembark." On the street again, he saw an ambulance zoom by. The driver was wearing a PPE suit. Everyone stopped to watch, petrified. This delighted Masood enormously. *It's starting to seep in, starting to saturate.*

He spent rush hour on the subway. He found a seat in the third car, picked up a discarded copy of the *Times,* and did his able best to act as though he were reading it. A lot of eye contact was being made; the air was thick with tension. It was as if everyone had abandoned hope of fending it off and simply decided it was only a matter of when. He had to work hard to suppress any coughs or sneezes here, as his final destination was coming up and he couldn't afford to get thrown off again.

Most of the other passengers were sporting the obligatory surgical mask and gloves. A few had taken it a step further with rubber masks and oxygen tanks. The tanks ranged from thermos-sized models to about the length of a standard fire extinguisher. Masood saw a commercial on television the night before where you could get even smaller ones—"Guaranteed twelve-hour supply!" the salesman raved, for the reasonable price of $340 plus shipping and tax. *Personalized oxygen tanks,* he thought, shaking his head. America's devotion to personalization never ceased to amaze him. The tanks would soon come in designer colors so they didn't clash with your outfit. Then you could get your initials engraved. After that there would be filling stations in case you ran low while you were still out. Then a subscription service where, for something like $39.99 a month, you could get unlimited refills. *Only in America.*

He reached into the side pocket of his coat and took out some loose change, which he pretended to count before replacing it. In truth, he was checking yet again to make sure the pump-spray bottle was still there. It was about the size of a roll of nickels, the plastic a transparent blue. And it was filled with a clear liquid.

He felt an upwelling of euphoria as the subway

zoomed along. He couldn't help but look at some of the other passengers, feeling an indescribable warmth at the knowledge of what was about to happen—and, more to the point, that he knew about it and they didn't. This was going to be a moment for the ages, one that would be written about for years to come, first in newspapers and blog sites, then in history books all over the world. Once everything was revealed—and it would, because that, too, was part of the plan—he would be lauded as a hero. They would revere him, utter his name with the deepest respect. Fathers would name their sons after him, encourage them to emulate his bravery and courage. His image would hang in homes; maybe he would even be mentioned during prayers. He always believed in his destiny, always felt a kind of certainty that he was headed for greatness. And he would achieve that greatness today. He would become immortal. *And it will be so easy. So easy . . .*

The subway car squealed to a halt at Union Square, and he rose to leave with the others. The platform, he was happy to see, was fairly busy. He was also relieved, although not surprised, that there were uniformed police everywhere. Their eyes were moving about restlessly, looking for anything suspicious. *Let's help them out,* Masood thought to himself.

In the thick of crowd, he pulled the spray bottle just far enough out of his pocket to expose the nozzle. Then, supporting it in his palm, he began pumping with his thumb. Little mist clouds appeared and just as quickly disappeared. He made every effort to be casual. This was crucial to the plan—*as though you're trying to hide it.* As much as he would like to yank the thing out of his pocket and blast someone square in the face—or, better yet, jam it up the nostril of one of these contemptible insects and fire repeatedly—he knew that would blow everything. So he walked along and just kept pumping. *At least I'll infect a few of them along the way,* he thought, regarding this as a kind of bonus.

He was almost to the stairs and started to worry that the sequence of events might not roll out as he'd hoped. But then it happened—he heard someone shout, *"Hey! That guy's spraying something!"* and in a matter of seconds, the scene descended into chaos. People began screaming, running in every direction. Some jumped like Olympians over the turnstiles; others stumbled back into the train. From the corner of his eye he saw a middle-aged man with a briefcase push aside a mother and her little boy, his tie flying ridiculously over his shoulder as he fled away.

He saw two of the transit cops come running at him, their eyes wide with fear over the cotton masks; they no doubt hated their jobs at the moment. Masood did his best to appear frightened, backpedaling before turning to run. But he let his feet twist around each other and fell to the smoothed concrete. He tried to squeeze out a few more spritzes, but some Good Samaritan—Masood couldn't help but admire him, all things considered—grabbed his wrist and jarred the bottle free. The cops were on him instantly, flipping him onto his stomach. One pulled his hands together and cuffed him; the other placed his booted foot on the spray bottle and ordered the Samaritan to stand back. Then he produced a plastic bag, rolled the bottle into it, and zipped it shut.

Masood was heaved to his feet and marched away. Of the few people who were left, several had their cell phones out and were taking pictures or making little movies. Masood made sure he appeared regretful, almost ashamed. But he wanted to smile. They would drink in his honor this night, and millions more would do the same for years to come.

It was just the beginning.

Andi sat on the grassy hill behind the cabin—knees raised, elbows on their peaks, hands together—and focused solely on her own, measured breathing. The moon looked down from its high place above the rip of the tree line, bathing everything in an eerie luminescence. And the near-perfect silence, which seemed peculiar in the dead of spring, was a godsend.

What would be an even greater godsend right now would be a cigarette, she thought decadently. She hadn't set one between her lips since she and Dennis were engagees. Even then it hadn't been much of a vice. Maybe one pack every two weeks. She'd never been one for addictions, wasn't an "addictive personality," as some liked to say. The worst was her senior year in college: about a pack and a half a week. She groped her memory for the name of the brand. *Parliaments—that was it.* It was a choice of convenience, as several of her friends smoked them, too. For all she knew, they had the most disagreeable flavor on the market. But she hadn't tried any other brand and had no intention of doing so. She knew she wouldn't be a smoker for long. She kicked the habit altogether when they decided to start a family. Cravings came once in a while, but never to the point of distraction. Most days she couldn't even believe she'd smoked at all. It was like remembering a detail from someone else's life.

Sure as hell wouldn't mind one now, though. I'd suck it down to the filter faster than a Shop-Vac.

The silence was broken by the metallic stretch of a rusted spring on the other side of the house. The fact that the door wasn't allowed to slap shut told Andi it was Dennis; he always guided doors to a close. Then the muted shuffle of his footsteps on the grass until he came up alongside her.

"They're in dreamland?" she asked.

"Out like lights."

"Good."

"It's amazing—they're only seven and five, yet they both snore like bears."

"Uh-huh."

He got down beside her and arranged himself in the same position. "I was prepared to read two stories each, but I didn't even finish one."

"It's been a long day."

"Yeah." He laughed humorlessly and shook his head.

"What's funny?"

"A 'long day.' It just sounds ridiculous. A long day here at our cabin, like we're early American settlers or something."

"Well, we did do a lot. I felt like *I* got things accomplished, anyway. I don't know about you."

"I did, I did."

"I had four phone interviews, sent out two emails making job offers, and got the payroll done. And all from my remote office here in the Hundred Acre Wood. Thank god for laptops."

"Is anyone even at the plant right now?"

"A couple of people. They don't stay long, though. The CEO doesn't want them there until this thing goes away. They're only doing what they have to do, no more."

The CEO of Andi's company was a fifty-three-year-old native of Denmark, where the company was headquartered. In the six years she'd been there, she was frequently startled by the degree of humanity he and the other executives displayed. It was a radical shift from the soulless band of savages who ran her last company—based in Texas—and masterfully guided it into insolvency.

"And everyone's still getting paid," Dennis said.

"That's right."

"Eddie just sent an email saying we wouldn't be given more than two weeks. After that, we had to start using our personal, sick, and vacation time."

Eddie Wells was Dennis's departmental supervisor. Forty-one and already divorced three times, he had four kids, crushing alimony and child-support payments, and—Dennis was fairly sure—a cocaine habit that he supported through casual dealing on the weekends. How the guy wasn't dead yet, either by his own hand, a drug contact, or one of the countless underlings who hated his guts, was a mystery.

"He's a piece of work," Andi said.

"He's a piece of something."

She giggled—a sound Dennis hadn't heard in what seemed like an eternity. Then she set her head on his shoulder, something else she hadn't done in forever. He caught the floral scent of her shampoo.

She let out a long sigh. "When do you think we'll be able to leave?" she asked. A few cicadas had begun chirring in the tall grass along the edge of the forest.

"I wouldn't even want to guess. A few weeks, maybe?"

"God, I hope it doesn't take that long."

"Me neither. Then again, I'm not in any rush to leave."

"Why do you say that?"

"I don't want to go back until we're absolutely certain the virus has been run out of town."

"I agree with that."

"I wonder if that's why Josiah wasn't there. Maybe he heard about people coming up here, and he left."

"Maybe."

His cabin had been locked tight, and there was no note on the door or any other indication of his present whereabouts.

"Just before I shut the laptop, I did a Google

search to see if there were any new cases in Carlton," Dennis said.

"And?"

"Yeah, plenty. One even had a YouTube video someone took with their cell phone. A biohazard team was carrying the victim out in a black body bag."

"Anyone we know?" She didn't really want to ask but couldn't help it.

"No. It was a retired man who lived by himself in that development over by the dam."

The dam was on the lowland side of town, the first area of Carlton settled in the mid-1700s, and was favored by the sixty-and-older crowd. Dennis and Andi had never spent any time there.

"But the report said he killed himself. They found empty bottles of both Jim Beam and Clorox bleach by his body."

"My God."

"And a brush, too."

"A brush?"

"A steel-bristled barbecue brush. Apparently he was using it to—"

"No—"

"—scratch off the blisters. I guess the itching was so bad, it drove him out of his mind."

Andi slowly shook her head. And although she was shocked by what she'd just heard, it was shock of a much milder wattage than it should have been. So many similar stories, so much suffering. Was she becoming desensitized? Any one of these reports would've sent her into a mild depression a week ago. Now it felt like each one was bouncing off her like tiny hailstones.

"The scariest part is that it could've just as easily been us," Dennis said. "*We* could've been the ones with the infection so deep, it would've made sense to use a wire brush."

"Yeah."

"What must that be like, to be pushed to the point where you think that way?"

"I don't know. I don't want to know."

"Me neither. That's why I say, no rush to leave here."

"No, no rush."

"I mean, I know the kids don't like being pulled out of their routine."

"No, they don't. All that school they're missing."

"Yeah. Well, at least they're doing some homework."

Which was true—the teachers had been trying their best to compensate for the educational blackout by posting lessons and homework online. Andi, who had seriously considered a career in teaching, enjoyed indulging this unfulfilled ambition. Classes were from eleven until two each day, with a half-hour break for lunch. Dennis, who handled the tech stuff on the computer, came up with the idea of taking pictures of their homework assignments with the digital camera and emailing them.

"But it's not the same," Andi said.

"I know."

She closed her eyes and exhaled slowly. "This is craziness."

"It sure as hell is."

"We're in the middle of the woods, for Pete's sake."

"But we're safe."

"Yeah."

Neither one said a word for the next ten minutes. At one point, Dennis thought Andi had fallen asleep. Then she started softly humming the Beatles' "I Saw Her Standing There," a song her parents had taught her as a child.

"You know what this reminds me of?" Dennis said.

"What?"

"The night of our first official date. Remember? After dinner we went to Indian Hill Park?"

Andi lifted her head—to Dennis's disappointment—and appraised her surroundings more carefully. "Yeah, a little bit. You mean the moonglow and the woody smell in the air?"

"Absolutely. Sitting on the swings?"

"Yeah."

He grinned. "You were hot that night, baby. Smokin'."

"You weren't so bad yourself, except for that ridiculous cologne."

He laughed. "The stuff I bought from JCPenney? It smelled great in the store."

"Not so much on you, though."

"No, not so much."

"Not exactly a good mix with your body chemistry."

Dennis turned and studied her for a long moment, taking in the delicate outline of her face and the pleasant curvature below it. He had told her a thousand times how beautiful she was. He knew she didn't believe him, but it had always been an honest assessment.

When Andi sensed what he was doing, she didn't return the look but merely raised her eyebrows. "Yes?"

"How about you? Do *you* think you'd mix well with my body chemistry?"

Now she did turn. "I think maybe we should find out."

"I think so, too."

The moon continued its slow glide across the pale night sky, a witness to the many agreeable things they did next.

NINE

The top to the convertible was up now; Beck had done it the day before. Top up, windows shut, vents closed. The car was sealed like a Tupperware container. This was every epidemiologist's nightmare—to be afraid of oxygen. If you were afraid of the water, you didn't have to swim. If you were afraid of wild animals, you didn't go into the woods. But how did you get away from air?

He drove slowly through Allendale on the way to another interview. An upscale, respectable town. There was a bistro, a bagel shop, a florist, a day spa. . . . The sign for the *Town Journal* bore the motto YOUR HOMETOWN NEWSPAPER. The Dairy Queen was a hangout for local teens, no doubt. And the Dog Boutique offered a special price on nail clipping, NO APPOINTMENT NEEDED.

But there was no life here. He came to a stop with the motor still chugging. He didn't bother to check the rearview mirror; no one was back there. The potted trees on the sidewalks were nodding in the wind, which was potentially deadly under the circumstances. A Burger King bag rolled and tumbled across the road and out of sight. One of the windows at Kammen's Jewelers had been smashed in, the alarm still going. A few doors down, a child's bicycle lay on its side. The pavement had been decorated—most likely by the bicycle's owner—in pastel colors. Beck couldn't make out what the pictures were, but the plastic tub of chubby chalk was still there.

He'd seen enough after a few minutes and started moving again. He passed out of Allendale's business district and into the residential area. A spray-painted sign on the side of the road read, THIS IS OUR PUNISHMENT FOR THE WAR IN IRAQ. A little ways down, a Dodge pickup had been driven into someone's front porch. Both doors were left open as the interior light slowly drained the battery. Just beyond that was Lyons Funeral Home. The lawn still looked as though it'd been cut with a pair of cuticle scissors, and there were several cars parked in the small back lot, so business appeared to be good. It reminded Beck of the conversation he'd had with Gillette the day before about how the corpses were piling up in local morgues, and what was being done with them. The state had ordered a minimum one-day postmortem hold before any family representatives could come and claim them. This was due to the rough determination that the virus lost its virulency in a body that had been dead for twenty-four hours. The rate of cremations versus burials had skyrocketed, had in fact become exclusive in almost all cases. In the rare event of a memorial service where the deceased was present, the bodies were rarely displayed. Beck had no trouble understanding this, as he doubted there were many people who wanted to see their beloved Aunt Martha for the last time after she'd had a fifteen-round bout with this particular contagion.

His mind turned back to the radio, which had been on for a while. He wasn't even sure which station, but it almost didn't matter—they were all broadcasting updates around the clock now. It reminded him of 9/11, when nearly every cable television channel in the area temporarily turned into a news network.

There was an up-to-the-minute estimate of 1,500 dead and at least another 3,000 infected. The illness had spread to nine states now, and President Obama finally ordered travel restrictions throughout the Northeast. Panic was widespread, bordering on hysteria. The media was doing a splendid job of scaring the daylights out of everyone, and Beck wondered what they'd say if they knew the full truth. The death toll was more in the area of 2,100, with at least 4,400 more acting as carriers—at least temporarily.

The virus also continued to be a problem for law enforcement. Police originally utilized the rubber-gloves-and-surgical-masks that had become standard gear for most everyone else, but the death toll among their ranks continued to rise. Every organization from the Fraternal Order of Police to the International Union of Police Associations cried foul, and many local unions ordered that their members answer no more outbreak-related calls unless given more appropriate protection. That led to the issuance of thousands of "escape hoods"—baggy head covering that makes the wearer look like a character in a sci-fi movie—with integrated air purifiers, either passive or active depending on each town's financial agility. These did reduce the number of fatalities, but not appreciably. A call to an infected site was still considered a date with death, and many towns simply stopped sending their officers into certain areas. Predictably, widespread looting became commonplace in these sectors, the thieves making the irrational decision to risk their lives by entering the homes of deceased residents in order to get their hands on one more diamond ring, flat-screen television, or whatever. Authorities reported the virus in twelve states for sure, and that number would likely double in the next few weeks, travel restrictions notwithstanding, if a vaccine wasn't discovered soon.

Sheila Abbott was in the hot seat. She was being assaulted by reporters day and night, and everyone from the president to countless spotlight-starved senators and congressmen were publicly demanding answers. She still managed to call both Beck and Gillette for updates every few hours, and she sounded reasonably sane on the surface. But Beck had known her too long, knew the strain was getting to her. He didn't talk about the media aspect of it, focused only on the matter at hand. Once, while discussing the frustratingly slow progress of the vaccine development, Abbott snapped and called Cara Porter, "that worthless assistant of yours." Beck, sitting stunned in his hotel room, offered no response, and the silence on the phone seemed to stretch on forever. Then Abbott apologized profusely.

Thinking of Porter at that moment, he put in his earpiece and gave her a call.

"What do you want?"

"Just to bother you," Beck said with a grin.

"Naturally. How are things going out there?"

"Well, I don't think I've ever felt so tired in my life. I've now conducted over a hundred and twenty interviews, resulting in more data than I think I've ever collected. Even with the other people in the field that Sheila hired to help collect samples and information for me, I'm still overwhelmed. Yet I don't feel any closer to finding answers."

"The frustration's running fairly high here at the lab, too."

"Yeah?"

"We're trying different things, but we're not getting anywhere. The virus's resistance to the antivirals we've fired at it so far is discouraging."

"Did you hear the name?"

"Name?"

"The name the press came up with?"

"No."

"They're calling it the 'Gemini virus.'"

"That sounds appropriately dramatic."

"Yeah, and it's starting to pick up steam, too."

"What's the rationale behind it?"

Beck laughed. "Some of it actually makes sense.

First, it's because the virus is so good at cloning—in other words, *twinning*—itself. Then there's those two lines it has on the head. In astrology, the mark of Gemini is essentially a Roman numeral two with its horizontal lines curved outward into half circles. But really, any two lines can represent the same basic symbol."

"I guess."

"The third reason—I know you'll like this—is because the outbreak began at the end of May, which is the start of the Gemini period on the calendar. May twenty-first to June twentieth to be exact, at least in tropical and Western astrology. The doomsayers are really having a field day about that part of it, saying all signs point to this being the end of the world and so on."

"Well, if we don't find a way to combat this thing, they might be right."

"Is it exhibiting genetic drift?" This was the process by which select bases in a virus's nucleic acid mutate to other bases, thereby restructuring itself in a defensive maneuver.

Porter said, "We don't have solid evidence of that yet, but it's certainly a possibility. Wouldn't that just be terrific, if it was capable of point mutations?"

"Or, even better, antigenic shift." Similar, it was a fundamental alteration in a virus's genome, essentially giving it an entirely new character.

"That's our worst nightmare—recombination or reassortment."

"A chameleon virus."

"Right. At this point, though, we're not seeing evidence of that, either. It's just one strain so far, thank goodness."

"That's something, I guess. So, no chance of viral sex, then?"

Porter laughed. "No, not yet. But we've all got our fingers crossed. We're a bunch of lonely, nerdy scientists, after all."

Separate strains of a viral species that possess a segmented genome had the ability to couple and produce offspring with unique traits. Due to the process's similarity to animal reproduction, it was referred to colloquially as *viral sex*.

"Microscopic porn," Porter went on. "Not much in the way of theatrics, but better than nothing."

"Uh-huh."

She sighed. "Anyway, we'll keep at it."

"I feel your pain, believe me."

"What about Ben? Anything?"

"He's just about finished mapping the virus's genome, after which he'll post the DNA sequences on the GenBank site to share with the virological community." GenBank was a massive online data repository for billions of genomic sequences, including more viruses, bacteria, and other pathogens. "Once that's done, there'll be a hundred professionals around the world working on the sequence, trying to find some common ancestry with another virus in GenBank's vast geography."

"It'll be scary if they can't."

"Yeah. The strain of H1N1 swine flu that zoomed

through North America in 2009 was mapped out, and the age and lineage determined, within a matter of days. That one was believed to be a hybrid of five separate viral elements from three different organisms—birds, pigs, and humans—and was so contagious because all five segments were types of influenza."

"And flu viruses, the little bastards, have the ability to adopt, adapt, and improve themselves each year, avoiding whatever treatments have been designed to combat them."

"Exactly. If that's the case here, this thing is going to be nearly unstoppable." *The Black Plague of the twenty-first century,* Beck thought. Someone had also used that phrase on television recently, on Fox News.

"Terrifying."

"Tell me about it."

"Is the mapping of a viral genome quicker than that of a mammal because of its size?"

"That's probably the biggest factor, yes. A viral genome has only a few thousand bases, whereas those of a full species will number in the billions. Even with the aid of computers, it's a considerable difference. Then there's the genomic diversity, which among viruses is enormous. A virus's nucleic acids can be DNA, RNA, or both. And viral size and shape variation is staggering. The shape can be circular, segmented, whatever. Single strands, double strands . . . positive sense, negative . . ."

"It's amazing, isn't it?"

"It really is. Within the relatively small size of their group, they have more structural diversity than almost anything else on Earth. We've cataloged around six thousand different viruses, but a lot of people don't realize there are millions more. That there is what's truly amazing—how much we don't know. What we've got on our hands here is just one more little creature we haven't met yet. And the most frightening part is that there are, undoubtedly, more out there like this one." He paused a moment, then said, "Sometimes I think there's a virus sitting out there somewhere, maybe in some rare plant deep in the Amazon or waiting to mutate in some cow that's headed for the dinner table, that we won't be able to stop. A pathogen that'll make this new one look like the common cold. And once it gets rolling, it'll sweep us off this planet like chess pieces."

"Now you're starting to sound like . . . well, me."

"Oh man, that's not good."

"No."

"Anyway, let me go. I just turned down the street where I'm supposed to be."

"Okay. Have a lucky day."

"You, too, kiddo."

He pulled up to the house where he was expected—421 Cypress Road. A modest ranch in pale yellow with white shutters. There was a small flower bed beneath the bay window, showing early signs of weed invasion since no one was coming to tend it anymore. A maroon Chrysler sedan sat in the driveway. It looked to be from the early or mid '90s. The car of an elderly woman on a fixed income.

Beck put on his surgical mask and gloves and got out. The silence was eerie in contrast to the bright and sunny afternoon. Birds chirped and cicadas trilled, but there was no sign of human life. He looked up and down the street at the other homes, the phone poles and fire hydrants, and the yellow intersection light flashing in the distance. It was the very model of contemporaneous suburban America, yet he was alone.

With notebook in hand, he went to the front door and rang the bell. No one answered. He stepped back to check the small black numbers on the side—*4-2-1*. That was correct. Fear stirred inside him. *Is this woman also dead?* Would he have to call the authorities and have them break in, only to find her hideous, blackened body lying—

The inside door finally opened a few inches; the vacuum effect sucked in the outer door as well. He could see an eye peering suspiciously through the dark. The woman looked him up and down, then said, "What do you want?"

"I'm Michael Beck, Mrs. Dylan. I talked to you on the phone this morning."

"Beck?" She didn't speak the name so much as she spat it—*Bechhh*.

"Yes, ma'am. I found your contact information in Katie Milligan's apartment. Remember?" Specifically, it appeared in the recently dialed calls memory of her cordless phone. "I'm from the CDC." He took his ID badge from his pocket and held it up. She studied it carefully, as if the area were swarming with people pretending to be epidemiologists.

"Okay," she said. When the door opened, Beck could see that she, too, was wearing a surgical mask and gloves. They looked ridiculous in contrast to the long housecoat—pink with embroidered flowers—and soft slippers.

She ushered him into the kitchen without greeting or ceremony, and with no reaction to the fact he was the same man who had been interviewed repeatedly on every major news channel over the last two weeks. Instead, she busied herself with something at the counter.

A quick survey of the home told Beck that his host had taken the time to read the circular on preventive measures that the Centers issued on Monday: two pages of instructions he had originally typed up in his hotel room and that had since been downloaded by more than a million people. Every window appeared to be shut and locked, every item in the house scrubbed to a sparkle, the trash cans kept outside. . . .

"I see you've taken the preventive steps the CDC outlined," Beck said in an attempt to be friendly. The air reeked of Vicks VapoRub and green tea.

"What was that?" Her voice was harsh and raspy, as if she'd spent a lifetime smoking unfiltered cigarettes. But Beck didn't think so—she looked too fit and alert for that. He pegged her for mid-eighties at the youngest, yet she appeared to be fairly spry.

Her skin was clear, her posture good. *This one's a survivor,* he decided with a certain admiration.

"I said you've taken the precautionary measures around the house that the CDC recommended."

She walked behind him and pulled out one of the chairs at the oval kitchen table, holding her hand above it as if to say, *Here, sit.* Then she took one on the other side, dropping into it somewhat abruptly.

"Yes, I did everything the CDC told me to do. Took me all of last night and most of this morning. I don't get around like I used to."

"Were the directions clear? Could you understand everything okay?"

"Why, did you write them?"

"Actually, yes."

"They were fine." She had her gloved hands clasped together and was looking around at everything but him.

"Well . . . okay, good," he said.

"And I'm staying inside as much as possible."

"That's a very good idea right n—"

"Yesterday we had an incident in the street." She motioned briefly in that direction. "Someone died out there."

"Out in the street?"

"Yes. Kenneth Hillman." She said the name as if Beck already knew him. Then, as if realizing this, she continued with, "He was the nineteen-year-old who lived in the house on the other side."

"And he died in the street?"

Dylan nodded. "The house was burning, and someone called the fire department. I was watching out the window when the trucks came. They started putting it out—you know, with those big hoses."

"Sure."

"And Kenneth came running out the front door. I saw the whole thing. He was—" She looked away and cleared her throat. Beck got the distinct impression—and was mildly surprised by it—that she was trying to squelch any reaction she might be having to the retelling of Hillman's death.

"He was on fire, too," she said, looking at Beck directly.

"Oh no."

"He was all in flames and screaming. I could hear him through the glass."

"And he died right there?"

"No. He was running toward the firemen, and at first they didn't seem to know what to do. Then one of them aimed the hose at *him* because Kenneth was going to run into him."

"My God."

"He moved around a little bit after that, lying on the ground, then went still. They found out later that he had the infection. He got it somehow."

This bit of information sent shock waves through Michael Beck. "Don't tell me he was—"

"He set *himself* on fire. Trying to get rid of it, I assume. And that caused the house to catch on fire, too."

"That's awful."

"He must have been out of his head."

"Extreme confusion and hysteria are among the symptoms."

"Yeah . . ."

She went glassy eyed at that point, staring into empty space. "He had been messed up with drugs, too," she said finally. "Had a lot of problems."

This, Beck realized, was her way of dealing with the incomprehensible horror of it—find a way to make the loss seem minimal, almost trivial. He had witnessed it many times. Again he thought, *This tough old broad's a survivor, all right.*

"So what did you want to ask me about?" she asked.

He opened his notebook and found a clean page. "If you don't mind my asking, how did you know Katie Milligan?"

"She was a student of mine."

"Oh? I didn't realize you were a teacher."

"Thirty-two years at Ramsey Middle School."

"Retired now?" He was going to add, *I assume?* but caught himself.

"Yep. Since 1997."

"And you and Ms. Milligan . . ." He wasn't sure how to word this. "You became friends after she was your student?"

"Yes. She was one of the best I ever had. Always behaved herself, never missed an assignment, never talked out of turn. I've stayed close with all the good ones." She still hadn't made eye contact, giving Beck the feeling he would've had little chance of being on her Good Ones list.

"That's nice," he said. "And when was the last time you spoke with her?"

"Two days before she died. Or, before they found her body, anyway."

Her eyes were fixed on the TV set in the living room now, which adjoined the kitchen without a dividing wall.

"I have no idea when she actually died," Mrs. Dylan added.

"And did she mention anything about her illness? Anything about, you know, feeling run down, or a rash, or—?"

"She said her sinuses were starting to bother her, and I could hear it, too. She was sneezing, blowing her nose." She turned to Beck and said, "She was supposed to come here the day after we talked, to help me do some gardening."

"Really?"

"That's right."

"If you don't mind my saying so, you're a very lucky woman, Mrs. Dylan. Had that happened, I doubt very much you'd still be here."

"No, probably not." She seemed nervous now, as if the thought of coming so close to death unsettled her. Beck had to admit he was impressed by this trait as well. The great majority of elderly people he had known possessed little or no fear of death. An elderly man he met during his final year of post-graduate school, who had pancreatic cancer and no more than three months left on the clock, had even said, "I consider death a friend. It doesn't scare me at all." Beck still hadn't reached the age where he began to feel that way. The thought of dying still filled him with dread and depression. He loved life and the manifold joys that could be found if one took the time to look for them. He *wanted* to be alive, absorbing and enjoying and experiencing as much as possible. And this woman seemed to be of similar mind.

"As I said on the phone, I'm trying to get a sense of where this outbreak started. And to do that, I have to do a lot of backtracking. So here's the million-dollar question: Did Katie say anything about where or how she got sick in the first place? Any sense of—?"

"I know exactly where she got it," Dylan said, and now there was anger in her voice.

"You do?"

"At the supermarket in Ramsey, standing in the checkout line."

Beck wrote this down. "Do you remember anything else she—?"

"She said he was sneezing and coughing like crazy."

"He? Who?"

"Right there in front of everybody."

"Who was it?"

She was shaking her head now. "Gotta lotta goddamn nerve, going out in public *sick* like that."

"Mrs. Dylan—"

"The most inconsiderate man in this godforsaken tow—"

"Mrs. *Dylan*."

She snapped out of her ramble and looked over at him. "What?"

He smiled and said quietly, "Who was it?"

"That no-good bastard *Bob Easton,*" she replied, "that's who."

The mere fact that they were all singing struck Dennis as so bizarre that it defied description. The four of them, making their way along the trail as they crooned a casual rendition of "The Muffin Man," was so peculiar under the circumstances that he wanted to laugh out loud. *Oh, do you know the muffin man, the muffin man, the muffin man?* . . . No one had suggested it; it just sort of happened. Chelsea started; Andi joined her. Billy tried to keep up, having heard it a thousand times back home. Then Dennis chimed in from the back of the line. He felt like an idiot—but loved it at the same time.

In spite of Andi's determination to import as much as their routine from home as possible, they were forging what she was now calling "a new kind of normal." Patterns were beginning to emerge from the chaos as each person found his or her niche. Chores were assigned, TV channels committed to memory, new meals prepared based on whatever was available to them. It was funny, he thought, how easily the fundamentals could be replaced. For example, instead of the local ShopRite, they now had Hall's General Store. They made the two-mile trip last Tuesday when, running low on the basics, they had to take a chance. Hall's was still a good five miles from Route 88; Dennis and Andi thought of 88 as the transitional point between their safe, isolated universe and the "real world." So if Hall's was closed . . .

Dennis pumped his fist when they pulled up and saw the black and orange OPEN sign in the window. Andi whispered *"Thank God."* As it turned out, they were even luckier than they thought—Old Man Hall said business had slowed so much, he was keeping the place open only five hours a day. Dennis found it amazing more people hadn't escaped to their vacation cabins.

He and Andi loaded up three carriages, everything from bread, milk, and toilet paper to eight DVDs, a dozen coloring books, and a Nerf basketball set. Hall hesitated when Dennis presented his Visa card. The crusty old bastard said he'd actually prefer cash, then pointed out the ATM machine wasn't working because he wouldn't permit anyone from the bank to come out and refill it. An argument was about to ensue, when Hall's wife appeared from the back and scolded her husband. She also gave free lollipops to Chelsea and Billy as they were leaving, to the old man's dismay.

Once they'd had enough of "The Muffin Man," Andi led them into "The Itsy Bitsy Spider." Billy, exhilarated by the fact that he knew all the words at the ripe old age of five, marched along enthusiastically, like a soldier in a parade. Dennis couldn't help but marvel at the three of them, especially Andi. He knew her stress level was still high and would remain there until they left this place. But she never let it show when they were around. Their emotional tone would be decided by hers, so she put on a brave face.

They reached the peak of a pebbly, wooded rise, the same point where Scooter had pulled at the leash the week before. He'd been running all over the place today, sniffing and exploring and doing his own thing. Dennis decided ultimately to set him free from now on, his rationale being driven in part by the purchase of a flea-and-tick medication he'd found on the shelf at Hall's. Scooter was now the happiest dog in the world, free to roam about at will.

When "The Itsy Bitsy Spider" was finished, Chelsea said, "Daddy, can I call Noelle when we get back?"

Both he and Andi had the same thought. *Damn . . .* They knew the question was coming sooner or later. Noelle Taylor was one of Chelsea's best friends. Last week, after enduring relentless wheedling, they decided to let her talk to one of her schoolmates. The challenge was figuring out which one. This led to a strange form of Russian roulette in which they took turns calling the parents to see who was . . . *available*. No one answered the first three numbers; the line had been disconnected on the fourth. Then Andi discovered the cell number of Noelle's mom, scribbled on the back of a business card she kept in her wallet. As it turned out, the Taylors had done something similar to the Jensens—they packed their minivan and hightailed it to a quiet area of West Virginia where some relative had a summer home overlooking a small pond. Dennis and Andi were pleased the Taylors had escaped unharmed; they always liked them.

The parents had talked first, of course, trading survival tips and obituary bulletins. Then came the inevitable back-home stories, dark and horrifying—the Sunoco station exploded . . . the strip mall burned to the ground . . . the elementary school's head janitor hanged himself from the flagpole out front. . . . No word on whether anyone had found ol' Jack McLaughlin on the Jensens' front lawn, though.

When Chelsea and Noelle finally got the chance to speak, their parents hovered by the phones to monitor the conversation. They rambled on about the usual stuff of interest to a pair of sevensomethings—television, music, video games, and so on. Andi's resolve weakened as she caught a powerfully nostalgic glimpse of normalcy—or, more to the point, a normalcy she was likely never to experience again. Two weeks ago, they would've had the same conversation and she'd pay it no mind. Now she was grateful for every word. It was a bright little piece of a life that seemed so distant now.

"We'll see, sweetheart," Andi said, stepping over a rotting cedar tree that had fallen across the trail. Chelsea knew this was the standard answer parents gave when they just didn't feel like dealing with the inevitable resistance that followed the word *no*. She groaned out loud.

"Mommy didn't say you couldn't," Dennis told her. "Just not right now. But we will, I promise."

"Sure," she said with tenuous conviction.

Dennis's cell phone rang at that moment, as if on cue.

"Is it Noelle?" Chelsea asked brightly.

"Wouldn't that be something?" Dennis said as he took it from the case clipped on his belt. He checked the caller ID before unfolding it. "Nope, sorry, kiddo. It's your aunt Elaine."

Chelsea made a face and turned back to her mother, who put an arm around her shoulders. Billy trotted up and tried to get Andi to do the same from the other side.

The three of them kept walking until Andi realized Dennis wasn't following. She stopped, turned back, saw him standing there, and knew right away something was wrong. His mouth hung open just slightly, his eyes a little wider than usual. He was also visibly pale, almost sick-looking.

"Honey, what is it?"

He said okay into the phone twice, then shut it with a snap. "We have to go back to the cabin. Something's happening."

Andi started in that direction. "What?"

"Elaine said the president is going to talk to the nation at eleven o'clock. It's supposed to be important."

Andi checked her watch. "That's twenty minutes from now. We'd better hurry."

"Quite." He scooped up Billy and began jogging. "Where's Scooter?"

"I don't know."

"Scooter! Come on, boy! Come on, Scoot!" Andi called for him, too.

He was about a hundred yards away, due east. He had located the source of the interesting odor from days ago—a large carcass lying on its side. It was only partially decayed, squirming with maggots and hazy with flies. The tongue hung out like a worm on a hook, blood dried around the mouth and between the teeth. Scooter sniffed it all over, pawed at the entrails that had been exposed by a hungry coyote the night before. Then he began licking whatever seemed appetizing. It wasn't overly flavorful, and when he heard the voices calling for him, he willingly abandoned the corpse and bounded off.

TEN

DAY 13

Sheila Abbott appeared on Meet the Press, *at the request of President Obama, to update the public. The president chose her over Secretary Sibelius so Americans would know they were getting the information directly from the CDC rather than feel it might be somehow filtered or otherwise interpreted through the Department of Health and Human Services. Obama also wanted to make sure the public focused on the medical points of the crisis rather than any potential geopolitical aspects. Neither he nor the State Department were anywhere near ready to address the country on that front.*

Host David Gregory was thoroughly professional in manner, but his line of inquiry was brutally direct. Abbott, looking haggard even in a new Donna Karan, coughed out the most up-to-date statistics she had at her disposal—4,211 deaths, and more than 7,800 further cases of exposure and infection. She admitted that neither the CDC nor the WHO was any closer to combating the virus than it had been at the beginning. It was now in seventeen states, and she fully expected it to reach more. When Gregory asked if the government suspected a terrorist connection, particularly in light of the capture of Abdulaziz Masood, Abbott said she was not aware of any such discussions. When Gregory asked if she was lying, the skin under her pearls quickly reddened. No, she said firmly, she was not.

In spite of her indignation, the American public was not ready to accept the notion that there was no element of foreign subterfuge involved. Word leaked out about Masood's possible ties to the Iranian government, and protesters held demonstrations around the country insisting that Obama launch a retaliatory attack. The president's most fervent and steadfast opponents had a field day reminding people that he had touted the election of Iranian reformist president Maziar Baraheri as a "turning point in the history of Iran, and thus a turning point in the history of Iranian–American relations." Obama's misplaced faith in Baraheri, they cawed, had now paid out its first ugly dividend. It should be a lesson to all those who, in the future, might entertain the foolish delusion of trying to make friends with leaders in the Middle East.

The Dow shed more than 15 percent of its total volume as business slowed in every sector. Restaurants, bars, malls, hotels, and supermarkets were empty or altogether shuttered in some areas. Phone and email usage skyrocketed as most people remained indoors, and Internet usage reached historic highs so the public could stay informed. The CDC posted a central page that quickly caused their server to crash due to unexpected volume. Domestic suppliers of surgical masks and rubber gloves were so overwhelmed by the sudden demand that they had to begin importing from overseas manufacturers. There were three separate arrests of relatively low-ranked hospital employees stealing boxes of one or the other and selling them on eBay. In a medical supply store, two young mothers got into a fistfight over the last carton of cotton masks and ended up going to the hospital anyway—one with a broken nose, the other with a deep bite in her left arm.

The virus reached Michigan through two Pennsylvania teenagers who were at a cheerleading meet and shared a joint with one of the hosting school's baseball players. They had already made his acquaintance online via Facebook. After the meet, he invited them back to his parents' house—a three-story Tudor in the better section of town—knowing his family wouldn't return until the following morning. They passed the J among themselves in the backyard, which was fully enclosed by a shadowy gathering of ancient cedars. Then they went inside and starting working through a bottle of vodka the boy had squirreled away for just such an occasion. He couldn't decide which of the two future debutantes he wanted more—the blonde with the skinny waist or the slightly heavier brunette with the jiggling rack. He settled on the blonde simply because she was more receptive to him. The fact that she seemed to have brought a cold with her was only of mild concern at first, and less so as the vodka diminished. They did it on the couch in the downstairs family room; then he sent both girls packing. He woke up just before noon the next day to the sound of the maid service's vacuum cleaners. His sinuses were stuffed to the rafters, and he felt sick to his stomach. Cursing the blonde, he took two Advil and returned to bed. When his mother roused him for dinner some hours later, a localized rash had joined the ensemble of symptoms. The next morning he was awoken by his own hand, which was scratching madly at his legs. An odor more foul than anything he had ever encountered in the boys' locker room seized his attention, pulling him sharply into the moment. He lifted the sheets to find a calico mess of blood and golden pus-oil. His eyes widened into large marbles as he inspected the gooey buildup under his fingernails. Then he heard a scream down the hall—it was his mother, as clear as a bell even from behind the heavy mahogany of her bedroom door. In that moment, all the pieces to the puzzle came together, and he began crying.

It got into Kansas from a hitchhiker who had also dropped it off in Kentucky and Missouri. The hitchhiker's name was Doug: Douglas Fairbanks Miller. His mother had insisted on the "Fairbanks" because she considered the former movie star from Hollywood's Golden Age the greatest male specimen ever to have graced this earth. She left Doug's father after a tequila-fueled, harsher-than-usual beating, then died a few years later in a motorcycle accident while riding with the last in a string of moron boyfriends. Since sperm-donor dad was nowhere to be found, sixteen-year-old Doug was left with the choice of either becoming a ward of the state or escaping. He chose the latter, and drifting became his profession. He picked up cash in odd jobs here and there, and when honest work was scarce, he wasn't above the petty-crime-and-pawnshops matrix. At the time he caught the virus, he was twenty-six and had been to every state on the continent. He had even spent a little time in that Mexican political curio known as Baja California—and returning there was, in fact, the reason he was working his way through the Midwest. He had liked Baja very much; Mexican laws weren't quite so voluminous or hard-assed as they were in America. Steady work could be found if you kept to yourself and were willing to show some productivity from time to time. The weather was beautiful and the women were easy. He entertained thoughts of even owning a home of some kind, maybe a little shack right along the Pacific shore. Something like that. He'd never been one for making plans, but then he'd never been in love before, either. And the first step, of course, was getting there. In spite of his bushy beard and hard-rock hairstyle, he'd never had trouble getting a lift. There was always someone, usually a trucker or some idiot college kid looking to piss off his parents or impress his friends. He had begun feeling ill after a six-hour stint in a FedEx rig that had carried him across the Missouri–Kansas border. Working his way along Route I-135, he felt the dizziness strike and decided to lie down for a while. There was a grove of cottonwood trees about a hundred yards from the shoulder, and he found a quiet spot to lie down. He woke several hours later to the distant roar of speeding vehicles and the more intimate calls of crickets, cicadas, and other benign critters of the night. When he tried to stand, the world spun around him and he went back down. Swaying gently on all fours with his unwashed hair hanging on either side of his face, he knew something was seriously wrong. Through his confused and diluted mind he managed to piece together a rudimentary plan—get a ride, then get to a hospital. He'd know where a hospital was when he saw the square blue sign with the white capital H *in the middle. They'd have to treat him even though he didn't have any money. That was the law, he thought. They'd take care of him, and someone else would pay for it. Good ol' America. He struggled to his feet again, steadied himself against the tree that he'd slept under, and staggered like a newborn foal back to the road. As the hours passed and the infection flooded into his brain tissue, thoughts became more difficult to hold together. The only one that recurred with any cohesion was that his skin seemed to be on fire and itched like a bastard. Just as dawn was creeping into the eastern sky, Douglas Fairbanks Miller stumbled unknowingly in front of an eighteen-wheeler that was carrying a packed load of appliances to a cluster of Best Buys in*

Wichita. The driver would later tell his wife through a purge of tears that, "the guy just . . . exploded."

It was imported into Wyoming via several large containers of coleslaw that had been infected in Nebraska before being shipped across state lines, where it was enthusiastically consumed during a community picnic. All sixty pounds were procured by a local wheeler-dealer named Chester D. "Chet" Maxwell. Quick with a laugh and a firm handshake, he was tall and handsome with the hairstyle all parents wished for their sons. He was an insurance salesman by trade, but his great love was his hometown, and the conduit through which he exercised that love was any organization associated with it—the Elks, the VFW, the church. In high school, he couldn't go a week without being mentioned or photographed in the local paper for one astonishing sports achievement or another. But he didn't have what it took to be a pro, and he knew it. Being involved in community affairs had been his way of staying in the spotlight. He was particularly proud of the coleslaw deal, from a vendor in Casper that no one had ever heard of. All the food at the picnic, in fact, was bought at phenomenal prices, keeping him within a budget that was already microscopic and, as a result, once again anointing him the hero. Sitting in the first-floor office of his comfortable home three days later, however, he found himself faced with the very real possibility of becoming the focus of the local media's wrath rather than its love. With a tenuous and sweaty grip on the phone, he listened with diminishing strength as the details of the outbreak's investigation were relayed. Six people were already dead, twenty-two others infected, and at least forty to fifty more—estimated conservatively—would follow in short order. One of the dead was a little boy whose parents had bought a fire-insurance policy from Chet some years back. Another was one of his former teachers. And it had come from the cut-rate coleslaw, the caller said; of that there was no remaining doubt. After Chet returned the phone gently to its cradle, he sat in stunned silence for a while. The phone rang again, but he didn't answer it that time. He hadn't eaten any of the slaw himself; he didn't like the stuff. But he had still been there that day, shaking hands and taking kisses on the cheek like the equally cut-rate politician he was. So he would have the infection soon, too—of that there was also no doubt. He rose from the chair in a daze, went upstairs into his bedroom, and got the revolver that he'd inherited from his father out of its locked box at the back of the closet. Then he nestled the barrel snugly beneath his chin and squeezed the trigger.

A couple that had attended the picnic, Willie and Lorraine Pryce, flew to San Francisco later that night to begin a fifteen-day cruise. They had been chattering about it to anyone at the picnic who would listen. It had been their dream to take a cruise on their honeymoon twelve years earlier, but they hadn't been able to afford it at the time. When they boarded the first day, they both felt fine. By the second night, however, Willie had begun to feel nauseated. After Lorraine had fallen asleep, he all but crawled into the bathroom—or rather the head, as he understand the nautical term to be—and involuntarily transferred the contents of his stomach into the small porcelain bowl. At first he thought it was seasickness, then rejected the idea on the basis that he had been on his boss's boat a half dozen times without so much as a stomach flutter. He stayed in the head wrapped in a blanket and curled close to the toilet because he didn't want to wake his wife during her dream vacation. He threw up three more times before finally drifting off to sleep. He was jarred awake a few hours later by the sound of the door being thrown open. Lorraine stood silhouetted by the gaining sunlight shining in from the row of portholes above their bed and was holding on to the doorway for support. At first Willie thought that look of terror on her face came from waking up and finding him gone. Then he realized she felt as awful as he did. She charged forward and just about made it to the throne in time to copycat his earlier performance. From his ringside seat, he got to see everything in Technicolor clarity, thinking her mouth looked like the end of a fire hose that was discharging water the color of cooked salmon. He put one hand on her back as a gesture of support and used the other for the multiple flushes he knew would be required. After some discussion, the couple decided the culprit had been the cruise's inaugural dinner from the night before. They then took showers, got dressed, and decided to soldier on. By the time they reached their first port of call, however—Acapulco—the rash had broken out and they were forced to seek medical attention. They were advised to return home by plane and did not argue. Meanwhile, the Sun-class cruiser and its nearly 1,800 passengers—several dozen of whom were now also infected—continued on its way, with scheduled stops in Huatulco, Puntarenas, Fuerte Amador, Cartagena, Aruba, and the Panama Canal Zone. . . .

President Obama was one of the few people in the Situation Room not wearing a military uniform. He was seated at the head of the table, and a map of the Middle East was on the screen at the far side. It felt as though he'd seen it a hundred times, and he thought many more presidents would see it in the future.

CIA Director Leon Panetta had delivered the grim news yesterday—the man identified as Abdulaziz Masood was directly connected to the government of Iran. The supporting evidence was overwhelming. There were names, phone numbers, and email addresses on Masood's hard drive. There was a bank account with several recent transfers from an offshore account known to be controlled by several past Iranian regimes. There were notes and letters found in a hollowed-out cavity behind a piece of molding along the kitchen floor. And there was Masood himself, Syrian-born but a resident of Tehran since 1988. When the clear liquid in Masood's spray bottle was analyzed, no one was surprised to find it contained the same virus in Masood's bloodstream.

What FBI and CIA investigators never suspected was that the Iranian connection was apocryphal. In this respect, Masood had done a truly masterful job. He got caught because he wanted to get caught. But any confession that might've revealed the truth behind the lie was impossible because Masood lost consciousness in the intensive care unit at Saint Vincent's less than two hours after he'd been apprehended and died shortly thereafter.

A distraught Obama listened stoically as his military advisers now had a conversation that was inevitable.

Admiral Thomas Teller, Chairman of the Joint Chiefs, said, "Iran's solid-fuel, Sejil-Two surface-to-surface missiles have a range of about twelve hundred miles, Mr. President." Teller looked more like a suburbanite from the 1950s than a military officer, the type who mowed his lawn every Saturday, then admired it on Sunday while cooking Delmonicos on the barbecue. He was sixty-two, soft-spoken, and on most days, upbeat and congenial. Not today, though.

"The Sejil series is a vast improvement over their Shahabs," he said, "which are liquid fueled. Sejils are much more accurate."

"And this is the best asset they've got?" Obama asked mechanically.

"Yes, although we're all but certain they're actively developing a two-stage rocket. That, of course, would allow for greater range with less fuel consumption."

"Let's not focus on what they haven't got," the president said.

"No, sir."

"Let's just stick to what they've got."

"Yes, sir."

"If we hit them, can they strike here? The American mainland?"

Teller shook his head, as did the others around the table.

"Not yet, Mr. President. Although I'm sure they'd like to. Chances are they'd strike our allies in the region, including Israel. That would be their way of exacting revenge."

"And then Israel would strike *them,*" a female vice admiral commented from the other end of the table.

"And the region would explode in all-out warfare," added a marine general across from her. "The Middle East conflict everyone's been expecting for years. It would be a bloodbath."

"Tom, who else would get involved if we attacked?" Obama asked. "Would Syria?"

"The Syrian ambassador has already made it clear through diplomatic back channels that any strike against Iran would be regarded as an act of war. If it came from Israel, there's not much doubt they'd stand alongside Iran in that instance. If it came from us—" He put his hands up. "—it's much harder to say. But they would spin it as a slap to the face of Islam rather than the Iranian government, and that could cause some problems."

"What about China?"

Teller nodded to one of his subordinates, a lieutenant general named Albright who'd been stationed in the region.

"China's ties to Iran have increased and strengthened in recent years, as you know, Mr. President," Jettick said. "As you know, Iran terminated most trade with Japan in the early 2000s, mostly because they didn't like the fact that Japan had become so friendly with us. So, China became one of their new customers. And thus far, I'm sorry to say, it has worked out nicely for both sides. Iran, for example, is a generous producer of hydrocarbons, and China is a voracious consumer."

Teller finished with, "As China's dependency on Iran grows, so will its motivation to feel protective."

Obama nodded. "Sally, what's your read on the Secretary General?"

Sally Kramer was the first female African American U.S. Ambassador to the UN, having been confirmed in the Senate by unanimous consent. A graduate of both Stanford and New College, she previously worked in President Clinton's National Security Council.

"His feeling is that any military action on Iran would have little support from the great majority of our allies. In spite of what appears to be an Iranian-funded attack on our citizenry, no one is eager for more American aggression in the Middle East."

Several in the room had the same thought at this moment: *If we hadn't invaded Iraq in 2003, we'd have the political cover we needed. . . .*

"And Russia?"

"It's very hard to gauge Russia's reaction at this point, Mr. President," Kramer replied. "There are still active trade relations between them and Iran, but due to Iran's inability to get their own economy fully stabilized, Russia is becoming more and more dependent upon us and other Western nations. Then again, they continue to provide Iran with most of their airplanes, both domestic and military. So it is a complicated situation. The Cold War is supposedly over, yet Russia keeps trying to delimit American influence in Central Asia, with China's help, through the Shanghai Cooperative. If we launched a strike against Iran, both Russia and China might very well feel the need to respond."

Obama nodded gravely. "The opening salvo to World War Three."

"And yet we can't do nothing," General Teller said. "We have to respond in some fashion, sir."

"I'm aware of that, Tommy."

"These people planned and carried out an attack on America, on our soil."

"I know."

"We've got over four thousand dead. Dead bodies are being found all over because no one wants to touch them. American bodies lying dead. The press knows about Masood and is running with the story, fueling public fear and outrage. Our economy is grinding to a halt, which means the global economy is next. And the CDC people can't stop this thing. We're speeding toward some kind of Armageddon scenario, and—"

"I *know,* Tommy."

The others fell silent as the president closed his eyes and massaged his temples. The tension in the room became asphyxiating.

Obama took a deep breath. "Give me a little time to think it through," he said softly.

"Yes, sir, Mr. President."

"Thank you."

The room emptied swiftly. When everyone else had gone, Obama shook his head and muttered one word to himself. *"Dammit . . ."*

Sitting in the lab's break room, Cara Porter thought, *Kathy and David don't know what they're talking about, but Russell and Craig do. They've got it right.*

"Greg Thomas is going to win the whole freakin' thing," Russell said, talking through a mouthful of tuna fish. He always brought his lunch from home, she had come to notice, usually a sandwich wrapped a bit too tightly in clear plastic. A piece of fresh fruit and a little juice box usually completed the meal, all carried in a vintage Van Halen lunchbox, as if he were in the third grade. Porter immediately picked up on the fact that this was part of Russell's big joke on the world. He was in his early thirties, married with two kids, and was one of the smartest virologists on the team. His unkempt curly hair, thick glasses, and habit of wearing concert

T-shirts under the white lab coat that he never kept buttoned made him easy to underestimate. She now believed that was exactly what he wanted.

"He's the next American Idol, so get used to it."

"He's a rocker," Kathy Chi said. "Rockers are a dime a dozen." Chi was the other midlevel virologist in the group. She was young, pretty, and single, and the latter was engineered, Porter had come to understand, because "career" came before "marriage" on what Chi called her Life List. She still had a few rungs to climb before she was ready to start targeting handsome young doctors. She sat cross-legged in a distinctly ladylike fashion, leaning slightly forward with her lab coat buttoned to the top, eating sushi. Her skill with chopsticks was something close to amazing. Porter found her bubbly personality a bit of an act, but she couldn't help admiring Chi's solemnity where the job was concerned. Like Russell, she was very good.

"He's the only one in the bunch who plays an instrument," Russell said emphatically. "Guitar, harmonica, piano, mandolin . . . Every week he's out there with something different. What's your girl play? The lottery?"

"Debbi Dixon has the best *voice,* and that's what the show's about, right? Singing?" Chi looked to the others fiercely, ready to pounce on the first dissenter.

"I think what Russell's saying is that Greg Thomas is more diverse. He's a more complete package." This was Dr. Kevin Little, the bushy-bearded team leader.

His easygoing nature and disheveled appearance belied a vast intelligence that bubbled just below the surface. If this was a college setting, he'd be the professor all the students liked, the one who managed to maintain a degree of order that his more hard-assed colleagues found frustratingly evasive. Porter particularly appreciated the way he never spoke to any of them in a condescending manner.

"What good is diversity if you don't have a phenomenal voice?" Cho argued back. "When I'm listening to an album, I don't care who's playing the instruments. I care about the person up front. The singer."

"Debbi Dixon really does have a terrific voice," said Nick Orton. He was one of two assistants, the youngest son in a medical family and just a few years out of Stanford. Porter thought he was a bit of a wimp, but a very cute wimp. She kept catching him staring at one part of her anatomy or another. Even though she wanted to lose about two dozen pounds, she knew she was still pretty; Orton's obvious interest confirmed this. He was as straight and clean-cut as they came, which would've turned her off in the past. Now, to her surprise, she had a vague sense of why someone would find this appealing. She gave no hint of her interest, however, as it was always better to be on the receiving end of a one-sided flirtation.

Russell made a face. "Ugh, she sounds like a damn bird."

"You mean melodic and beautiful?" Chi said.

"No, I mean she *squawks*. If her register was any higher, it'd disappear to an imperceptible wavelength." He then added, "Not that I'd mind."

"What about you, Cara?" Little asked. "Wanna get in on this?"

All eyes turned to her, and for a fleeting moment her stomach tightened. Then it relaxed again, and she intuitively understood why—she *liked* these people. Yes, Kathy Chi was a little annoying. But not prohibitively so. And the others were actually pretty cool. *My God, am I displaying signs of normal socialization?* she ruminated, stifling the urge to laugh. *Would Michael believe this? Would anyone who knew me?*

"I think I'm on shaky diplomatic ground here. Do you guys want me to be politically sensitive, or honest?" The disorganized group response unanimously indicated the latter. "Okay, well, I'm afraid I have to go with Russell and Kevin on this. Sorry, Kathy. Sorry, David. In my mind, the harder the sound, the better. And I'm talking about music when I say that, by the way." She shot a quick glance at David, whose cheeks, to her great delight, warmed to a bright crimson. The others laughed at this unabashed smuttiness, which also pleased her to no end. *They like me.*

Now that Porter's position on the issue was established, the debate began rolling again. She returned to the sidelines as an observer rather than a participant, and after a while she shifted her attention to the last person in the room—a young woman named Cherise, who sat curled up in a chair in one corner, reading a virology textbook while absently nibbling on the fingernail of her left pinkie. Like David, she was one of the lab assistants with a freshly minted undergrad degree. And also like David, she was shy almost to the point of paralysis. While Porter suspected this to be feelings of intimidation and inferiority in David's case, Cherise's introversion was due more to external factors. According to the others, she'd had a nightmare childhood courtesy of an alcoholic father and an embittered mother. How she managed to work around it and get into college in the first place, much less pay for it, Porter could not fathom. But she quickly came to admire the girl.

She slid down the bench and said, "Hey, whatcha reading? Anything good?"

Cherise looked up briefly, her eyes glazed with concentration. "The chapter on retroviruses. Converting RNA to DNA and so on."

"Interesting stuff."

"It is."

"Do you have any questions about anything?"

"I'm on the part about structural proteins, and I'm not clear on the protein that makes up the capsids. It's separate from the virus's main protein, right?"

"Yes, it's called a 'gag' protein. The name comes from the phrase 'group-specific antigen.' Some retroviruses, though not all, have capsid proteins that induce cross-reactive antibodies."

"And these capsids contain critical enzymes?"

"Yes, but only copies of those enzymes. Spares, you might say—protease, integrase, and reverse transcriptase pol. They're crucial for the virus's ability to infect the host cells early in the process."

Cherise nodded. "Okay, thank you."

"Sure."

Porter smiled as Cherise went back to the book. Teaching, she'd recently discovered through her interactions with both Cherise and David, was a practice she enjoyed. The notion of becoming an educator had struck her as absurd in years past, when the only image she associated with it was of a roomful of screaming, obstinate children. But when she encountered someone like these two—attentive, driven, eager to learn—such a career seemed very satisfying.

Kevin Little checked his watch—a behemoth waterproof thing with a knobby band—and clapped his hands together. "Okay, everybody," he said, "time to get back to the salt mines. Remember the new cases we heard about this morning." Eleven more fatalities in the surrounding area, including a family of four found in their home, strangled to death by the mother, who then hanged herself in the garage. Little had a friend on the police force who gave him daily updates, and he used them to keep his team focused. "The sooner we get to the bottom of this, the sooner it all stops."

The group rose in unison. Little's choice of metaphor echoed in Porter's mind as they filed toward the door. *Back to the salt mines. Sounds like a Michaelism. Old men and their funny sayings . . .*

"Cara," Little called out as they went down the hallway, "I have wonderful news. You've pulled cage duty this evening."

The others cackled like monkeys—"cage duty" was the unpleasant task of cleaning out the enclosures occupied by the experiment animals. It was disgusting at best, but unavoidable since budgetary constraints precluded the hiring of a lackey. Until now, Porter had been deeply thankful she hadn't drawn this card.

While the others continued ogling, her stomach tightened into a hard knot, one that would endure and worsen as the day dragged on. She suddenly felt ill, nearly nauseated. She also felt a dim anger toward the man who had burdened her with this grim assignment.

Regardless, she managed to reply with a hoarse, "Okay," hoping the rage she felt had no presence in her tone.

ELEVEN

If it's going to rain, I wish it would just do it, Dennis thought as he stared through the kitchen window again. It had been gray and gloomy for two days, yet not a drop had fallen.

The scrambled eggs sizzled and popped in the grill pan in front of him. He kept prodding them with the spatula, trying to get them evenly cooked and finely chopped. Billy sat in his chair, waiting. He was playing with a pair of little toy trucks, crashing them together in slow motion while adding his own sound effects. Scooter watched him from a sitting position, his tail sweeping the floor every time Billy giggled.

Dennis sang along softly to Dave Matthews's "Too Much," which was playing on the under-cabinet stereo. *"Oooh, traffic jam got more cars than a beach got sand. . . ."* He remembered how much he liked the song, and that he kept a copy of Matthews's *Crash* CD here, when he spoke with Elaine on the phone about an hour earlier and it was playing in the background on her car system. She was on her way to work after a luxuriant six hours' sleep and giving him updates. He and Andi had also been following reports via radio and the Internet. Over six thousand dead in twenty-three states, the American economy slowing down, and the possibility of an Iranian connection. *If this keeps up, we'll be living here forever,* he thought, and shuddered at the prospect of that actually happening. *We'll also be the only ones left alive.* That was utterly ridiculous, he told himself. Of course it was. *But the fact that you even thought it. . . .* There was a time when such an idea wouldn't even have materialized on the most distant edges of his consciousness.

"Daddy . . ."

"Huh? Oh, sorry. Sorry."

He dug under the eggs and flipped them one more time. They had browned on the bottom as the last of the butter evaporated, but at least they weren't burnt. Billy wouldn't complain either way, as he had a most agreeable attitude toward food for a five-year-old. But Chelsea would—she expected eggs to be *yellow,* not brown. She was that way about everything she ate—if what was on that plate wasn't precisely what she envisioned, she'd either cut and pick off the parts she didn't like or wouldn't eat at all. She didn't whine, though, and Dennis was grateful for that. She might make a face, but—thank merciful God—she wasn't much of a whiner compared to the average second-grader. Still, he planned to make her eggs next, so he had to be careful. After that, an omelet for Andi. She loved a good egg-and-cheese omelet.

Andi and Chelsea had apparently decided to sleep in this morning. It was going on seven thirty, and the door to their bedroom still hadn't opened. Technically, of course, it was Dennis and Andi's bedroom, but the buddy system had been reworked due to a thunderstorm that began in the middle of the night. One parent slept with one child because neither of the latter was willing to sleep "alone." So it was Dennis and Billy in the kids' room, and Andi and Chelsea, along with Scooter most nights, in the adults' room. It was the first time Dennis had slept without his wife beside him since they were married—and he didn't have the heart to tell Andi he'd never felt so rested. There were two single beds in there, so he was by himself. He couldn't remember the last time he'd slept so deeply or felt so refreshed. He even began having vivid dreams again.

He heard Billy coughing behind him, and in that strange way the human body sometimes responds to the ailments of others, a cough coalesced in his own chest and rose to the surface.

"You can thank your father for that," he said as he lifted the frypan from the coil, whose orange glow was fading quickly. "I've got the allergies in the family. The pollen up here is unbelievable." He tried to inhale through his nostrils, but they were both clogged. "Mold, too. So I guess we can thank Mother Nature as well."

He shoveled a portion of the scrambled eggs onto Billy's Styrofoam plate, then put the rest on his own. The bacon was already done and being sweated of its excess grease in a folded paper towel. He took a test bite of one slice, deemed it suitable, then gave two to his son. Billy looked at him adoringly; he loved bacon. It was hardly nutritional, but today was Sunday—what the Jensens liked to call "Bacon Day." Everyone got to eat whatever they wanted for breakfast and hang the health considerations. Bacon was a staple because they all loved it, although Chelsea sometimes deviated to hash browns or—best of all, when her parents bought them—pork sausages.

Dennis was halfway through his meal when another coughing jag came over Billy. The little boy's face twisted with pain as bits of phlegm—pale and tinted green, Dennis noticed with alarm—flew out. Then he began turning an ashy shade of grayish blue. Dennis, thinking he was choking, jumped out of his seat. He knocked his orange juice over in the process.

"Billy? Are you okay? Hey—"

The child was leaning forward with his mouth open, and there was a peculiar expression on his face—more confusion than fear, as if he was puzzled by what was happening and waiting to see what came next. Then a thin string of blood came out, extending from Billy's mouth to the egg heap with the laziness of a spider on a thread.

Dennis thumped him on the back with his open hand. "Billy? *Billy!*" He tried again, then a third time. What dropped out after the last blow was a revolting package of phlegm, blood, scrambled eggs, and warm milk. The boy gasped for air, refilling his lungs in great and noisy heaves.

"Oh, thank God," Dennis said, his hand on his chest as his heart rate slowly diminished. "Thank G—"

Then the screams—*"Dennis!* DENNIS!*"*

They were muffled, distant, and he instantly understood why—they were coming from behind a closed door.

Upstairs . . .

*"*DENNIS!*"*

He was up the rough-hewn steps in seconds. The door was just to the right, and he pushed it back roughly. Andi and Chelsea were sitting together with their knees raised, holding each other tight, and crying wildly.

They were covered with rashes.

Porter had waited until everyone else left before she cleaned out the cages that night; it gave her the privacy she needed to fire a line of profanities in the general direction of Kevin Little. If there was one aspect of lab work she had always hated with a passion, it was experimenting on animals. She knew it was necessary to infect them so their physiological reactions could be observed, recorded, and studied . . . but to see them suffer, even if it was for a greater good, was unbearable. She had a professor in college, handsome like a model in a cologne ad, who grinned with his perfect teeth and told her soothingly that she'd get used to it. But she never did. Even if watching one mouse endure the agonies of cancer led to the finding of an across-the-board cure, she still felt there was something wrong with it. For this alone, she seriously considered joining Beck in the field of epidemiology and leaving virology to those who had the stomach for it.

She kept her focus on the large computer screen, on the ultramagnified images of one sample after another, in the hope that she'd see something significant: some sign that one of the many treatments they were trying would prove effective. Information was flying around the world between the eight labs that were now working nonstop, via computer, fax, and telephone. No one had made any progress, and frustration was mounting. Since this was a new virus, they were having trouble building a foundation upon which to attack it. Exhaustive examination of Ben Gillette's gene map had gleaned little. One of the CDC people believed there might be an influenza connection, although none of the drugs geared in that direction had made an impact. With the media, the politicians, and the general public putting pressure on the Centers to produce results at any cost, out-of-the-box thinking was now being encouraged, albeit quietly and indirectly. Porter shivered when she'd heard this, as she knew what it meant—*anything goes*. A part of her wanted to lock the animal room and hide the keys. But then she reminded herself of the necessity of it all. . . .

She was studying a blood sample taken from

one of the chickens—they had six different specimens on hand—when her cell phone jingled. She put the small Bluetooth device in her ear and pressed the button.

"Cara Porter."

"Hello, Cara Porter, this is Michael Beck. How's it been going?"

"Less than stellar."

"Yeah, I heard. I assume you guys are trying pretty much everything at this point."

"You name it, we're trying it. Amantadine, ribovirin, penciclovir, interferon type one, even ganciclovir, which only works with herpes . . . We're not getting anywhere."

"Always the problem with antivirals. What works with one doesn't work with any other."

Since antiviral drugs were designed to interrupt the viruses at a certain stage in their life cycle, each one had to be essentially tailor-made for the virus it was designed to target. Success in producing such a medication required exhaustive testing and experimentation due to the unique characteristics of each pathogen. In some instances, for example, a virus was best stifled in the preentry stage, before it had the chance to subjugate the host cell. One effective way to achieve that was by providing mimicking agents that misled the virus into attacking "decoy" cells. Another was to prevent the virus from binding with the host cell's receptor molecules—an approach that had worked with some success in the treatment of HIV and AIDS. A second approach was to disrupt the virus after it had invaded the host cell. Again, deceiving the pathogen was the most effective strategy. One, known as reverse transcription, provided nucleoanalogues that acted as RNA/DNA building blocks but would instead shut down the virus's sythesizing enzymes. Another, the protease inhibitor, prevented a virus from reassembling protein chains before new viruses could be created. Protease inhibitors had shown great promise in spite of some troubling side effects, and research on their improvement had continued unabated. A few antivirals focused on the assembly and release phases of the viral life cycle, and a handful bypassed the replication process altogether and worked to stimulate the immune system.

"We'll keep at it, though, and try everything we can," Porter said. "Every drug we can get our hands on. We just need some bell bottoms and lava lamps and it's Haight-Ashbury all over again."

Beck chuckled. "Except without the free love."

"Considering how much tension there is over here, it couldn't hurt."

"Now, now, let's remember you're a lady."

"Up yours."

"Right. Hey, listen, I understand someone in Atlanta thinks there might be an influenza connection?"

"Yeah. Gregory Cox thought he saw something in the gene sequence that was similar. Everyone else is taking a look."

"Hmm . . . well, I guess it's a start. Now that they've mapped out the whole thing, they're sure it's not in the pox family?"

"No, that's still a possibility. But it isn't smallpox. They did a side-by-side with *Variola*."

Beck said, "I hope Sheila releases that information soon. The press just won't let go of it. All someone has to do is read up on smallpox and they'd know. Even if it's a relative, it's *not* smallpox. It's obviously much deadlier."

"Let's lay odds on someone at home taking the time to conduct that research."

"I know, but the public is scared out of their wits, and they have every right to be."

"I'll tell you one thing," Porter said, "it seems to me that the virus is pretty stable. I've been throwing some foreign genetic bits and pieces at it, and none of them have stuck. That's good news, I guess. It reduces the chance of it turning into something else."

"You've been doing this research on your own?"

"Yeah, pretty much. Someone's going to have to do it anyway, so I figured I'd get the ball rolling."

The viruses with the greatest likelihood of changing form and developing drug resistance were those with lesser stability. They could more easily swap genetic material with other pathogens, essentially creating altogether new organisms on the fly.

"The little detective in you."

"Something like that. The instability of the H1N1 virus was what had health officials so concerned in '09, right?"

"Right. It didn't turn into anything more virulent, but there seemed to be a fairly good chance that it would. Even to this day, a lot of people in the CDC, WHO, and elsewhere are waiting for that to happen."

Porter tapped her keyboard and switched to another sample. "Speaking of that, how's the Hardy Boys stuff going?"

Now Beck sighed. "One lead brings me to another, then to another, and then another. I can't find the beginning of this thing. Maybe I never will. It's like that movie we watched on DVD last year, *National Treasure,* where Jon Voight says to Nicolas Cage, 'And that clue will lead to another clue. Don't you see? There *is* no treasure.' "

"That was a good movie," Porter said, ignoring the fact that she'd complained all the way to and from the rental store.

"Yeah, but this isn't a movie. This is real. We've *got* to find the treasure."

"Nicolas Cage found the treasure, remember?"

"Optimism? From you?"

"I just want to get my picture in the paper."

"Ah, of course."

"Where are you headed now?"

"To the home of a guy named Bob Easton. More backtracking, and this after doing nothing *but* backtracking and following narrow leads for the better part of two days. Pure drudgery."

"I know, you've been busy as hell."

"Yeah. And worst of all, this is probably another dead end."

"So to speak."

"Yes, so to speak. He had the infection and gave it to his wife. Apparently he killed her before drowning himself in their pool."

"Lovely."

"The fun part of this job."

Porter thought about the animals being tortured in the glass-walled room directly behind her and shuddered. *Of the two professions, I think I'd prefer the one that has me finding people in swimming pools.* "Well, you enjoy that. Let me know if you find anything. Any treasure."

"I will."

She ended the call and dropped the earpiece back into the pocket of her lab coat.

After a few more samples, she decided to get up and walk through the halls for a few minutes. She'd been sitting for over two hours and her eyes were burning.

Halfway to the door, she couldn't resist the urge to at least glance into the animal room. One of the white rats was lying on its side, trembling and looking terrified.

She fought back the urge to scream and kept moving.

TWELVE

The room in President Baraheri's Tehran residence where he liked to hold these meetings was spare and humble, with white walls, plain brown carpet, and a collection of antique furniture. The Iranian flag stood in one corner, and a framed photo of the Supreme Leader—technically, as the highest authority in both politics and religion, Iran's most powerful man—hung on the wall, more for its diplomatic value than anything else.

Maziar Baraheri sat on a gold couch near a pair of heavy curtains. His neat silver hair, steel-rimmed glasses, and pleasant face made him look more like a scientist than like a political leader. The election was almost half a year in the past now, yet he was still a complete stranger—the official International Man of Mystery of global politics.

When Iran's last presidential campaign began, it appeared as though the only two candidates of consequence were the incumbent, conservative Mahmoud Ahmadinejad, and the president before him, moderate Mohammad Khatami. After years of Ahmadinejad's incendiary policies toward the West, verbal abuse of Israel, and failure to improve the nation's economy, Khatami found himself with a tremendous lead in the polls, much to the excitement of his many supporters at home and abroad—including the American government. However, he dropped out of the race just two months before the summer election, citing the belief that those in other powerful positions would block him from making the reforms he felt were necessary. Critics and analysts believed another factor was the refusal by Ahmadinejad's government to allow Khatami to hold rallies in key locations, plus their nocturnal habit of removing Khatami posters from public places.

With less than sixty days to go, Khatami threw his support behind Baraheri, a former two-term mayor from the Shia province of Kerman. Totally unknown outside his obscure hometown, Baraheri endeared himself to the Iranian public with his calm demeanor, seemingly boundless knowledge of the Koran, promise of a "sensible government that works in the best interests of all our people," and his reputation as a uniter. Khatami campaigned vigorously for him, creating the illusion that Baraheri was equally moderate and thus the two were interchangeable. But mostly, Khatami simply wanted to dethrone Ahmadinejad, which in turn would move Iran closer to a position of sanity on the world stage.

The Iranian people spoke on June 12, and

Baraheri took 63 percent of the popular vote—a landslide by any definition. Ahmadinejad's people did their best to squelch it, but in the end he had no choice but to vacate his office, and the rest of the world breathed a sigh of relief. Baraheri's first address to the public was rambling and unfocused, leaving other world leaders scratching their heads. It was as if the man was purposely trying to avoid a hard stance on any issue. With rumors rampant that he had written the text himself, most dismissed it as the awkward first effort of an amateur. In time, however, they would realize this "nonimage" was carefully sculpted, suggesting there was more to him than previously estimated. He was unpredictable and subtly manipulative, leaving those around him unsure of whether he was their ally or their enemy, yet he made significant progress on both domestic and foreign fronts. Nevertheless, he did not speak to the media, avoided being photographed, and rarely traveled outside the country.

The only other man in the room with him asked, "The conversation did not go well, I assume?"

Sanjar Hejazi was still handsome and boyish in his fifties, with large eyes and a pile of dark hair on top. He had been friends with Baraheri since childhood. They rose through the political ranks together, with Baraheri always out front and Hejazi behind the curtain working the controls. Baraheri could not have gone far without him and trusted him completely.

"No, it did not," Baraheri said, exhaling deeply.

"I am surprised he was so swift to condemn you. I thought the two of you were making progress on a personal basis."

"We were."

And I genuinely liked the man, too, Baraheri thought, recalling the previous conversation he'd had with Barack Obama. It was only their third since Baraheri's election, yet it was three more than anyone else in the world would've thought possible. They had even moved beyond politics and discussed casual personal matters—for example, First Lady Michelle's love of reading and gardening, and the fact that Baraheri's late wife, Donya, had been an admirer of the American television program *The West Wing*. Baraheri had ended that last call feeling more enthusiastic than ever, excited at the prospect of a renewed relationship with the United States. *This is a man I can work with,* he had told Hejazi that night. *We can make good things happen together.*

And then the call a few hours ago . . . an openly irate Obama, feeling deceived and misled. He was straightforward with his diction, but Baraheri could detect the underlying sentiment.

"He made demands?" Hejazi asked.

Baraheri nodded. "He has given me forty-eight hours to cease any further attempts to spread the virus, to provide detailed information on how it was created, arrest all people associated with Masood currently being harbored in Iran, and provide American intelligence services with the necessary information to do the same concerning whatever members continued to operate on American soil."

"And if not?"

Baraheri looked at his old friend. "He said he would have no choice but to take military action."

After a pause, Hejazi said, "Do you think he means it?"

Baraheri leaned forward with his elbows on his knees. This was a question he had been considering since the call ended two hours ago. He decided to leave it alone for the moment. "Do you have any idea who might be behind this?"

"There are several groups, I believe. Several individuals who have tried from time to time. We know this. American intelligence know this."

"So that's why they think it was us?"

"Very likely."

"But do any have the *means* to orchestrate something so intricate, then execute it?"

"Possibly."

"This is not simple science here, my friend. Creating a virus with this kind of power requires time, money, research, expertise. . . . Then having it delivered to the American mainland and creating false evidence pointing to us. Who would—?"

Baraheri's eyes widened. "Do you truly think it could be Shalizeh?"

"I do," Hejazi replied. "In my heart, I do."

"Do we have any idea of his whereabouts?"

Hejazi was already getting up. "I'll check into it at once."

"Thank you. And Sanjar?"

Hejazi was at the door. He stopped and turned. "Yes?"

"Quickly."

"Of course."

It was called Little Nelly's Little Deli—a name that Cara Porter had characterized as "grating on my nerves like a phone solicitor." But it also served its purpose quite adequately, at least in her and Ben's and Michael's eyes. It was their new hideaway, tucked into the quiet town of Riverdale, about twenty minutes west of Ramsey, in a dainty strip mall. And in spite of the town's proximity to the outbreak, it seemed oddly isolated, as if there were a protective force field around it, and the citizens weren't aware of the crisis unfolding beyond their borders.

They found Nelly's purely by chance three days ago. Ben suggested they all get together for lunch, preferably someplace where they were unlikely to encounter members of the media. This was in response not just to their rapidly diminishing patience but also Sheila Abbott's declaration that she alone would be the official distributor of public information. "The more obscure, the better," Ben had said, setting down the search criteria. Michael suggested they look in Riverdale based on the statistical evidence that it had gone relatively unaffected. There seemed to be one anomalous area in every outbreak that fell into this category. So they piled into Ben's car—writers and photographers had already identified Michael's convertible—and drove around until Nelly's caught their attention. SOUPS AND SANDWICHES AND SO MUCH MORE! blared the cheerful subtitle, to Cara's further irritation.

The inside was inviting and well kept, but hardly unique. There were a dozen cramped booths, a long meat case, an overhead menu board, and a Coca-Cola cooler with sliding doors. A pair of ceiling fans spun at low speed, efficiently distributing the scents of fresh ham, hot tomato soup, and toasted garlic bread. The actual Nelly was an aging hippie with a ponytail and narrow rectangular glasses. She wore a white apron tied at the back, ran both the meat slicer and the cash register, and smiled unceasingly.

Cara watched her with tepid interest from booth number 6, situated next to the snack rack and well away from the panoramic front window. This was the third straight day they'd come here, the most notable difference this time being that Michael was absent; he had to interview a newlywed couple in West Milford and was planning to eat on the run.

"*Spaceballs* was funny," she said, turning back to the roast beef sub lying on the plate in front of her. "That's one I liked."

Ben nodded enthusiastically as he guided a dangling shred of lettuce back into his mouth. "That was one of the best."

"Michael insisted I watch it, and I admit it was good."

The topic of the moment was Mel Brooks movies. Michael and Ben had OD'd on them in their Chapel Hill days. What topic came next was impossible to predict; the only rule, they had agreed, was no shop talk. This was the only break they got from it during their waking hours. Cara was particularly adamant about this now that most of the once-healthy animals in the lab were in advanced stages of the illnesses their human hosts had given them and were suffering horribly.

"*The Producers* was maybe his best," Ben said.

"Didn't catch that one."

"No?"

"No, but it's on the list. The one Michael made for me."

"It's worth seeing, believe me. What about *Young Frankenstein?*"

"That was the only one I'd seen already. A friend in college rented it. We sat in her dorm room and watched it on a Friday night."

Ben grinned. "So you don't remember much of it, right? Bombed out of your skull, were you?"

Cara did not return the smile; the thought of someone assuming she was a typical drunken college kid struck her as deeply offensive. She never cared much for alcohol and hadn't touched a drop all through her time at the University of Chicago.

"No, I watched it to the end. It wasn't too bad. My mind was on other things, though. I was studying all the time."

At first she didn't know why she'd added this last proclamation. Then she did—her aunt Beverly and uncle Sid had gone into crippling debt to see that she received the best education available, and there was no way she was going to blow it by getting blasted every weekend like most of those losers. She wanted to make sure that was perfectly clear to Ben. She liked him—liked him a lot, in fact. But she wanted to be sure he understood she wasn't the type who wasted her time, money, and brain cells on booze, nor someone who took a cavalier attitude toward precious opportunities provided by saintly relatives.

Ben picked up on this and promptly said, "I know, I was just kidding around. Michael told me a long time ago that you were an excellent student."

"Three-point-eight GPA and a regular on the Dean's List, baby."

"Very impressive."

"Mmm . . . thanks."

He got the feeling she wanted to say something else, something like *Damn right* or *Better believe it,* but then erred on the side of diplomacy. *Did Michael teach her that, too?* he wondered, studying her. She wasn't an easy read; she had thicker walls than Fort Knox. He had a pretty good idea why, too. In the year and a half that she'd been Michael's assistant, Ben had learned a few things. Michael hadn't received much of the information directly, of course; she was predictably stingy when it came to personal details. But there had been an interview process, and there were records.

First there was the agonizing death of her father, a dedicated and idealistic physician who went to

Africa to combat the Marburg virus. Somehow, in spite of meticulous precautions, he caught it himself and was dead after two weeks of unimaginable suffering. Then her mother, who was consumed in the wake of depression and never recovered, leaving fourteen-year-old Cara to fend for herself. She inevitably hooked up with the wrong crowd, leading to a nightmarish odyssey of excessive drinking, hardcore drugs, unprotected sex, and other horrors. That phase of her life resulted in two arrests and one near-fatal accident involving a stolen car.

With the aid of her kindhearted aunt and uncle, she restacked her priorities and gained acceptance into medical school. There she discovered a natural gift for research, an inherited trait from her late father, and blossomed into one of the school's outstanding students. Exuberant letters from professors and counselors coalesced into a lavish chorus of praise. Their only reservations, predictably, concerned her ongoing emotional withdrawal. *But Michael has been working on that, too,* Ben decided. *He's one of the most patient and generous people on this earth, and he's the perfect mentor for her.* Then he thought, *And she might be perfect for him, too, in some ways. . . .*

"No, seriously," he said, "Chicago is a tough school. A lot of kids don't make it through."

She nodded, the anger forgotten. "I saw that happen a lot."

"Do you miss being there? Do you miss your friends?"

"Sometimes. I didn't like the city that much. Not Chicago in particular, just cities in general."

"More of a suburban type?" he asked. She made a face, which amused him to no end. "Vacuum cleaners, washing machines, hot dinners on the table when hubby gets home—" She was sticking her finger in her mouth in a gagging gesture. "Babies crawling everywhere, loading up their diapers." He was shaking with laughter now, enjoying the escalating absurdity of it.

"Yeah, that's me. 'Yes, dear,' and 'Whatever you say, honey,' and 'Stop calling your brother a penis, Jonathan.' That sounds great."

"I'd love to see it."

"Just shoot me now."

"No husband? No kids? Never?"

She drew a sip of her soda. "I never say 'never' to anything, but I've got no such plans at present."

"It's not a bad deal if you find the right person."

"That's what I hear. What about you? Do you think you'll ever find the right person?"

"Haven't yet," he replied. Cara took note of his demeanor and saw nothing, either in the way he answered the question or in the subtleties of his body language, to suggest the kind of discomfort natural to someone who had gone to great pains to hide his homosexuality. *And the mystery continues,* she thought.

"But my parents had a great marriage," he said, "so I believe it's possible."

"I agree with that. I don't think it's im*possible*."

She took another bite of her sub, chewed it contemplatively, then said, "And what about Michael? What's his deal with marriage?"

Ben's smile fell like a Venetian blind whose clutch had snapped. Cara noticed this and realized she was on to something.

"Come on, I know you know stuff." She lowered her voice. "He won't tell me anything. He gets tighter than a clam's butt."

"I know a little," Ben said somberly, breaking eye contact. "But nothing I should share."

"Please?"

He toyed with his salad before shaking his head. "No, I'm sorry. That's Michael's business."

Now it was Cara's turn to do the studying. Ben was serious; that much was obvious. She'd never seen him so sensitive about anything, and she was mildly surprised by it. It seemed to run counter to his easygoing reputation.

"I guess it's a touchy subject," she said, hoping to sound casual enough to wave off some of the tension.

"Yeah," Ben said, "you could say that."

Whenever he thought about this aspect of Michael's life, his mind always reached for the same memory. It was in June of 1982, less than a year after Michael's return from Yambuku. Ben had been invited to attend a banquet where Michael was due to receive the Outstanding Contributions to Epidemiology Methods Award from the American College of Epidemiology. It was in recognition of the field strategies he had conceived to make the

Africa trip more efficient, resulting in the discovery of the virus's origin in an unusually short time. It was remarkable for someone so young to be given such an honor.

Michael did not appear at the ceremony, and every one of the 234 attendees knew why. With no choice, Ben had to accept the award in his place, speaking off the cuff as he gave the most difficult speech of his life. After that night, the epidemiological world did not hear from Michael Beck again for nearly sixteen months. And when he emerged from his self-imposed exile, he was treated not with scorn but with admiration, sympathy, and a collective sigh of relief.

"I wouldn't dig too deep," Ben counseled.

"I won't."

"Professionally, he is a true genius in every sense of the word. He never forgets a stat, learns faster than anyone I've ever seen, and processes information like a computer. And what's more, he's so natural at it that he makes it look *easy*. But that's the working side of the man. The other half, well . . . He thinks the world of you, but I wouldn't push it."

"I'm sorry I brought it up."

Ben smiled again. "No, don't be sorry. It's natural to be curious. You just have to remember one thing about Michael Beck—and this is all I'm going to say."

"What's that?"

"He's *haunted*, okay? And haunted men are . . . well, delicate."

"I understand."

"Okay."

From there the conversation quickly returned to the filmography of Mel Brooks, then petered out when the latest casualty updates crawled across the bottom of the flat-screen monitor that was showing CNN high in one corner of the room.

THIRTEEN

Andrea Jensen was no longer able to look at herself, and not just because she had covered the cheval mirror in the bedroom with a large blanket. The blisters and pustules were everywhere now and becoming engorged with fluid. The swelling, too—her hands, legs, and face looked as though they'd been inflated with an air pump. The facial enlargement was occurring disproportionally, giving her a freakishly lopsided look. Her left eye was shrinking into a hill of pus-bloated tissue, and the right cheek was beginning to sag. She was in Stage Two—and so was Chelsea, who was sitting in cool-water bath down the hall and sobbing loudly.

Dennis stood there with the cell phone pressed to his ear. He was coughing every few seconds and sweating continuously.

"Come on, come on! . . ."

He snapped the phone shut and walked in a small circle by the bed. Andi was sitting on the other side, watching him.

"Where the hell *is* she?"

He hadn't been able to get his sister for the last two hours. He tried her station number on the third floor of Brick Memorial, her home number, and her cell. She had never been the type to dodge a call, and certainly never from him. *Something's wrong,* he thought. *Something's happened.* He kept pacing and cursed under his breath, enraged that everything in his world had fallen apart so swiftly. In times like this, he seriously wondered if recognizing God's existence was a matter of faith or folly. He knew that sounded childish, but he couldn't stop from being angry about the unfairness of it. He had played it straight all his life—worked hard and kept within reasonable ethical boundaries, gave an abundance of love and attention to his children, never fooled around on his wife, paid his taxes, always crossed at the green . . . and yet this had happened. *Being a good person has really paid off,* he told himself, one bitter sentiment amid a swirl of others. His mind was racing right now, throwing out hundreds of random thoughts. When he considered what Andi and Chelsea were going through, he felt a fury that bordered on madness.

"We can't sit and do nothing," Andi said, her speech slightly distorted by the heavy cheek and likely to get worse. "We should go to Catskills Regional *now*."

"I know . . . but they still don't have any treatment or vaccine or anything. What are they going to *do*?"

They had tried every radio and TV station, surfed through every major website, yet there was no news of a breakthrough. No vaccine, no medication, nothing to ease the suffering. Professionals working on the infection all around the world, investing thousands of hours and millions of dollars—and still nothing.

"They said they were letting people try different things if they wanted," Andi reminded him. "If you signed the waivers, you could have some experimental drugs."

"Great. Our family turned into human guinea pigs." He leaned down, hands on his thighs, and coughed mightily. Some greenish spittle flew out and landed in a cluster of prim little dots on the rug. After he'd wiped his mouth with a handkerchief that was looking increasingly vile, he said, "I don't want the kids to become lab specimens."

They couldn't hear Billy over Chelsea's persistent wailing, but Dennis went in every ten minutes or so to check on him. He had vomited puddles of phlegm twice now and had a fever of 102 degrees F; a number that would likely move up before it went down. Now he was lying in his room with his favorite blanket, his stuffed Ernie doll, and his third pair of pajamas. Scooter lay on the floor beside him, his paws primly together and his brown eyes wide and watchful as he absorbed the tension.

"What are the options?" Andi said. "We sit here and just wait? We just *let it happen*?"

Dennis covered his face with his hands and took a deep breath. He was having trouble concentrating, a problem with which he was not familiar. At work, he could focus with such intensity that he usually had to be jarred out of it. Now, though, he couldn't seem to put his thoughts in a straight line.

He was just about to respond, when Chelsea came into the room, dripping wet and wrapped in a towel. The cool bath had robbed her of all color, leaving her skin a ghostly white in vibrant contrast to the broad red splotches. The facial swelling in her case had started around the lower jaw, and her bottom lip protruded to the point where it looked as though she were pretending to be an old man.

"Are we going to see Aunt Elaine?" she asked between snivels. In spite of the swollen lip, she was able to enunciate this clearly enough.

"No, sweetheart," Andi said, stroking her wet hair, "we're probably just going to go the hospital near here. Aunt Elaine's hospital is too far, and she's very busy with all the new cases coming in. She's been working around the clock."

"But I want to see Aunt *Elaine*."

"I'm sorry, honey, but it's too—"

Chelsea stomped the floor with her heel. "I want Aunt Elaine!"

"Chelsea, we—"

"Aunt Elaine!"

"Honey . . ."

"Aunt E—"

Dennis exploded—"goddammit enough!"

Chelsea jumped as if poked with an electric prod, then ran from the room bawling.

Andi got to her feet quickly. "It's not her fault, Dennis!"

"I know it's not her fault, but when she gets like that, do you have to patronize her?"

"She's *scared*!"

"Do you think I'm not?"

The last few words broke apart as tears began streaming down his own face. In the silence that followed, he put his hands on his hips and looked out the window, his chest heaving.

"I'm sorry, I'm sorry. You're absolutely right, I shouldn't have yelled."

"It's okay," Andi said softly.

"I just . . . I don't know what to do. I mean, what is there to *do*?" He began choking out little breaths and coughing worse than ever.

His wife crawled across the bed and took his hand.

"I'm supposed to be protecting all of you," he said, his voice rising to a squeal. "That's why we came up here. It's my job to protect you."

"It's my job, too," Andi said.

"Yeah, well . . ." He fell to his knees, striking the dusty boards with a thud. His wife held him against her chest and kissed the top of his head.

"If we go now," she said, "at least there's some chance. If we stay—think about what they're going to go through. Think about it, Dennis."

He knew all too well, had thought about it a few thousand times already. The excruciating physical agony, the dementia leading to extreme confusion and violence. He had tried to block out the lurid images that came into his mind, but it was becoming more difficult as each moment ticked by—and the nightmare moved closer to crossing the border into reality.

With a voice that she could no longer keep steady, she whispered the most chilling thing he ever heard. "At least they can keep Chelsea and Billy sedated."

They held each other and cried aloud for what felt like an eternity. There was no other communication between them, just a flood of tears and the impotent emptiness of resignation.

Finally, he nodded. "Yeah, all right. Let's just get going and maybe . . . I don't know. Let's just go."

"Okay."

They began throwing a few basic things into a bag—another change of clothes for each of them, some toys for the kids, snacks for the ride. They decidedly ignored the fact that all of this was just stage work and totally unnecessary.

Then Dennis came across his gun. It felt like it weighed a hundred pounds. That meant the magazine was still fully loaded. Only one slug short, in fact—the one that was probably still lodged in Jack McLaughlin's shoulder.

Still fully loaded . . .

He and Andi looked at each other, and the idea they shared at that moment was too dreadful to articulate.

But it was there.

FOURTEEN

"Dr. Beck? I'm Mark Hollis."

Beck reached out to shake hands, both of which were wrapped in pale surgical gloves. "Good to meet you."

"I'm sorry, but can I see some ID, please? I have to ask."

"Sure, no problem."

He seemed like a nice kid, Beck thought. Mid-twenties at the oldest. Dark brown hair, green eyes. Couldn't tell much else because of the mask. Beck was getting used to seeing them, which was unsettling in its own way. The only other facts he knew about Hollis were that he was a police officer, as told by the uniform, and that he was not happy being one at the moment. Hollis belonged to the same department as the two cops who'd gone to Katie Milligan's apartment and died shortly thereafter, not to mention nearly a dozen others who'd perished in the line of duty over the past two weeks. He looked like he'd rather be anywhere else right now.

Beck took his CDC identification from his wallet and handed it over.

Hollis studied it for a moment before returning it. "All right, Dr. Beck, thank you. Please follow me."

It was yet another modest home in the middle of a typical suburban grid. This one was a bit nicer than most, with extensive landscaping, a two-car garage, and what appeared to be a freshly laid driveway. Beck also knew there was a large in-ground swimming pool around back. Bob Easton had done well for himself. The report Ben had emailed him said he'd been earning six figures since the late '90s. He had two children, but they were both grown and gone. And his mortgage was paid off. He and his wife had been living well until Fate pointed its crooked finger in their direction.

Hollis unwrapped the yellow crime-scene tape that blocked the porch and allowed Beck to pass. "I unlocked the door already. You can go in."

Beck looked at him, saw the pleading in those youthful eyes, and didn't bother asking if Hollis was coming along. Law enforcement had finally found a way to carry out its duties in connection with the outbreak without risking what had become almost certain death—by exercising only what the police unions came to call "first line of defense only." In the event of an emergency call, officers would report to the scene as usual. But at the first sign of possible infection, they were then required to withdraw and contact local biohazard units. The bio teams were better equipped, police leadership reasoned, and therefore represented the "second line." After the death of more than five hundred officers nationwide, no one argued with this approach.

"Call me if you need anything," Hollis said. *But don't need anything,* was the unspoken caveat.

"Sure," Beck replied. "Thanks."

He pulled up his own cotton mask and stepped inside. His first impression was that the house had been well kept—there seemed to be a place for everything, and most everything was still in its place. There were no cobwebs hanging from the ceiling, no dust bunnies along the edge of the floor. At the same time, however, there were the unmistakable signs of domestic violence, driven by dementia though it may have been. A large gilded mirror had been smashed and was now facedown on the beige carpet in the hallway. The easy chair in the living room had been heaved into the giant flat-screen television, breaking the latter in half like a cracker. And, of course, there were smears of pus-encrusted blood everywhere: on the walls, counters, tabletops . . .

He went down the hall, stepping over what remained of the mirror, and opened the bedroom door. This, the report said, was where the wife's body was found. Other than examine the room and remove the corpse, they left everything untouched. The sheets were surprisingly neat, considering the nature of the crime. They were folded down in a near-perfect angle on her side, and altogether undisturbed on his. *She was sleeping when he killed her,* Beck realized. *She had gone to bed early, and he came in later*. He saw the blood-painted pillow and winced. There was a funnel-hole marking the direction of the bullet. The blood had pooled there and coagulated over time. The windows were all shut and locked, he noticed. It was a considerate gesture by the Eastons, as none of their neighbors had become infected. In fact, only one other individual on the street had caught it—a Mr. Ted Lewis, six doors down on the opposite side. Why him and no one else was puzzling to Beck. It may have had to do with the fact that he and Bob Easton were buddies. That's what Easton's oldest daughter had said.

He returned to the hallway and went into the kitchen, digging gingerly through the garbage can and then checking the fridge. It was remarkable how many viral and bacterial infections began with food; he had dealt with dozens of such cases and knew of hundreds more. But he didn't see anything unusual here. He would order that samples of everything be removed and tested, just in case, but he was doubtful anything would come of it.

He opened one of the sliding-glass doors and went out on the deck. The water in the swimming pool was sparkling. Whether it had been sanitized by the Realtors or the automatic pump, he didn't know. But this was where they'd found Bob Easton, dead and bloated at the bottom after chaining himself to a statue of the Roman god Neptune that previously stood at the southeast corner of the walkway.

According to the police report, Easton tied the chain around his midsection, securing it around back with a padlock, then tipped the statue forward until it tumbled in. The latter was still lying on the pool floor, the broken chain lying around it like an untied bow on a gift box.

He went back inside and found the Eastons' office, a tiny room with a desk, computer, and two-tiered filing cabinet. There was no damage in here: no broken glass, no crusted stains. It was a room they didn't use much, he figured. For paying bills and doing taxes. It seemed to be somehow detached from everything else, a tiny universe all its own.

When he returned to the main hallway, a feeling of weary frustration crept into him. This visit was turning into another dead end. Over two hundred interviews now, a few zillion megabytes of hard data, and he was nowhere. *Just like in that movie—one clue leads to another, but there is no treasure.* He was exhausted, discouraged, even depressed. An optimist by nature, he wasn't comfortable with these emotions. Fighting off the sense of failure was beginning to require some effort. The more he dug, the more confused and dispirited he became. *Thousands of people are counting on me. Millions . . .* His education, training, experience, and reputation meant nothing right now. This was strictly a what-have-you-done-for-me-lately profession. Past victories held no value. All that counted was tackling the problem at hand—and in that regard, he simply wasn't getting it done.

He was yanked violently from this miserable train of thought the moment he opened the basement door. The thick, wretched stench that emanated from the hollows below struck him like a punch to the face. He shuddered briefly and his eyes bulged.

"My *God,*" he said out loud.

He had been around his share of foul odors. Everything from sliced-open bodies in autopsy rooms to synthesized chemicals designed to produce instant vomiting—and this was easily a candidate for the top ten list—top five, even. It made him feel light-headed, seasickish. *What the hell is down there?*

At first he thought the obvious—another dead body. But no, he reasoned, the police would've found it in their search. *An animal, maybe?* Possibly. Perhaps a squirrel or a raccoon had come in through one of the windows, couldn't get back out, and was now lying on its side with its tongue hanging out.

Whatever it was, he was obligated to check.

He flicked on the light and went down. The pungency seemed to increase exponentially with each step. By the time he reached the bottom, he was covering his nose with both hands. But even that plus the mask wasn't getting it done.

It was a simple cellar, essentially a huge rectangle that covered a little less area than the house above it. The stairs put you down in the middle, and the single bare bulb illuminated almost everything. He looked to the left and saw a furnace and a weight bench. Then he looked right and found a free-standing clothes rack. Shirts and dresses, all neatly pressed. Shoes for both of them were lined up along the bottom. Certainly nothing there that would produce an aroma of such dizzying strength.

Then he saw a partitioned area with a closed door. There was a small, rectangular sign on the door—KEEP OUT. As he moved in that direction, he realized he was drawing closer to the source. His heart began pounding; his throat went dry and tightened up. *This is like something out of a Stephen King story,* he thought crazily, wondering if a zombie or a vampire was waiting for him in the darkness. He opened the door and pulled the hanging string that fired another bulb. There was a worktable, a variety of tools hanging neatly on Peg-Board, and a stack of woodworking magazines on a shelf. He also spotted a smaller table in one corner—and that's where he found it. For the first time in a forgotten number of years, he screamed.

When it was brand new, it had been a large Coleman ice chest, royal blue with a white lid. Now it was a home for thousands of chubby maggots, moving about as busily as commuters. They covered the chest completely, with extended populations running along the edge of the sink and up the wall. The smell at this close range was beyond description. Beck felt his stomach lurch and prayed he wouldn't lose his lunch.

There was a long screwdriver hanging from one of the Peg-Board hooks. He took it down and used it to prop open the lid. A large portion of the maggot population fell away with a grotesque sliding sound. Many of them tumbled into the unlit area behind the table with the unsteady patter of a rainstorm. Clenching his teeth, he took one step forward and retrieved a penlight from his back pocket. He clicked it on and shone it into the compact void.

Oh, man . . .

There were several large pieces of shriveled meat, cut in formless shapes with ragged edges. Due to the decay and the increased maggot concentration, he couldn't make out what type it was—beef, pork, lamb, et cetera. But judging by the shallow pool of water at the bottom, Beck concluded that Bob Easton brought them home packed in ice that had long since melted, presumably with the plan of wrapping them up and storing them in the freezer upstairs. *But he was already feeling sick by then, and he forgot about it,* Beck theorized. *This could be it. Maybe, just maybe . . .*

He turned to go back out, his forbearance nearly exhausted. He would order samples be taken and tested immediately. If the virus was there, the store that sold Easton the meat would be shuttered. It'd never reopen, either. Even if the outbreak truly hadn't been its fault, even if there was no intentional wrongdoing, the general public wouldn't go near the place. Years of honest business practice couldn't outweigh one mistake when the public was your jury, Beck knew. He'd seen it enough times.

He was almost to the stairs when the adjusted realization struck. The whole picture, bright and colorful, flashed through his mind. *The meat . . . the other neighbor . . . the lantern . . .* There had been a large Coleman lantern next to the ice chest, which the maggots had more or less ignored. *The shotgun . . . the one he used to kill his wife . . .*

Beck took off running, bounding up the stairs two at a time. He was shouting for Hollis before he even reached the front door.

FIFTEEN

Cara Porter slipped another grid into the electron microscope and peered into the viewer at the image produced by the electron-dense. Today she would use the microscope's tiny screen; tomorrow she'd view everything on a larger desktop computer.

She had seen the virus so many times now that she could draw it from memory. Even the fascination of coming face-to-face with the very thing that was causing so much suffering and discord had faded. She and her colleagues—there were twenty others in this lab, divided into teams of seven in three shifts—were trying everything from orthodox to bizarre and getting nowhere; none of the potential medications were having any effect. And the people working on the vaccine weren't doing any better. It was becoming a long and costly battle, and all they had to show for it was the frustration of being toyed with by a far-superior adversary.

She pulled away from the microscope, closed her eyes, and set her chin in her hands. This lab had become her second home. She had tried endless combinations of drugs, studied thousands of samples, and entered a zillion bits of data into the online repositories. She had grown used to these tasks, grown used to her colleagues, grown used to the long hours and the headaches. She'd grown used to everything . . . except the animals.

She looked at them without really wanting to, then just as quickly looked away. Some were suffering so badly, whining and groaning and scratching at their cage doors. How could the others go about their business and barely notice? They ran tests, wrote reports, even talked and laughed with one another, all against the lachrymose cacophony of their torment; it was amazing. For her own part, she brought along her iPod every day and played it nonstop. And she made sure it was charged every night at the hotel before she went to sleep; she didn't want to have to make the decision of not coming in because it wasn't ready.

She opened her eyes and saw that it was nearly eleven—time to leave. Everyone else was gone. She would go back to the hotel, put the iPod in its charger, slip a DVD into her laptop, and fall asleep during the first fifteen minutes. Then she'd dream of reaching the end of this crisis and taking a vacation. Maybe Rome or Paris. Perhaps São Paulo. She'd heard Brazil was interesting.

With Led Zeppelin's "Kashmir" chugging in her head, she removed her lab coat, grabbed her bag, and headed out. She willed herself not to look directly at the animal room, but then something caught her attention—the ferret in cage 32 was lying on its side, motionless. Porter turned and saw that it was dead. Not surprising, considering the poor thing had been twisting and screeching for the past twenty-four hours.

She couldn't just let it lie there. The next shift might not bother with it right away. They were the worst. There were some mornings when she came in and found animals who had died during the night but had been ignored. At best, the techs would cut them open, record whatever data they needed, then toss their carcasses into the incinerator. One time she found a severed mouse head stuck to the top of a pencil. It was propped in the animal room with a Post-it Note that read, YOU COULD BE NEXT. Bunch of comedians, those guys.

She put on her protective gear and stepped inside. The iPod's volume was maxed out, which was painful enough but better than the alternative. She opened the cage door and lifted out the lifeless body. It was still warm and somewhat pliable, which meant it had died during her shift. Something about this was particularly depressing. She set the body into a plastic bag, zipped it shut, and put it in the freezer at the far end of the room. She'd leave a note outside so they'd know.

As she closed the empty cage, she noticed that the ferret above it was sticking its little pink nose through the tiny chrome bars. When Porter looked up, the animal sneezed explosively.

As the moisture sprayed onto her face, a grim realization struck. *My goggles aren't on. Oh my good God . . .*

She didn't have to turn around to know where she'd left them—on the table by the electron microscope; she had to remove them to look into the eyepieces. She spent so much time training herself not to look from the workstation to the animal room. Now she was unable to do the reverse.

She dashed into the decontamination area, stripped off the protective gear with much less delicacy than was recommended, and turned on both faucets at the scrub sink. There was an official eyewashing station in the prep room outside and down the hall, but there was no time for that.

She took the plastic bottle of sanitizer from its little pedestal above the spigot and squeezed a generous portion into her palm. As the shuffle engine in her iPod followed "Kashmir" with "Black Country Woman," she rubbed her hands together like a mad scientist, took a deep breath, then forced her eyes to open as wide as they would go and slapped the gel into them. The scream that followed was like something out of a horror movie. Nevertheless, she rubbed the gel in harder, then leaned down and washed it all out with clumsy, frantic movements. She kept splashing water in there long after all the sanitizer was gone, making bovine grunting noises with each shot.

She found the roll of paper towels and dried her face. Then she willed herself to look into the small mirror hanging on the wall by the garbage can. A doctor might think she had the worst case of pinkeye in history, or maybe she'd been beaten up pretty good by her boyfriend. She began crying, and a part of her thought this was good—maybe the tears would wash out any remaining contagion.

She returned to the workstation, whispering in a quivering voice. *Please, God, please don't let this happen. Please, I'll do anything . . . anything you want.*

Then she picked up her cell phone.

SIXTEEN

DAY 16

MSNBC had the numbers correct thanks to a single sheet of paper handed to Dr. Nancy Snyderman, its chief medical editor, just as a commercial break was ending—roughly 12,700 dead and more than 31,000 infected. This was according to the CDC, which was now updating its dedicated webpage every twenty minutes. The webmaster resisted the urge to put up a counter, feeling it would be a bit too game show–esque, and instead continued to embed all new information within ordinary text.

The virus had found a home in thirty-seven states, and few had any doubt it would run the table in the continental United States. Alaska and Hawaii were still unaffected, the latter suffering dearly for minimizing all commercial air travel from the mainland. Tourism constituted the bulk of its revenue, and some experts were already predicting the island group would not recover from the losses for at least a decade.

Deaths were also being reported for the first time in other countries, spreading the fear worldwide and sparking continuing talk of the infection being "the Black Plague of the twenty-first century."

Almost all the cases in Mexico were traced back to the Pryce couple and other passengers from the Princess Line cruise. Some, however, likely also came in through Texas, California, Arizona, and New Mexico, ultimately driving the Mexican government, somewhat ironically, to close the border.

In China, all commercial flights from the United States were banned after an infected couple from Maine was discovered at the Zhaolong Hotel in Beijing. The hotel was subsequently sealed until all other guests could be screened. In spite of these efforts, cases began appearing almost immediately in the surrounding area, then spreading quickly outward.

In Japan, commercial airline flights were permitted to continue, but incoming passengers had to submit to a twenty-four-hour quarantine period. While this caused great consternation among travelers, it did also appear to have the desired effect—nineteen infected individuals were identified before they could enter Japan's greater population, the latter of whom also protected themselves through the use of gloves and masks. Commercial shipping ports were also rigidly monitored in spite of the loss of billions in trade revenue on both sides.

The first case in Canada involved a single mother and her two-month-old son, who lived in St. Catharines, Ontario, and had recently returned after a brief visit with relatives in Buffalo, New York. They showed up at the local hospital already well into Stage Two, the baby barely able to breathe. He died hours later of cardiac arrest, and the mother passed away the next evening. The Canadian government immediately dispatched hundreds of health-care workers to all border crossings, but within a week, more than fifty new cases had been confirmed.

The first six victims in England were reported in Guildford, just southwest of London, by the European Centre for Disease Prevention and Control. In typically civilized fashion, little public furor resulted as the patients were quietly removed from the population and kept comfortable. Meanwhile, health officials requested that anyone else exhibiting symptoms of the disease kindly report to the nearest hospital for "interview and treatment." Seventy-two individuals would do so.

The American media continued its relentless coverage of all developments, gradually stripping away each layer of editorial integrity until the daily reports seemed more like scenes from a horror movie. Bodies were shown lying in streets in broad daylight, disfigured and decomposed, because no one wanted to go near them. In Mississippi, someone took a blurry cell phone clip of a corpse being torn apart by a pack of coyotes in the wooded stretch behind a convenience store. In the Bronx, the dead body of a black woman lay slumped out the window of her ninth-story apartment all night long. She was noticed early the following morning by a jogger.

The suicides had also become particularly grisly. A thirty-four-year-old Delaware man rammed the paired prongs of a geared rotisserie wheel into his eyes. A Maine woman of about the same age swallowed every pill in her bathroom cabinet, then got on her knees and drank from the bottles of cleaning fluid under the sink until she went into convulsions. A night watchman in a Tennessee junkyard sat in his beloved '69 Mustang convertible while the crusher reduced it to the size of a washing machine. No one witnessed the incident, but it took the local fire department nearly an hour to hose away all the blood.

One Miami newspaper ran what it called a "local interest story" about an elderly widower who, once he realized he had acquired the infection, decided to spend his remaining three days running through a bizarre bucket list—he smoked a joint, wrote an anonymous note to the woman next door telling her about the affair her husband was having, called the IRS to say he had cheated on his taxes more than a dozen times and wished them good luck in getting the money, and recorded a video for YouTube confessing his love for Kirsten Dunst. When the symptoms began, he journaled the illness on his computer until he was no longer able, leaving the message that the information should be sent to the CDC in case it might be useful.

At exactly 3:36 A.M. local time in Tehran, a Saipa 141 sedan—one of thousands seen on Iranian roads every day—pulled into a dimly lit backstreet two blocks from the Presidential Palace. The driver, the only one in the car, got out and didn't bother to lock it. He walked at a steady, deliberate pace, hunched slightly forward with his hands in his pockets. His appearance was as unremarkable as the vehicle: just another local going about his business. There was no one else around. If there had been, they might have noticed the way his eyes moved about restlessly, surveying everything.

He reached the rear entrance to the palace, where two guards were milling about. When they saw him approach, they paused. They did not, however, demand that he identify himself; they were expecting him. He passed between them wordlessly, continued through the courtyard, and was greeted on the back portico by Sanjar Hejazi, a man he'd known only a few months but had come to like enormously.

Sanjar brought him up a winding staircase to the second floor, then into an ornately decorated room with tall curtains, gilded chandeliers, and a magnificent silk rug that covered almost the entire floor. President Baraheri was sitting in an antique chair reading a copy of *The New York Times*.

The president rose when he saw his guest. "Good evening, Mushir. What have you learned?"

Mushir Garoussi had spent the first sixteen years of his adult life in the Army of the Guardians of the Islamic Revolution. He distinguished himself in the Iran–Iraq War through extensive undercover work and was afterward moved to Iran's Intelligence Ministry. He rose to a midlevel position before internal politics slowed his progress, mostly due to his superiors' suspicion that he was, at heart, a moderate rather than a fundamentalist. He climbed a few more rungs during President Khatami's reformist administration, then hit another snag when Khatami was replaced by hardliner Ahmadinejad in 2005. When Baraheri succeeded Ahmadinejad following his startling dark horse victory, he appointed Garoussi head of the Intelligence Ministry. Garoussi had not even heard of Baraheri prior to the election, much less expected anything from him. But he had come to learn there was a great deal more to the man than a cursory examination would suggest. He was, in Garoussi's opinion, Iran's only hope for the future.

"We discovered Shalizeh's old laboratory, Mr. President. It was an abandoned house on the northern edge of the Darakeh neighborhood. We broke down the front door and found papers strewn about everywhere, mold growing throughout the kitchen, and about a million flies. There were bare mattresses in almost every room, stained and disgusting. There were two computers on the first floor, which we took away for examination." Garoussi shivered. "Then we went into the basement. . . ."

The equipment was still there—the microscopes, syringes, scissors, jars of paraffin and hard resin, a variety of irradiators, a vacuum infiltrator, and a cryostat. In the center of one room, under a light with a huge chrome hood, was a slightly tilted necropsy table. The leather straps were rotted and hanging loose. There were still bloodstains on the surface, the sides, and the floor. A glass-enclosed chamber had rows of animal cages. Some held skeletons lying on their sides, the flesh rotted away or chewed off by maggots that were also long gone.

"There were also three more computers, as well as a cabinet with dozens of notebooks. What became clear is that they had no idea what they were doing. They were just experimenting, completely at random. Different viruses, different drugs, different effects. And then . . . then we found some notes that led us to the back of the property."

"This is the part you didn't want to tell me about on the phone?" Hejazi asked.

Garoussi nodded. "Yes. We found the spot in a clearing. It had become a large depression because the loosened soil had settled back down. We began digging, and it didn't take long to find the first carcass—a medium-sized dog. Then two more. Finally, we discovered the first human victim—a female, mid-thirties at the oldest, very badly decayed. But . . . the horror was still visible on her face. No sooner had we removed her corpse than another was found underneath."

Baraheri shook his head slowly; Hejazi cursed under his breath.

"In total, there were seventy-two corpses," Garoussi said. "Forty-one were animals, the other thirty-one human, including eleven children and fourteen women."

"Savages, absolute savages," Baraheri said. "Men without souls."

"The children were all kidnap victims, the women

prostitutes. The males . . . they came from a variety of places. We are contacting the families now. It is a most unpleasant business."

"I would imagine." Baraheri took a deep breath and then let it out slowly. "So, it appears Shalizeh really is behind this. I can't believe he actually managed to engineer a vir—"

"No, Mr. President," Garoussi said, then surprised them by smiling.

"What?"

"According to the records we found, he never succeeded in creating a virus that could be used as a weapon."

Baraheri's eyes widened. "Are you certain of this?"

"Yes, most definitely. All the notes and computer files indicate that none of the experiments produced a virus of appreciable virulency. Also, there was nothing to make us believe he ever obtained samples of the smallpox virus from the Russians. No evidence whatsoever."

Baraheri turned to Hejazi, who appeared to be just as bewildered.

"Then what's this thing that's spreading through America?"

"Impossible to say at this point," Garoussi replied. "But there is nothing to indicate that it came from Shalizeh."

"So we were wrong in assuming he had anything to do with it."

"No, that's not quite true either, sir," Garoussi said. "He *was* involved, but in a very different way."

"I don't understand."

Garoussi told him.

Baraheri was on the phone within minutes.

In Washington, President Obama was walking down the second-floor hallway of the Executive Mansion carrying a pair of white towels. He was heading for the bathroom, where his younger daughter was about to be told it was time to get out of the tub and get ready for bed. He was still in his suit pants and white shirt, but his tie and jacket had been removed. Just as he reached the door, his BlackBerry trilled and vibrated at the same time.

"Let's go, ladies," he said, setting the towels on the basin and then removing the device from his pocket. It was a text message from his chief of staff. He read it twice to make sure he wasn't imagining it.

Calling back immediately, he said, "Is this for real?"

It was.

SEVENTEEN

The Jensen family was given a private room at Catskills Regional shortly after they arrived. A heavyset nurse with her hair twirled up like soft ice cream came down to the receiving area and led them away. An elevator ride and two hallways later, she showed them in. There were two large mechanical beds, which she rolled together, and a HEPA filter already humming away. Her name was Melanie, and she sat with them in her protective gear and patiently filled out their paperwork, sparing them the tedium of doing it in the lobby downstairs.

This didn't spare them from a number of ghastly sights, however. Two sheet-covered corpses were wheeled by when they came up, one downstairs and one in the hallway. The sheets were splotched with pus, so heavily in some places that you could vaguely see what was underneath. Relatives in protective gear were coming and going, most of them bawling like babies. In one room, they caught a glimpse of a screaming woman holding a small child in her arms just before the door drifted shut. They would later learn that the woman's two-year-old son had died the day before, but she refused to let the body go.

Dennis doubted Andi and Chelsea had taken much note of any of this; they were in their own little world now. But he noticed all of it. He saw and absorbed every detail, and he thought, *We're part of it now. We're in the middle of it.* He hated himself with a seething intensity, hated that he had been unable to protect them from it. It was his job, as a father and husband, to protect his family from harm. Maybe that sounded corny or old-fashioned, but he believed in it. And he'd failed—when it mattered most, he failed. As he watched Andi and Chelsea go down the hallway in front of him, their arms wrapped tight around each other, he felt nothing but guilt and self-loathing. *After they're gone,* he thought, *I hope it lingers a long time in me. I hope I really suffer.*

They had not left the room since Mel, as they had come to know her, got them settled. The top half of the beds were raised to a forty-five-degree angle, and she brought them cold drinks and snacks. She told them several other couples and their children were in the same situation, and the hospital administrators had agreed to let them stay in their rooms until the inevitable occurred. Dennis and Andi did not even entertain the idea of seeking out any of these families, to commiserate or offer comfort. There was no comfort to be found here, and they had enough to deal with in their own suffering; the last thing they wanted to do was share someone else's.

Dennis called Elaine and gave her the news. She sobbed into the phone and said she was coming up immediately. That was yesterday evening, shortly after they'd arrived. He stayed on the phone with her for a long time, talking about a variety of things. He told her he loved her, which she already knew, and that he would not have wanted anyone else for a sister. It struck him at that moment how natural it seemed to be undertaking final, wrapping-up kinds of things. Calling people to say good-bye (without really saying it), filling out papers to make sure everything would be in order after they were all gone, even *thinking* final thoughts. It was as if he'd stepped into a previously unseen current of reality. Everything around him was colored by a different meaning now, a different value. The money they had in the bank, for which they had worked so very hard, was as important to him as the pile of used tissues that clogged the little plastic wastebasket. Their home, their two nice cars . . . irrelevant. Andi said it should be split up evenly between their respective families, and Dennis agreed. Everybody would get something, and everyone would get what they wanted. Because it was material, it was immaterial. Their world was this tiny room now, with the pale green walls and polished tile floor and softly humming fluorescent lights. *This is where it ends*, he thought. *When Mel brought us through that door, she brought us through a gateway—from this world into whichever one is next.*

Not long after they arrived, he put Nickelodeon on the TV for Billy. The little boy sat there, attention fully trained on the set, scratching his arms and legs absentmindedly as pediatric sedatives and painkillers coursed through his five-year-old body. It wasn't long before they were all watching. No one said anything about what was on; they simply went with it. When the kids slept, Dennis and Andi switched to PBS for *Sesame Street* and *Mister Rogers' Neighborhood*—programs they had watched as children. This also seemed like a natural thing to do, as if they were coming full circle in their lives. Back to the beginning . . .

They talked as they hadn't talked in years, like in the early days of their relationship. Dennis told her again that she was the love of his life, something he had thought often but, to his regret, felt he had not expressed enough. He said she had made his life worthwhile, gave it real meaning and substance. Andi listened to every word and cried frequently, holding him close and offering her own, similar sentiments. He was the only man she'd ever truly loved, the one who made her realize what love really was. In this one respect, she said, she would die satisfied. Dennis then apologized profusely for anything he ever did to hurt or upset her, and he begged for her forgiveness. She gave it without hesitation.

As the last of the sunlight faded on the second day, and with both kids fast asleep, Andi whispered to Dennis, "When will it start?" The *it*, as Dennis already knew, was the onset of Stage Three—blurred vision, slurred speech, and general confusion. It would last about six to eight hours, followed by dementia and episodic violence, plus the systemic bleeding from the meltdown of internal organs. You were stripped of everything that mattered—your personality, your identity, and your dignity.

Dennis glanced briefly at the clock on the wall. It was of the basic variety seen in hospitals, classrooms, and police stations all over the world.

"It should be any time," he said, his voice so dry that the first words came up like embers through a chimney.

"I guess we . . . we should have Mel start using the sedatives now."

They looked at each other for a long time, the torment clear on their faces. They knew the sedatives would be, for all practical purposes, the end of the road. As the infection progressed, the drugs would be the only mercy they would receive. By administering them, the kids would be spared most of the suffering. But they would also be close to a vegetative state, drifting through a mindless haze until death finally came for them.

"I suppose," Dennis said, his voice faltering. He leaned over and stroked Chelsea's hair, then kissed her gently on the top of the head. "I guess it's the right . . . the best thing to do." Then, his lower lip trembling, he said in a sharp whisper. "Mother of God, she's only *seven*. . . ." He buried his face in a pillow and broke down, his body trembling as the grief took over. Andi put her arm around him and kissed him on the back of the neck.

Mel came into the room thirty minutes later

with the syringe. The fluid was clear and loose, almost like water. The Jensens didn't know what it was, didn't really care. Andi held Chelsea against her; Dennis continued to stroke her hair with one hand while balling the other into a fist and pressing it against his mouth.

Talking softly to the child even though she was asleep, Mel pulled up the sleeve of her cotton shirt to search for a vein, as she had done with over two dozen other children in the last week alone.

Then she stopped. "What the—?"

Dennis and Andi turned their heads at precisely the same moment, as if they'd rehearsed the move.

"What?" Andi said—then she saw it, too. "Oh my God . . ."

The pustules had shrunk. The rash had faded.

Dennis gently lifted the sleeve of her other arm. "No way . . ."

Same thing.

Then, with the excruciating daintiness that any decent father reserves for his daughter, he lifted her gown to just above her knees.

"It's disappearing!" Andi said, the tiniest of smiles appearing on her face for the first time in weeks. "Mel! It's disa—"

But Mel had already fled the room to find the nearest doctor.

EIGHTEEN

Beck was in the middle of nowhere, on a sandy trail that slithered through the green wilderness of the Catskills. The rented convertible had not been built for off-road travel, and he prayed it wouldn't shake apart. He was also praying that *he* would hold together—pain waves were radiating through his back from the bumping and jostling. He had pulled off Route 88 nearly an hour ago. According to the handwritten notes lying on the passenger seat, he should reach his destination any minute now.

Neither Bob Easton nor any of his three friends survived after their last trip here. That was significant. All three had more of the same hunks of raggedly cut meat in their homes. One had apparently cooked and eaten some the same night he brought it back. The other two put it in their freezers. Sure enough, the mystery virus was present in all of them. The final piece to the puzzle came to Beck when he interviewed a fifth man, a friend of theirs from the local VFW, who was supposed to go on the trip but couldn't make it due to, of all things, an illness. He was a widower, and he'd left town when the outbreak began to stay with a son in Vermont. Over the phone, he told Beck where the others had been. It was their favorite spot, especially at the start of the season. Beck jotted down the rough directions and hoped he could divine the location. Neither MapQuest nor his GPS would do much good out here.

The trail finally smoothed out and cut through a colorful, flower-filled glade, then led into a hallway of fir and pine trees. A few hundred yards farther on, it terminated abruptly in a sandy, circular clearing: a natural cul-de-sac. He parked and got out, gloves, mask, and goggles in place. He also carried a kit with a variety of instruments and containers, plus a digital camera in a black leather case. Both were small enough to clip onto his belt.

Others had been here recently, as evidenced by the tire tracks printed in the sand. There were footprints, too. Or, more specifically, what appeared to be boot prints. They led down the narrow trail Beck had been told to follow. It seemed that this "favorite spot" wasn't exclusive to Bob Easton and company after all.

The trail led Beck through the forest for about a half hour. He liked the wild; under normal circumstances the isolation and quiet would have a calming effect on him. It was a beautiful day, and this was a beautiful place—the kind of place where he might do a little hiking, maybe find a waterway and bring a kayak. Under normal circumstances . . .

He found one of Easton's hunting stands; it looked like a tree fort on stilts. It was wide enough to fit several grown men, and there was a ladder leading up to a trapdoor in the bottom. The door was hanging down, the hook darkened with rust. Plastic shotgun shells were scattered in the dried leaves, along with a few beer cans: Miller Lite and Budweiser.

Farther along he found another stand, more basic than the first—a group of two-by-fours nailed together in a tree to create a serviceable single-person platform. He crossed a tiny stream in a lowland area. Then the trail ran up again, meeting a second path that bisected it in perfect right angles, creating a four-way intersection. Beck turned left, never realizing the other way would have taken him to the Jensens' cabin.

A few minutes later he found himself at the peak of a pebbly ridge. Through the leafy canopy he could see the mountains and valleys beyond. Then the smell hit him, different from the one in Easton's basement, but just as heavy.

Beck stopped, looked around, saw nothing. The odor disappeared . . . then it was there again. *The wind,* he realized.

He watched the trees intently for a moment. When another gust rustled through, he left the trail and moved hurriedly in the direction from which it came. The odor became stronger, more invasive. Some characteristics were familiar to him, triggering all sorts of unpleasant memories. The stench of rot and disease and decay. *And death* . . .

He found the first deer lying in a shallow, open space among a cluster of trees. It was a whitetail, a young male judging by the relatively small size of its horns. Its eyes were puffed shut, and black eruptions that looked like giant zits mottled most of its face. The mouth was open slightly, frozen that way when the rigor mortis set in. Dried blood was still present, caked onto the animal's tiny teeth. Flies buzzed noisily around the carcass, so thick by the gutted torso that they formed a scant cloud. Beck doubted this was the one from which Easton and his friends had taken their meat. It hadn't been cut open—it'd been *ripped.* Clawed by some hungry predator—or, more likely, a pack of them. He took a sample of the dried blood and transferred it to a rubbed-capped vial. He labeled the vial and put it back in the case. Then he took out the camera and clicked a few pictures.

About twenty yards on, he found another corpse. It had been decaying longer than the first, the hair dry-matted to the bones, half the skull exposed. Beck scraped off a few tissue samples into a plastic bag. The third body was at the peak of a small hill to the right, and from there Beck could see four more. Two were lying side by side, as if they'd killed each other in close combat.

By the time he got back to the convertible, he had collected material from more than twenty of them. He took a portable test kit from the trunk and used sterile tweezers to immerse several tissue samples into small reaction tubes of greenish liquid. Within thirty seconds, the viral proteins changed the color of the fluid from green to red—the polymerase chain reaction he was hoping for. He knew it wasn't conclusive by any means; field kits could be notoriously unreliable. This one in particular, although capable of testing beyond a single-pathogen regime and with an industry reputation for minimal false positives or negatives, was intended to detect common respiratory contagion during cold and flu season. Also, the samples were usually of human origin—nasopharyngeal aspirates and swabs, and bronchoalveolar lavage. So he needed confirmation in a lab setting before he could take the next step.

But still . . .

This is it. I'd bet my life on it.

He yanked his cell phone from his pocket and was about to dial, but the screen displayed an icon of a phone inside a circle with a line through it, and underneath it read, SERVICE UNAVAILABLE.

"Damn."

He packed everything quickly and got back in the car.

NINETEEN

It was a montage of colorful, soft-edged images. They seemed to be coming randomly now—Dennis sitting in the science lab of his elementary school, watching Mr. Matheson use potassium nitrate to make little smoke bombs . . . checking himself over in the mirror on the night of his senior prom, looking fairly sharp in his white tuxedo . . . racing BMX bikes around an impromptu track that had been etched through a local construction site. The tractors responsible for it were sitting idle along the fringes because one of the site owners had been arrested for something called embezzlement. There was also a memory of him and Elaine at the Jersey Shore, crouching down in the wet surf trying to dig up "sandbugs"—opaque, beetle-like creatures that buried themselves a few inches below the surface. His parents—both long dead now—stood nearby. Dad, so gangly-thin that you could count each rib from twenty paces, was puffing on one of the Pall Malls that had contributed to the diminishment of his existence. Mom sat nearby in a beach chair reading a glamour magazine, the cancer in her uterus still a few years away from taking shape.

The image that shuddered through the darkness and then brightened to full clarity was of him lying in his bed on a Saturday morning while the comforting scents of summer blew through the half-open windows. He was about ten or eleven and looked every bit of it. He was being slowly awoken by someone who was trying to do it diplomatically. A hand had been set on his bare arm—he always slept without a shirt in the summer—and was now shaking him so gently that it felt like he was on a raft in a swimming pool. The lids of one eye slowly peeled apart. It was Elaine again, dressed in shorts and a T-shirt, ready to go. Blond-haired, blue-eyed, pretty like a character in an L. M. Montgomery novel. Those eyes were wide with both excitement and fear. The excitement came from deep within, where she had a natural wellspring of it. She had always been that way—thrilled about life, about *being* alive, and the shiny possibilities each day held. The fear . . . well, that was Dennis's fault, and he knew it. He wasn't a "morning person" as a kid, and he particularly hated getting up on weekends one minute earlier than his Circadian rhythms required. He snapped at her many times for this travesty, and she had become gun-shy about it. Nevertheless . . . she wanted someone to play with, and she just adored her older brother. So her compromise was to wake him in as inoffensive a manner as possible.

"Den," she said, her voice echoey in the dream,

"come on, wake up. I want to do something, Dennis. Come on . . ."

Except that she didn't say *I want to do something* in the dream—what she said was, *You* need *to do something.* And her voice didn't have that hint of terror in it. It was still soft and delicate, but it wasn't the voice of a child.

His eyes fluttered open, and he turned to see her hovering nearby. It was the grown-up version of her now. As his mind swam back to the present, some distant part of it took note of the hand that had been carefully set on his bare arm. It was kind of funny, he thought—more than thirty years later, and she still woke him like she was defusing a bomb.

"What's going on?" he said, or at least tried to—the words crumbled in a dry hiss. He cleared his throat and tried again—"Hey, what's up?"

"Someone's here to see you guys," she said, smiling and looking toward the front of the room. Dennis noticed for the first time that his sister was wearing a surgical mask.

He followed her gaze and found Mel standing there. Her nurse's scrubs were the color of raspberry sherbet, but her mask was baby blue like Elaine's. *They don't match . . . what would Stacy and Clinton of* What Not to Wear *have to say about that?* This bizarre thought inspired him to make a real effort to get with it.

He turned and found Andi sitting there with her arms crossed, grinning at him.

"It's about time," she said. "We've been waiting nearly twenty minutes."

"You were snoring like a hog in a barn," Mel added, driving the other two into a fit of laughter. The kids lay next to their mother on their sides, snoozing away.

Andi noticed the look of bewilderment on his face and said, "Mel gave them each a sedative. They need the rest."

Dennis felt a jolt of alarm—*A sedative?*... Then he saw the fading blisters on his daughter's arms, pinkish now as opposed to the angry red they were twenty-four hours ago. Same with those on Andi's arms, as well as the swelling around her face. The original features were beginning to reemerge, restoring the simple-but-natural beauty that always stirred him.

"Are you with us now?" Mel asked.

"Yeah, sorry." He cleared his throat again and repositioned himself. "I'm here. What's up?"

"Well, I wanted to tell you all that the serum is *working*."

"That's wonderful," Andi said.

"Awesome," Elaine added.

"Yes. Thirty-two patients have seen reduced symptoms, and I'm sure there will be more."

"*Excellent!*" Andi said with a liveliness Dennis had thought he would never hear again.

Mel was nodding. "There are a lot of people in this hospital who have put you on their Christmas list, that's for sure. If it wasn't for Dr. Petti's strict orders that you should all be left alone to rest, there'd be a stampede to this room, believe me."

Andi looked to her sister-in-law, then back to

Mel. "How is the serum being made so fast, and in enough quantities for so many people?" she asked. "There hasn't been that much blood taken from us, and you couldn't use it on everyone anyway."

"They're taking your immune system cells and growing them in a culture," Elaine said. "They're the ones producing the protective antibodies."

"The ones neutralizing the effect of the virus," Mel said.

"That's right. Once they're cultured, the antibodies are ready for injection into other patients. Some are also left behind to grow more cultures, and then production becomes exponential."

"That's fantastic," Andi said. "And it all sounds relatively simple, too."

"Well . . . there are some snags," Mel said. "It's not *that* simple."

"Such as?"

"Like human cells in a culture divide only every twenty hours or so, so it takes time to produce more antibodies. We can't make nature go faster."

It didn't take a mathematician to figure out what this meant. "So some people who can be saved simply won't get the serum in time?"

"That's right," Mel said. "It's like the day they find a cure for cancer. Even if they get it to every person in the world who needs it, some will die while it's in the mail."

"Is there any way to make serum faster?"

"There's an experimental approach that's been discussed," Elaine said, "and I think the government might try it. It goes like this—a high-tech company that specializes in rapid sequencing may be able to quickly map out the DNA that encodes the antibody's dual chains. Then the DNA is placed in a bacterial expression system, where it could then, theoretically, be replicated in large quantities."

Mel chuckled. "Did anyone in the room understand that besides the two of us?"

"Synthesis," Andi said. This made Dennis suddenly remember her fascination for all things science. It had always been a mystery why she didn't choose a scientific discipline for a career.

"That's right."

"It sounds unstable, though. Unpredictable. A lot of variables that can fall the wrong way."

"That's why it's experimental," Elaine told her. "Plus, the legalities if someone is injected and it doesn't work, or their condition worsens. . . ."

"So then the best approach is the one they're already doing?" Andi asked. "Based on our cells?"

"That's right," Mel said. "The good stuff floating around in your body is not only going to be made into a serum, but the attenuated virus will be used to create a vaccine."

"And they're optimistic it'll work, too," Elaine added. "It's just like the cowpox relationship to smallpox. Once someone was injected with cowpox, smallpox did not have as dramatic an effect on them. That's where the original vaccine for smallpox came from—the cowpox virus. Now, the attenuated virus in the four of you will be the basis for the vaccine for this new virus."

"Attenuated?" Andi repeated. "You mean weakened?"

"That's right. You have a weakened form of the poxvirus that's affecting everyone else."

"Where did we get it from?" Dennis asked. "We were in the middle of nowhere."

Elaine's smile widened. She looked to Mel and said, "Do you want to tell them or can I?"

"Go ahead."

She turned back to her brother. "From Scooter," she said.

"*What?*"

"Your dog saved your life," Elaine replied. "Somehow he caught the original—they're still trying to figure out where and when—and his system produced a weaker version."

"That's unbelievable," Andi said.

"Actually, it isn't. It's not unusual for a virus to become attenuated after it has passed through a different species."

"Not unusual at all," Mel said, shaking her head.

"Viruses that are dangerous to one animal are very often harmless to another. The one that's been claiming so many human lives apparently has no effect on dogs. But dogs have a very interesting effect on the virus. When the virus adopts to their system, its virulency toward the human system is significantly weakened."

"So, is that another way people can save themselves?" Andi said. "By having their dogs get it?"

"It's possible," Elaine told her. "It worked for

you, so it could work for others. But I don't know how many people want to become infected through their dogs just for the sake of finding out."

"Yeah."

"Did you get Scooter back?" Dennis asked. "Was he all right?"

"He was just fine," Elaine said. "Happy to see me, that's for sure. But he was fine."

Dennis had told her Scooter was still in the cabin, where they'd left him with two huge bowls of dry food and a bathtub full of water. He made his sister promise to take care of him after. . . .

"So anyway," Mel said, "that's the big news for today. Once word gets out, you guys are going to be heroes."

"Scooter, too," Dennis added.

"Of course."

"Does the CDC know yet?" Andi asked.

"Yes, the director's been told. And I'm sure the president knows by now, too." She reached down and patted Andi on the ankle. "So I'll come back in and check on you in a little while. I've got some rounds to make."

Mel turned and went out. As the door glided to a close, Elaine said, "She also told me you guys should be discharged in two or three days."

"Thank God," Andi said. "Real food again."

Dennis looked all around the little room—a room he was sure he and his family would be leaving one at a time, on gurneys with sheets pulled over their heads. He had traveled to the very edge of mortality, seen the yawning darkness beyond.

"What are you guys going to do when you get out of here?" Elaine asked, snapping him from his trance.

The house, he thought dimly. *Carlton Lakes.* They couldn't stay away forever. Sooner or later, they had to go back and face whatever awaited them.

"Go home, I guess," he replied.

Andi turned and looked at him pensively. She knew what he was thinking. She could feel it.

Maybe the nightmare wasn't over yet.

•

The six-person technician team was waiting for Beck when he burst through the lab's double doors.

"Here, quickly!"

The samples were immediately taken from him and prepared while he put on his protective gear. The others worked together as a group, but they knew Beck only by reputation. He'd been here twice since the outbreak began, and on those two occasions he spoke exclusively to Kevin Little. Both times Beck struck Little as being uncommonly pleasant.

When the samples were ready, Little inserted them into the electron microscope. Magnification was pushed to 4000X. They had many from alternative sources, human and otherwise, to use for comparison.

Little said, "I believe these are one and the same."

"Yeah?"

"Uh-huh."

Beck felt a surge of excitement. "Okay, now I'm going to ask you to use the big gun. Let's take a look at it with the AFM."

Atomic force microscopes were the most advanced instruments ever created for viewing minute particles. Developed in the 1980s, they utilized a probe consisting of a cantilevered silicon tip that reacted to piezoelectric energy created by the tip's close proximity with a sample, such as capillary or electrostatic forces. From these minute movements, a computer image was drawn with resolution on a nanometric scale—more than a thousand times more detailed than that of optical diffraction microscopes—and with true tridimensionality. The resulting pictures had startling clarity, with the particles in question often bearing beautiful geometric shapes that defied their deadly nature. AFMs also had the advantages of requiring no stains or heavy metal coatings—thus doing no damage to the sample material—and could be used without the expense or trouble of a vacuum environment.

Little grinned. "Trying to get the virus to smile for the public?"

"Well, that, and I also want to make certain the match is beyond question. In this case, good enough isn't going to be good enough."

"I dig."

"And I want an image to send to Sheila Abbott. She'll want to see it."

"You got it."

"With a little luck, it'll end up on CNN or something."

Little chuckled. "I'll make sure the virus combs its hair."

The AFM sat on a square table in one corner and looked similar to an old portable record player with its lid raised. It even had a large silver disk in the center. Little fired up the computer and ordered everyone to put their masks back on. Six samples were set carefully under the conical tip—two from Beck's Catskills find, two from infected lab animals, and two from separate human victims. The whole process took about an hour, and no one in the group spoke a word as they waited for the images to unfold on the screen. Once that happened, all remaining doubt evaporated. The inconsistently shaped spheres, the rods and cylinders with their peculiar DNA cases, the graceful tail fibers . . .

"Bingo," Beck said.

"Sweet," one of the assistants whispered.

"I'll be damned," Little said. "By Jove, Beck, you've done it again."

"Yeah, I guess so. And it's very unlikely that this one was artificially engineered."

"No way anyone could produce this with modern technology. This was Mother Nature's recipe."

"A new mutant of some kind, that has a deadly effect on both deer and humans."

"Appears so. Just showed up in nature one day."

"That's how it usually happens," Beck said. Then he smiled broadly. "At last we have some answers. Can we get a few JPEG images together?"

"Most certainly."

"Thanks."

He was in the locker room five minutes later, removing his gear. Then he was in the parking lot, putting his earpiece in place.

"Sheila? It's me."

"What's happening with the tests?"

"You've got to call the president immediately."

"It's a match?"

"Perfect."

"My God, you're sure?"

"Yes, no doubt. I'm having the lab send pictures to you."

He got into the car, started the engine, and glanced only briefly in the rearview mirror before backing out.

"So you're certain this isn't a terrorist creation?"

"The kind of equipment they'd need, not to mention the advanced knowledge of how to do it . . . and maybe most important, it's pretty ridiculous to think they'd start the spread of it by infecting a population of deer in the Catskills."

"Yeah, okay . . . I'll let him know right away."

"Good. By the way, have you heard from Cara?"

"No, why?"

"She wasn't at the lab." He checked his watch. "Maybe she's getting something to eat."

"I don't know. I have to go, Michael."

"Right. Talk to you later."

"Bye."

TWENTY

DAY 18

As word of the serum spread, the government was forced to prioritize who would receive it—and, perhaps more significant, who would not—while the manufacturing process expanded in excruciating increments. In many instances, children were first in line, then their parents. Beyond those two categories—kids and parents—the key metric was age, with seniors at the bottom of the list if they made the list at all.

It didn't take long for the public to discover that the original antibodies came from the Catskills hospital, although the staff did an admirable job of keeping the Jensens' identity a secret. People showed up day and night, demanding doses either for themselves or their loved ones. Bribes were offered, threats made. Amazingly, no contraband samples found their way online. One vial, however, was successfully smuggled out by a young nurse who had cut a deal with a local stockbroker. The agreed price was $100,000—in cash, of course—and the dose was given to the man's twelve-year-old daughter. It *was an unusual incident in that all sides walked away happy—the child made a complete and uneventful recovery, and the nurse eventually put the money toward medical school, which had previously been little more than a pipe dream.*

As more laboratories began to manufacture doses, the federal government sent out military units to protect them, and boxes of finished serum were shipped to various hospitals via military transports. Security was also increased around President Obama, Secretary Napolitano, and Sheila Abbott after it leaked that they had made the decisions concerning recipient prioritization.

Lawsuits were filed by the thousands; everyone had a reason why they deserved treatment ahead of everyone else. There were also reports of infected people trying to pass the virus to their dogs in the hope of producing their own attenuated version, unaware that it worked with the Jensens' dog only because he had received the infectious agent from its original source.

The CDC and WHO made repeated assurances that new doses were being produced as quickly as possible, but it seemed to make little difference in light of the fact that the fatality count had now topped eighteen thousand in the United States alone and was continuing to rise.

William "Buster" Patterson sat in his home office, the huge Macintosh screen glowing into his beefy face, and yawned so hard, he shuddered. He'd been staring at the same Adobe Illustrator document for the last two hours—a meticulously crafted false passport—and was now bored of it. He had already scanned the eventual recipient's tiny photograph and set it in place. The name he'd been told to use was Kalil Hejazi. Age: 32. Occupation: International Sales Rep Company: MCM Steel. Location: Dubai. Patterson had no idea what Hejazi's real name was, and he didn't really care. He was being paid ten grand for the job: a passport and some other papers. He got that much because he was good at it, but also because he didn't ask questions.

He liked to think of himself as a Reality Adjuster. He didn't tell any of his clients that, didn't have it printed on a business card. But the description was accurate enough. He erased truths and manufactured fantasies. It began in the late '80s when a seven-year career in government intelligence ended with his getting caught, along with six others, for plotting to steal nearly half a million dollars in seized drug money. One of the other six, his superior, reduced his own sentence by ratting out the rest of the team, and Patterson spent four years in the federal tank before being quietly released on probation. He found legitimate employment difficult, so he turned to the dark side and utilized the artistic talents he'd had since childhood. He began by counterfeiting various foreign currencies, then went into documents that ranged from birth and death certificates to social security cards and diplomas. By the time he branched into computer hacking, his reputation had begun to grow. Terrorists became frequent clients, as they paid well and didn't waste time trying to get friendly. They also mentioned him to their friends, and he was always happy to get more work. Anything to stick it to Uncle Sam.

He adjusted Hejazi's picture—a nice-looking Arabic young man who, Patterson was sure, was on some government watch list somewhere—and then yawned again and got up. A quick glance at his Movado told him it was almost one in the morning. He thought about going down to Darklands and picking up one of the stragglers, Betsy or Tina or Cherise. One of them usually had trouble finding someone to go home with. Barstool warriors with too much makeup and spongy, sagging breasts. But he knew them and they knew him, and everyone woke up reasonably satisfied in the morning.

As he went down the hallway and into the kitchen, he made the decision to watch something on the Playboy Channel instead. He opened the fridge and removed a bottle of Schaefer from its cardboard carrier. His profession had netted him more than three million dollars over the years, and he still had about half of it sitting in an offshore account. In spite of that, plus the nice condo, the convertible Jaguar, the club memberships, the rest of the Movados, and a whole slew of other crap, he couldn't acquire a taste for fine wine or Dom Pérignon or anything of that. Just beer, and none of that gourmet garbage, either.

He twisted the cap and tossed it into the sink, then shuffled his large frame into the bathroom. He tilted the bottle back as he stood before the bowl pissing away, and the irony was not lost on him. *You never own beer, you just rent it,* he thought, remembering something he'd heard in a men's room ages ago. He set the bottle down on the marble shell-basin so he could shake out the last few drops. That's when the front door was kicked in.

It sounded like a WWE character being slammed to the mat—boom! Then the announcement that chilled his bones—*"FBI, don't move!"*

Others voices followed—many, in fact. Patterson sprang into action, following a plan he'd gone over a thousand times in his mind but prayed he'd never have to use. He streaked down the hallway and into the office, his hands already out and ready to apply the four-key combination he'd programmed to erase *everything*. It was a dangerous protocol—if he accidentally hit them during the course of an ordinary day, the paired hard drives in his CPU would be completely erased. But it was a necessary evil in his line of work.

He came to a halt at the doorway—another agent was crawling through the window that he'd foolishly left open to enjoy the night breeze. Typical FBI kid—muscular and handsome, with leather gloves, jackboots, goggles, a Kevlar vest. . . . He already had his weapon out and was pointing it directly at Patterson's chest, but his eyes were shifting between his target and the computer. In that instant, Patterson realized, they knew who he was, what he did . . . everything.

"Down on the floor, now!" the kid barked, now fully inside and blocking the way to the keyboard.

Patterson dodged to the right and continued down the darkened hall. More voices were shouting behind him. He scurried into his bedroom, was relieved to find no one coming through those windows, and locked the door. In spite of his size—he had topped 260 pounds the week before and vowed to do something about it—he dived over the bed onto the floor, then slipped his hand under the pillow and grabbed his own gun. Finding it unusually light, he realized the clip wasn't inserted and cursed loudly.

He pulled back the drawer on the nightstand as the pounding began. The magazine was, almost comically, under a pile of magazines. His shaking hands managed to ram it into the butt just as the door exploded off its hinges and a wave of agents poured in.

"Gun down!" one of them screamed. Patterson wasn't stupid enough to fire at any of them, but he had no intention of going back to prison, either.

He set the barrel on his temple and fired. He had thought often about death but never quite decided what to expect. Darkness and silence? Floating dreamily through time and space? A red-skinned demon with an arrowtail and a pitchfork?

What the hell—?

In a split second, he realized he hadn't fired—someone else had. The gun was now out of his hand. In fact, a sizable portion of his hand was no longer there. The pain followed a millisecond later with ferocious intensity, and he began screaming as blood sprayed from the severed vessels.

The sharpshooter replaced his pistol in his belt as four agents grabbed Patterson and threw him on the bed. That's when he realized they had been ordered to take him alive.

"I won't tell you a thing! Not a damn thing!*"* he howled. His guests didn't take any notice.

Within two hours, agents found the original computer files Patterson had created at the request of Ahmed Aaban el Shalizeh for the purpose of fabricating a link between Abdulaziz Masood and the Iranian government.

TWENTY-ONE

Beck was lying on his hotel bed the following morning, still fully dressed and covered with papers, when his cell phone rang. He dug it out of his pocket and answered on the fourth ring.

"Yeah?"

"Michael, it's Ben."

Still half asleep, Beck managed a smile. "Hey, did you hear about the serum? I got a call last night from—"

"No, Michael, listen."

"Someone's *dog* caught the virus, and it was—"

"Michael, wait."

"That's the coolest thing about stuff like this. You just never—"

"Michael."

Beck stopped. "Huh? What's the matter?"

There was a brief silence, followed by Gillette reporting the details about Cara's accident. At first Beck didn't understand. Gillette repeated it, almost breaking down. When he finished, there was more silence.

Then Beck was in his car.

"When are the first serum samples supposed to be delivered?" he asked, moving swiftly down the hospital corridor. Ben was having trouble keeping up. The fact that they were both wearing PPE suits didn't help.

"I don't know, they won't tell me."

"They won't *tell* you?"

"Not exactly."

"Not exactly? What does that mean, Ben?"

"They said they would, but only about an hour before they were due to arrive. They don't want word getting out, because they're afraid people will mob the place."

"But this facility has to be at the top of the distribution priority list. We're right in the heart of the damn outbreak."

"Yes, we know that much. But they're being paranoid. They've got guards around the hospital in the Catskills and the facility in Nutley where they're manufacturing it. *Armed* guards, for God's sake."

"Well . . . okay, whatever."

He mumbled something else as they turned a corner, but Gillette didn't hear it. When they reached the observation window outside Porter's room, Beck came to an abrupt stop.

She lay motionless, her head tilted slightly to one

side, eyes closed. Her arms were at her sides on the white sheet, covered to the wrists by a cotton shirt. She looked peaceful enough. But the large, red-rimmed blisters had begun erupting all over her hands and face. Her left eye, in particular, was being surrounded by a nest of them.

Gillette looked to Beck, who was staring through the glass. His eyebrows were raised in an expression that underscored his anxiety. *He doesn't know what to do,* Gillette thought. *He feels completely helpless . . . again.*

"She's in Stage Two," Beck said hoarsely. It wasn't really a question.

"For a few hours now."

"And the serum works only up to a point in this stage, right?"

"That's correct. It's nearly one hundred percent effective during the incubation period, and more than ninety percent during Stage One. But it's unpredictable in Stage Two. Based on the stats we've gathered so far, the rule of thumb is 'the earlier, the better,' obviously."

"So we really don't have time to wait for this stuff to show up."

Ben looked at him plaintively. "No, not really."

"Does she know about it? Does she know there's a treatment?"

"No. I've been ordered by the administrators not to tell any of the patients. Like I said, I don't know when we'll be getting our supply. If everyone knows it's out there, it'll be pandemonium."

"They're going to find out sooner or later."

"I know, and they know that. But they want to hold off the mayhem for as long as possible."

"Uh-huh," Beck said without a trace of sincerity.

He went inside, Gillette trailing. The emotional pressure became greater with each step closer to Porter's bedside. He tried to force his mind to be more clinical, to think in scientific terms, but it was no use. He drifted into a feeling of unreality, of being detached and outside himself. His stomach tightened into a granite knot, and a light chill crawled along his skin. He had never been able to fully unplug himself from these situations. On the other side of the world, watching babies die right in front of him as their parents became disabled by grief, he could not help but feel some measure of empathy. But even then he was able to *function*. He felt no such ability now. His legs were unsteady, and it took the supreme effort of his life to keep from collapsing.

"She came in early this morning," Gillette said quietly. "She called me after she tried to call you. She went to her hotel room after the incident at the lab. She didn't want to come straight here, because she was afraid she'd catch it if she didn't already have it. So she went to her room to wait and see."

He paused for Beck to say something at this point, but he didn't.

"When she starting exhibiting symptoms, I had her come right in. Then I arranged for this room, and we started treating her immediately. She's been kept comfortable."

"Okay," Beck said almost inaudibly.

He stepped alongside her and very gently lifted the edge of her sleeve. The blisters were becoming fluid-laden; soon they would begin to burst on their own. Then the crusting . . . then the loss of perception and rationality . . . then the meltdown of internal organs . . .

Dammit.

He noticed the iPod for the first time. It was a Nano, long and thin. She'd wanted one with greater capacity but didn't have the money. He was going to give her the biggest one Apple had for her birthday, which was just over two months away. It lay on the bed above her shoulder, the threadlike cables running in wavy lines to her ears. There was a second, heavier cable, Beck noticed, leading away from the bottom of the unit. He followed it visually and saw that it went into one of the electrical outlets. It was the charger, to keep the battery from running down. Beck turned the Nano over gently to make sure it was firmly connected and getting the juice it needed. In doing so, he caught sight of the album she'd put on—an iTunes Essentials compilation called *'70s Memories*. The song playing at that moment was "Brandy (You're a Fine Girl)" by Looking Glass.

His eyes reddened and his hands began to shake. He tried to set the iPod down again, but it slipped away. Porter stirred, her right eye fluttering. The other was sealed shut.

"No, no," he said softly. "Cara, stay asleep—"

The left eye finally broke open, and she surveyed

her surroundings. The confusion was plain in her face, a product of both sleep and medication. When she saw Beck, she managed a tiny smile. "Hey," she said with an airy raspiness. "I heard you figured out the mystery." She reached up slowly and removed the earbuds one at a time. "I guess I really can call you Holmes now."

Beck forced a smile of his own. "I guess so."

She went to say something else, then stopped. Her smile faded, and her eyes began darting around the room. They were absorbing more details, Beck realized, and a chilling thought struck him. *She forgot where she is and why she's here.*

When the impossible truth of it finally seeped in, she looked back to him. The smile vanished, and the beautiful young face clouded with fear. She held out her hand, and her lower lip began trembling.

"Oh my God," she said unevenly. Beck leaned down and held her, the material in his PPE suit crinkling like a paper bag. "Oh my God . . ."

She cried long and hard. Gillette moved to the other side of the bed, pulled over a chair, and set his hand on her shoulder.

"I screwed up," she said finally. "I'm so sorry. I screwed up royally."

"No, you didn't. You didn't screw anything up."

"I should've known better. I never should've done something like that."

"No, it's okay. It's perfectly okay."

"I'm so sorry."

"Don't be sorry."

When she paused to catch her breath, Beck pulled back and said, "There's a serum, Cara."

Gillette turned toward him, eyes wide, but said nothing.

"What?"

"A serum. A family came in with the infection, but it faded before Stage Three. They caught an attenuated version of the virus from their dog."

"Has it been working?"

"Yes, but . . ."

"But what?" She studied him carefully and caught the hesitation in his eyes. "Michael, what?"

"It has to be given no later than Stage Two . . . and the earlier, the better."

Her hands had tightened around his at the mention of the serum. Now they went limp again. "You mean it won't work on me." There was a heavy wash of dark sarcasm in her tone. *Of course not. I've been on the wrong side of luck all my life. Why should today be any different?*

"I don't know," Beck replied. "It's too new to say for sure."

"You could up the dosage, or the concentration," she said.

"That's risky," Gillette told her.

"But if we don't try, then . . . then I'm going to go for sure, right?"

Beck and Gillette glanced briefly at each other. *This is something they've already discussed,* she realized.

"Right?"

Beck slid off the bed and stood. A thousand

words flowed between them: words that could not be spoken aloud, for all sorts of reasons.

"I'll be right back," he said.

"You promise?"

"I promise."

TWENTY-TWO

Zooming down the winding back roads that led to the Hoffman-LaRoche campus, Beck focused on the plan he had hastily formulated while pushing aside unsavory thoughts concerning several other subjects—not the least of which was, *If I screw this up, I'm absolutely finished in this business.* The plan, he kept telling himself . . . *focus on the plan.* He'd hung up with Sheila Abbott ten minutes ago, and the name she gave him was Dr. Brian Childress. He was the laboratory chief in the immunogenetics section. Thank God she hadn't asked why he wanted to know this.

He reached the entrance, which had a small guardhouse and a candy-striped gate at the front of the long driveway. The lawn on the property was immaculate, covering the gently rolling hills like a green carpet.

The uniformed employee inside the guardhouse looked fearful enough—a young, broad-shouldered man with a stubbly beard who should've been playing professional football instead of checking

ID tags. But what really caught Beck's attention were the two National Guardsmen lingering outside. They were dressed in camouflage and holding their machine guns to their chests. He had no doubt they had been given the proper authorization to use them at their discretion.

The uniformed man came out. "Can I help you?" he said. There was no attempt to sound hospitable.

Beck had already put the lanyard holding his CDC credentials around his neck. He held up the two plastic cards for the guard to inspect.

"Take it off, please," he said, holding his hand out and sighing.

"Oh, sorry. Here you go. . . ."

The guy looked at both IDs carefully, then back to Beck to make sure the photos matched. He had a permanently pissed-off air, as if life hadn't shaped up quite the way he'd hoped, and he since decided it was everyone else's fault.

"What are you here for?"

"To see Dr. Childress. Brian Childress, lab chief of the immuno—"

"I know who Dr. Childress is. Does he know you're coming?"

The last thing Beck expected was for this guy to be throwing questions at him. Never a good liar, he became nervous. "Yeah, of course. I called half an hour ago."

The guy kept studying the ID cards, looking for some signs of forgery.

Offense is the best defense, Beck thought, remembering an adage his mother had once taught him. Funny how those things surfaced in your mind at precisely the moments when you needed them.

"I'm sorry, I don't mean to be rude, but this is a very important matter and time is of the essence. Unless you're going to call Brian right now, I really do need to get in there."

This earned him a dirty look—one that would've had him peeing his pants if he'd bumped into the guy in a dark alley—then returned the IDs, took one step back, and motioned for the guardsmen to lift the gate. Beck mumbled a thank you and zipped through.

Step one, he thought, his heart pounding.

Hoffman-LaRoche was a massive health-care organization with facilities in the United States, Switzerland, Germany, and China. It specialized in both pharmaceuticals and diagnostics, investing nearly $10 billion a year into research and development alone. It had over sixty-five thousand employees worldwide and was responsible for such brand-name drugs as Boniva, Tamiflu, and Valium. Due to its state-of-the-art New Jersey facilities and proximity to the epicenter of the outbreak, it had been contracted by the CDC to undertake the mass-production upscaling of the serum.

Beck followed the cottage road signs to the main laboratory building. There were more National Guardsmen in jackboots in camouflage, including an older man with a standard-issue eight-point cap instead of a helmet. As he approached, Beck realized he was a colonel by the spread-eagle insignia on his lapel. The stripe above his left breast pocket read CRAWFORD in military letters.

Beck stuck with the same story, figuring the guy wouldn't know Brian Childress from a hole in the wall. To Beck's surprise, Colonel Crawford seemed considerably less concerned than the guy at the guardhouse. He spent all of two seconds examining Beck's credentials before passing them back and grunting, "Go ahead."

At the front security desk, a heavyset man in a blue blazer eyed him up and down suspiciously.

"Yes?"

"I'm here to see Dr. Brian Childress. I'm Michael Beck from the CDC." Once again the IDs came out.

"Do you have an appointment?"

"I believe one was set up for me, yes."

That was a good line, he thought. It left wiggle room when the guy inevitably discovered that, in fact, no appointment had been made—*What? My secretary didn't take care of it? Damn her. . . .*

Blue blazer dropped his considerable butt into his chair, which creaked in protest, and fingered through his calendar book. "There's nothing on here."

"There should be. I'm supposed to make sure the production schedule is being kept."

"Production schedule?"

An obvious lie, no doubt on the orders of his superiors. *If anyone asks, you don't know anything.*

"On the serum. The one that originated at Catskills Regional."

The man became considerably more interested in his visitor now. "Oh, that," he said lamely. "Okay, well, let me call Dr. Childress and see if he's free."

As casually as he could, Beck said, "Sounds good."

The guard spoke to Childress in an easy manner, as if he had called up an old college friend. *Childress is a softie,* Beck realized. *Thank God.* He was a little surprised that someone of this nature would be elected overlord of such a sensitive project, but he wasn't about to argue.

The guard finished the dialogue and held the phone out. "He wants to speak with you."

"Sure." Beck took the receiver and summoned his inner diplomat.

Childress began with a friendly, "Good afternoon, Dr. Beck," and expressed unabashed honor at being visited by such a renowned figure. He apologized for not realizing Beck was coming, then asked him to come up to the office. Security concerns were never mentioned.

As Beck stood in an otherwise empty elevator, he allowed himself to relax slightly. The doors opened as Childress was coming down the hall. He was in his mid to late fifties, tall and slim, with his brown hair conservatively short and combed to perfection. Steel-rimmed glasses completed the picture, making him look more like a corporate officer than like a scientist. His clothing, too, was flawless, from the polished shoes and long white lab coat to the tightly knotted tie that was visible only at his throat.

As Beck stepped into the air-conditioned hallway, the two men smiled at each other.

"I'm Michael Beck," he said again, and Childress shook his hand enthusiastically. "Thank you for seeing me on short notice."

"You're most welcome, Dr. Beck. We're very busy today, as I'm sure you can imagine, so I'm afraid my time is limited. How can I be of service to you?"

The story he had prepared was that he was supposed to check on the progress of the serum production as part of his ongoing investigation. He was also gathering stats on how effective the serum had been so far, plus where the next shipments would be, in what quantities, and so on; that is, a general overview of the situation that could be relayed to his superiors. He took pains to point out that he did not consider himself to be here in any kind of authoritative capacity, and that no one was obligated to answer to him, and so forth. His function was purely for the purposes of fact-finding and observation.

Accepting all of this without hesitation, Childress took him into the main production laboratory. It was expansive and brightly lit, with several giant stainless steel kettles in the center. A dozen or so pipes ran to and from each one, then disappeared either into the floor or the ceiling. Workers milled about at various stations, in masks, gloves, and shower caps, nodding and smiling as Childress passed. He led Beck along the fringes, staying within a walkway that was demarcated by a painted yellow line on the floor.

"We're producing roughly three hundred doses an hour."

Beck didn't need a calculator to figure out how inadequate this was—there were over thirty thousand people infected at last estimation, and that number would continue growing over the next few weeks. The key was to make the immunization rate higher than the rate of the infection's spread—and the CDC was still having difficulty determining exactly how to achieve that.

"You're using monoclonal cell cultures, correct?"

"Yes. Unfortunately, we cannot increase the process exponentially. We have to adhere to a fixed rate."

"Where are the finished doses being stored?" he asked, staying focused on the time factor. "In a safe place, I hope."

"Yes, quite safe," Childress replied. At the end of the walkway was a large metal door similar to those on restaurant freezers. Beck was surprised to find it wasn't locked—Childress simply grabbed the chrome handle and pulled. Then he realized that, under normal circumstances, they wouldn't need that much security here. A locking refrigeration chamber was more common in military facilities.

As the door swung back, they were enveloped by a frigid fog. Stepping through it, Beck found himself surrounded by rows of steel racks. There were thousands of vials representing a variety of medications. Most were neatly and formally labeled; others had handwritten stickers.

Toward the back, on a middle shelf on the left side, was a stack of six white polypropylene racks. Each held fifty small vials, and in each vial was a dark red fluid that looked like cherry Kool-Aid.

"That's it," Childress said, nodding.

Beck found himself temporarily distracted by the magnitude of the moment. *That's the stuff that's going to stop this thing. Right there, within those two square feet of space . . . the curative for the virus that could've driven the human race to extinction.*

It seemed so insubstantial: a few squirts of liquid in a cluster of glass tubes. It was being manufactured in the room right outside, like putting cars together on an assembly line. *And yet how many people would sell their loved ones into slavery to be standing where I am right now? How many wouldn't hesitate to break Brian Childress's neck if that's what it took to get one of those vials and fire that magical fluid into their bloodstream?*

"This is the latest batch?" he asked, for no other reason than because he felt he had to say something.

"Yes. It was finished about ten minutes before you arrived."

Beck looked around at the other drugs. "And these are the only dosages in here?"

"Yes. They don't stay around long. In fact, someone should be along shortly to prepare them for shipping, which the military is handling for the obvious reasons."

"Okay, good." Beck nodded as if all of this met his approval. "Now, I have just a few more questions, then I'll leave you alone. Can we talk somewhere?"

"Sure. Follow me."

Childress's office was as tidy as the man himself. Personal effects included a few framed photographs of what Beck assumed was his family, an impressive collection of awards in the form of plaques and certificates, and a Velcro dart board. Every other item in the room existed to serve his employer. Piles of papers had been neatly squared off. Three clipboards hung in an even row on the wall by the chair. Even the mouse sat in what appeared to be the perfect geometric center of its pad, making Beck think Childress left it that way on purpose each time he was finished using the computer. *And the Nobel Prize for Anal Retention goes to . . .*

Taking his notepad from his pocket, he fired off questions from the top of his head. How many doses had been sent out already? What has the success rate been so far? Have there been any adverse reactions? Do you plan to start producing it in your California site as well?

Then he asked, "Where on the priority list is Valley Hospital in Ridgewood?"

It was a clumsy attempt to slip the question into the conversation, and Childress seemed slightly taken aback. "Excuse me?"

"I'm based in Ramsey right now, and Valley Hospital in Ridgewood is nearby. They've been overflowing with cases."

"Many hospitals have been overflowing with cases."

"Sure, I realize that. But if Valley is due for their delivery, I'd be happy to take it back with me. I'm not exactly driving an armored vehicle, but I don't think anyone will be looking in my direction."

Childress still had his affable smile in place, but it seemed slightly forced now.

"I'm headed to Valley next," Beck added. "That's the only reason I bring it up."

"Dr. Beck, you know I can't do that."

"I'm sorry?"

"I cannot do that. I can't simply hand it over to someone. There is a procedure to these things."

"Right, I know. But it's not as if I haven't handled vaccines before."

"Of course, but this situation is different. It's very sensitive."

Beck nodded amiably. *I'm quite aware of the sensitivity of the situation, chump,* he wanted to say, but there would be no productive value in dragging the conversation down to that level. For all his warmth and affability, Childress was, at heart, a bureaucrat, hopelessly enamored with procedure and protocol. Revealing Cara's condition at this point would do no good—it would expose Beck's visit as the charade that it was, and since Cara was already in Stage Two, Childress would be justified in refusing her a dose due to its unpredictability at that point. But most important, telling this prim little hard-ass about Cara would reduce the odds of pulling off Plan B, which had to be launched into action immediately.

"All right, well, I appreciate your time very much, Brian." Beck rose somewhat abruptly, which caused his host to do the same. Then they shook hands again.

"My pleasure. I hope you got all the information you came for."

"I certainly did. Thank you."

"Any time, Dr. Beck."

As Beck reached the door, he turned back and said, "Oh, one last question. Could you please tell me where the bathroom is?" He put on an embarrassed smile. "I've been on the road all day and I think I'm gonna pop."

Childress said it was down the hall, then right, second door on the left. Beck thanked him one last time and walked out.

He reached the bathroom and kept going, quickening his pace. *This is crazy, this is crazy . . .*, his mind kept repeating. *If you get caught, it's all over. You'll be lucky if you're not indicted.*

He slowed when he reached the lab. He took his notepad out again, flipped the cover, made sure the pen was in the other hand. It was all about looking right. He opened the door and walked casually inside. A few of the workers, he saw from the corner of his periphery, took notice of him. But no one approached. They'd just seen him fifteen minutes earlier with their boss, so he was okay.

He stopped twice on the way to the freezer and looked around, scribbling in the notepad. When he opened the freezer door, he didn't go inside right away but instead jotted down a few more observations. *Don't look too eager.*

When he stepped inside, the door glided to a close and the overhead lights came on. He had never felt such relief as when he saw the six polypropylene racks sitting there; no one had taken them away for shipping yet.

He lifted five of the six racks and set them aside. Then he carefully withdrew a vial from the center of the group, stored it in his jacket pocket, and returned the five racks to the original position.

He stepped out as casually as he had stepped in, scribbling in his pad again. No one took any notice of him. He glanced around quickly, begging God for Brian Childress to be nowhere in sight. He got his wish and exhaled slowly.

Hands trembling and heart pounding, he reached the hallway and walked swiftly to the fire stairs.

This was when Childress spotted him.

It would be another fifteen minutes before he discovered the missing vial.

Then he made a call to Washington.

In her office, Sheila Abbott quietly set the phone back into its cradle. The seriousness of Childress's accusation was inarguable. What Michael Beck had done went well beyond the limits of unprofessionalism. It bordered on the criminal. If convicted, he would lose his medical license, be shunned by his peers, incur massive fines, and possibly spend time in prison. His career would be over, and his life reduced to ruin. Childress knew all this and pushed for Abbott to act anyway. She promised she would. She assured him she would formulate an appropriate punishment and see that it was carried out. Then, at just the right moment, she told Childress about Porter. Childress went quiet, as she knew he would. Then—also as she expected—he tried to salvage his pride with a flaccid continuation of the assault. Abbott permitted this. When he was finished, she reiterated her intention to see that Beck be reprimanded for his actions. Childress hastily thanked her and was gone.

She returned to her priorities and never gave the incident another thought.

TWENTY-THREE

Cara Porter was sitting up in bed, a notebook on her knees, when Beck and Gillette returned in fresh PPE suits. Beck led the way, holding a small steel tray by its tiny handles. The contents of the tray were covered by a white sheet, although it wasn't tough to figure out what was under there. Porter brightened when they made eye contact, but Beck did not—her condition had advanced in the hours since he'd been gone. The swelling around her face was more noticeable, causing increased crookedness to her formerly symmetrical features. And the vesicles on her hands had filled with more fluid, turning some of them into sagging, paper-thin bags of flesh. Beck's stomach tightened as he remembered the other victims he'd seen in this very room a few weeks ago.

Porter set the notebook on the nightstand and removed her earbuds. *She likes to draw,* Beck thought. *To relax.* She told him that once, something about not being very good at it, but she liked doing it anyway. They were on an investigation in

Arizona: a group of people who'd fallen ill at a church picnic. She had a sketchbook with her at the hotel. She didn't show him any of her work, though. The scared kid that she was, afraid to reveal anything to anyone. *How wonderfully life has treated her,* Beck reminded himself, and for a moment he felt murderously angry.

"So, you didn't get arrested?" she asked. Her speech was slightly slurred.

"No, but I honestly thought I might." He set the tray on the wheeled table next to the bed and removed the sheet. One syringe, one vial. They looked ominous somehow, like instruments of torture.

"Is that it?" Porter asked.

"Yes."

"Well, let's go. Load me up."

Beck didn't move. He simply stood there, staring down at the tray.

"Michael? What's wrong?"

His eyes went to Gillette, then back. "Cara, Ben did some digging while I was gone. He got on the computer and found some data about the treatment." He paused again.

"And?"

Clearing his throat, Gillette stepped forward and said, "At the stage you're in, I'm afraid the antibody is having almost no effect."

Her smile faded instantly. "Oh."

"You are, of course, more than welcome to try it," Gillette added quickly, then felt like an idiot.

What a strange thing to say—"more than welcome," like I'm inviting her to come use my swimming pool while I'm on vacation. "But . . ."

Beck sat on the edge of the bed and took her hand. She barely seemed to notice the gesture.

"What if we increase the dosage?" she asked. "Give me the full vial?"

Beck and Gillette looked at each other.

"You talked about that, too?"

"We don't know what might happen," Gillette said. "The dosage they've been giving people has been relatively low. Because this is a new treatment, there's a lot we don't know about it. For people in later stages, the antibody doesn't seem to do much at all."

"Increasing the dose could pose certain dangers," Beck added.

"But what choice is there?" she asked.

Beck looked to Gillette again; then his eyes found the floor and stayed there.

Porter slid her hand out of Beck's and went to work. She loaded the syringe and injected half of it into a generous vein running along the inside of her left elbow. She flexed her fingers several times to encourage blood flow.

Then she reached for the syringe again. Beck tried once to stop her, but she gingerly removed his hand and said, "Michael, it's my choice." It was her tone that surprised them the most, possessing a sagelike maturity neither of them realized she had.

With her thumb on the plunger, she paused to

look up at Beck. Neither of them spoke, yet there was some kind of communication going on. Gillette could sense it. Then she pressed down on the plunger until the barrel was empty.

A moment passed. Then another. Porter eased the needle out of her arm and set it on the tray.

"Now let's see what happens," she said, mostly to herself. She was trying hard to be casual about the situation.

"So, how'd you get the stuff?" she asked Beck. "Just walk in and someone handed it to you?"

"Huh? Oh, no. Not exactly."

"I didn't think so."

Still watching her carefully, he got to his feet and said, "You would've been proud of me. I did a little lying, indulged in some con-artistry."

"Wow, that does make me proud. I'm also impressed that you pulled it off without getting caught."

"Well, I wouldn't go quite that far."

"What do you mean?"

"There was this guy there. . . ." Beck turned to Gillette. "Do you know Brian Childress?"

Gillette thought for a moment. "The name doesn't sound familiar."

"I didn't know him, either. Sheila did, of course. Anyway, he—"

The beeping cut him off. They turned to see a red light flashing on one of the monitors. Porter was still lying in the same position, but something wasn't right.

"Her pressure's dropping," Gillette said, hurrying to her side. "Oh hell . . ."

Her eyes were wide open but staring blankly at the ceiling. There was an adjustable light over the headboard. Beck flicked it on and shone it directly into her face.

"Pupils are dilated."

"She's in shock!" Gillette said. *"Dammit!"*

Beck picked up the phone, hit one of the memory keys, and called for a crash team. This would take some time, though, and he knew it—they had to put on their own PPE suits, and that couldn't be rushed. Emergency or not, healthy employees were not expected to put their own lives at risk.

Porter began choking, although her hands did not go to her throat.

"Oh God, anaphylaxis," Beck said. "Ben, do you have any—?"

"Getting it now!"

Gillette threw the cabinets open and found an EpiPen—an autoinjector preloaded with adrenaline. He tore apart the protective envelope and administered the shot in the same location Porter had used. The adrenaline was supposed to slow the constriction of the airways as well as reelevate blood pressure.

But it didn't seem to work—Porter's blood pressure continued to drop, and her choking became more convulsive.

"Get a respirator!" Beck said. "Fast! Let's go!"

Gillette found one on the top shelf. Beck took it from him and put it over Porter's nose and mouth, then began frantically squeezing the rubber bladder.

Her blood pressure kept dropping.

"Oh please . . . no, please don't." Beck's eyes filled with tears and began streaming down his face, dampening the PPE mask. "Cara, come on! Come *on*!"

He continued pumping until the monitor issued a steady electronic note. Beck looked up to see the double zeros on the screen.

"NO!"

He pumped faster now, begging and pleading with the gods for mercy, but to no avail. After a time, Gillette stepped in and took the respirator out of his hands.

Beck stared into Porter's eyes, still wide open, and searched for a sign—any sign. When it became obvious there would be none, he set his head down on hers and wept mightily.

She was pronounced dead by the leader of the crash team five minutes later.

TWENTY-FOUR

". . . wake up, wake up!"

Shalizeh lay in his private tent on his side, lost in a thick and dreamless sleep, as the desert winds howled outside. The one who came in to rouse him was named Khalil. He was the youngest member of Lashkar and had been around for only a few months. He was cocky as hell, which irritated some of the older members. But he was immunized because Shalizeh liked him. Confidence and arrogance would serve the boy well, Shalizeh thought—and, if properly manipulated, could be a useful asset at the right time.

"My leader, please!"

Shalizeh's good eye popped open first, followed by the dead one at a gruesomely slower pace. The good one shifted wildly about while he regained his bearing on reality.

He turned abruptly, as if shocked. "What? What do you wake me for?"

"Vehicles are approaching from the south! Look, please!"

The boy held out a pair of night goggles. Shalizeh threw off his blankets and took them. Peering through the slit in the tent, he saw it—a military convoy led by four Hummers and two covered troop trucks, then a few more too blurry to identify.

"Wake the others, tell them to prepare for battle."

"Yes, right away. What will you do?"

Khalil instantly regretted the question—it was not his place to ask such a thing, and he knew that before he had a chance to stop the words from spilling out. He prayed Shalizeh would understand he was asking only out of concern for the man he admired so deeply.

Shalizeh sensed this and smiled. "I am going to retrieve the rest of the weapons and explosives. If we are to go down, we will take as many of them with us as possible."

There was a flicker of uncertainty in Khalil's eyes, as if "going down" wasn't exactly what he'd signed up for. Then he smiled back, and the arrogant sparkle came into his youthful eyes. "Yes, absolutely."

"Good. I will return in a moment."

Shalizeh hurried outside, crossed the compound, and kept on until he reached the river. He did not hesitate before wading in, ignoring the fact that he and his men pissed and crapped in it every day. Once on the other side, he continued through the underbrush until he reached the foothills. The entrance to the cavernous network was slightly larger than an ordinary doorway and obscured by a pair of acacia trees. He turned and took one last look—in the neon glow of the tilted moon he could see his men hastily loading their rifles and crouching behind the gentle ridge that drew a perimeter around the southern edge of the settlement. The convoy was close now, and he wondered how in hell they finally figured out where he was.

He ducked in, the air thick with an earthy pungency, and began down the main passage. There was a flashlight on a ledge, and he grabbed it. The armory was about thirty yards along, in a chamber on the right. He'd had his men dig it out until it was large enough to hold everything they brought, plus extra space for assets that he planned to acquire but never did.

He went past it without so much as a glance.

A few minutes later he came to a sharp right-hand turn, then a second that went left. Fifty feet farther on was a final curve. *Almost there* . . . He pivoted sharply and broke into a run. He began laughing out loud, unable to help himself.

Then he stopped.

The second entrance—which he thought of more as a private exit he hoped he would never need—had been filled in. Large stones, hundreds of them, now blocked the way. He appraised it with the light beam several times, up and down, up and down. His heart began pounding. *How did this happen?* . . .

No time to think about it now. He turned and began running as fast as his robes would permit. If he could get back to the first entrance, he might be able to crawl through the underbrush until he reached the other side of the mountain. If need be, he could grab a few grenades and a rifle on the way.

As he came up to the armory, he heard the discordant rattle of gunfire, then caught the acrid scent of carbonite. Spotlights swirled in and out of view from the opening. He froze, afraid to move any closer.

Then came the low, grinding roar of a large motor. It seemed to be very close. *Impossible,* he thought. *How could any of those vehicles cross the river?* This was denial, and he knew it—the river was no more than two feet deep in this area, and the Hummers, at the very least, could roll through it with no problem.

A much louder noise filled the tunnel, and he lifted his flashlight to see more stones being pushed into the entryway with what appeared to be a bulldozer.

Shalizeh ran forward, screaming, "*NO! NO!*"

The stones kept piling up, the excess spilling inside like pudding, until only a small hole at the top remained. Then the bulldozer roar suddenly dropped to a low hum.

Shalizeh waited, listening. For a few moments there was nothing. Then, the crunching of footsteps just outside.

"A gift from America," someone said in a refined Farsi dialect. Then the sound of shattering glass inside.

Shalizeh shone the beam in that direction. There were glittering shards everywhere—and three small orange objects. He came closer, and this time both eyes widened. They were rubber stoppers, the kind used on medical vials.

My God . . .

The notes of the bulldozer's engine went up an octave again, and Shalizeh, as if trying to outdo it, screamed at the top of his lungs. It took only a moment to finish the job.

Outside, Mushir Garoussi stood nearby, watching passively. When the last stones were in place and the entrance fully sealed, he wiped his hands together and said, "Okay, good." He then checked his watch. "I give it less than two minutes."

A young corporal standing behind him said, "I'm sorry, sir, but you give *what* two min—?"

In spite of the solid rock that separated Garoussi and his men from their prisoner, the single gunshot Shalizeh used to take his own life pierced the night air with chilling clarity.

The corporal jumped; Garoussi just smiled. "Does that answer your question?"

"Yes, sir."

He turned to the bulldozer operator. "Okay, Rashid, dig him out now. We'll need the body for identification."

Rashid nodded and moved the rig forward again. As he did, the corporal found he had another question—"Are you not concerned about being infected?"

"By distilled water?" Garoussi replied. "No, not really."

Then he laughed out loud.

TWENTY-FIVE

Beck stood toward the back of the small crowd, hearing the priest yet not hearing him. A faint voice in a faraway place, as if in another room.

"There is an appointed time for everything, and a time for every affair under the heavens."

He was reading from Ecclesiastes; Beck knew the passage well. He'd heard it growing up in Sunday school, heard it at his mother's funeral, and heard it during a dozen other services around the world. All part of his ongoing flirtation with death, in a profession that often required him to walk the nether-line between mortality and the endless deep that lay beyond.

"A time to be born, and a time to die; a time to plant, and a time to harvest."

He and Cara had never talked about religion, he realized while sitting on the airplane this morning. Of the myriad topics they covered, religion was one they simply never got around to. It seemed to be her job to launch the conversations about life and philosophy and all that. They had spent a fair share of Sundays together, and she showed no inclination toward worship. She didn't wear any religious jewelry, didn't carry a copy of the Holy Bible or the Torah or the Koran in her suitcase, like some people he knew. Once, while investigating an outbreak at a wedding in Arizona, she seemed to regard the church as any other structure. She didn't dip her fingers in the holy water font when she entered, didn't bow before the altar at the end of the center aisle. Just moved in and out as needed; it may as well have been a garden shed. *Had religion let her down, too?* he wondered. *Why not, everything else had. . . .*

It had befallen him to call her relatives. This was never formally discussed between him, Ben, and Sheila; it was simply assumed he would be the one to do it. Tracking them down hadn't been easy. He was unsurprised to learn they were scattered across the country and rarely kept in touch with one another. Indifferent, insensitive people in a disjointed mass of dysfunctionality. Most of them barely remembered her, gave their condolences over the phone but wouldn't commit to anything more. One cousin in California cut the call short because he had a boat race to prepare for. Beck immediately put him on his Biggest Jerks I've Ever Met list. Cara's stepfather was more dumbfounded than anything else. Her mother had passed away several years before, and the new husband had never been interested in the daughter. He wanted a relationship based on more traditional features, like beer and sex. He didn't know how to handle the situation—or, rather, how to get out of it with the least amount of hassle—so Beck helped by simply relaying the details of the funeral then hanging up.

The uncle who helped raise Cara had died around the same time as her mother, but Aunt Eleanor was still alive and well. She was the only relation Cara ever talked about, and Beck soon realized why—she was the only one who resembled a normal human being. Over the last three days, he got to know her quite well. Sixty-seven, small, with a cloud of silver hair and lively green eyes that had lost little of their youthful sparkle. She was a ball of energy, as sharp and quick-witted as anyone he knew. She still worked part-time, ran her local church guild, and played cards with her friends on Saturday nights. Her opinion of the rest of the family was even lower than Beck's, calling the stepfather a "useless moron," then summing up her feelings about the wealthy California cousin by saying, "You can put a turd in a tuxedo, but it'll still stink." Beck could see why Cara adored her—and why she regarded the woman as her lifeline to sanity.

The priest rambled on, standing rod-straight in his long robes before the open grave. A total of twelve people attended the service, including a college roommate, two of Cara's elementary school teachers, a social worker who had helped her through her teenage years, and a childhood friend who had apparently kept in sporadic contact by email. They were all strangers to Beck, and it made him realize how much about her he never knew. Aunt Eleanor filled in many gaps the night before, when the two of them sat in her living room and burned away the hours, alternating between laughter and tears.

Ben and Sheila also came. Ben did his best to retain his composure, and each time he broke down, he tried to cover it up by coughing into his fist. Sheila wore a magnificent Louis Vuitton dress and white pearls, which only served to make her look as though she'd stumbled into the wrong funeral. She stood several yards away from the crowd due to the incessant vibrating of her cell phone. It was disgusting, of course, but Beck knew she couldn't turn it off. At least she seemed genuinely irritated by it. Whether she really was or not, he didn't give a damn.

"What is now has already been. What is to be, already is. And God restores what would otherwise be displaced."

He felt as though he should be crying along with the others, moved in some profound way. But there was nothing at the moment: just nothing. He cried long and hard in the hotel the night following her death, alternated between that and taking long slugs of vodka. He'd never been much of a drinker and didn't turn to a bottle in times of distress. He didn't even like the taste of hard alcohol. But this had been unbearable.

Then the dreams came, as he knew they would. Unlike so many other things in life, they never failed. The Ebola victims again, the smoking corpses, the infant that died in his arms, his tiny head falling back after his last shuddered breath. A macabre variation of *This Is Your Life*. The donated cadavers from medical school, the rows of jarred organs. And then, of course, Amy. Fresh-faced and all of seventeen when they first met at Stanford, they got married one year after graduation. Then he was offered the chance to go to Yambuku. She wanted to go back to school and begin studying for her Ph.D., but he pleaded with her. He was driven by a romantic vision—the two of them valiantly fighting disease and suffering together. What a way to start off their partnership. Maybe they'd open a clinic someday. The Becks, international saviors, respected and adored by millions. Maybe even a Nobel Prize. Then Amy appeared in the canvas tent one unforgettably humid evening, the tears on her face shining in the fitful light of the oil lamp, to tell him she'd become infected. She didn't know how, and he never did figure it out. But she was gone within two weeks, consumed by one of the ghastliest diseases ever known. And the baby went with her, the one she hadn't told him about at first because she wanted it to be a surprise.

Now there was a new set of images to add to the show, another scar cut across the flesh of his heart. And more dark thoughts to be buried down deep, sunk into a well of black water that, he was sure, would sooner or later become too full and begin to overflow. What would happen then, he couldn't say. Hopefully he'd be too close to his own end for it to matter. In the meantime, the dreams would keep coming. Of that he had no doubt.

"Both go to the same place. Both were made from the dust, and to the dust they shall return."

The crowd formed into a line and started forward. They stopped at the gleaming pewter-colored coffin one at a time, touching it, setting down flowers. Beck glanced over at Sheila Abbott, who was on the phone again and not paying attention. He went to the coffin last, where he lay a single red rose. For the briefest moment, he felt something stir inside. Then it passed.

Sheila caught up with him as he reached the new rental car, the one he was sharing with Ben. "Michael?"

He turned. "Yes?"

"Um . . . I know you need some time. Of course. But do you have any idea when you'll be back?"

He stared at her. "No," he said.

He climbed into the passenger seat without another word. Gillette had already started the engine. He also found an oldies station on the radio that was playing '70s hits.

Beck switched it off.

TWENTY-SIX

DAY 21

The CDC and WHO jointly announced for the first time that the surge of fatalities as well as new cases had begun to slow. They attributed this mostly to the discovery of the antibody, but also to the rapid response of local medical teams and law-enforcement agencies as well as widespread education of the public. During an interview on 60 Minutes, *Sheila Abbott reminded viewers that no such reversal is ever possible with a one-dimensional strategy, and that the outbreak could easily have killed hundreds of thousands or even millions if it had occurred in the previous generation. "Modern technology is the real hero here," she said, pointing to the Internet-aided efforts not only of the CDC and WHO but also researchers and other health practioners around the globe. "If the Net had existed in the fourteenth century, the Black Death might have wiped out only a few villages in Central Asia rather than half of the population of Europe." Abbott also announced that the virus, which she believed to be a new mutation of one that had existed for thousands of year, had been assigned its own Latin taxon,* Cervipox trimortumdiei, *with the genus coming from the family name for deer—Cervidae—and the species meaning "three-day death." The name it received from the media, however—the Gemini Virus—would sustain in popular usage, for years to come.*

Interviewer Lesley Stahl asked when Abbott thought she could claim the virus was completely eradicated. Abbott paused before saying there would likely be at least a thousand more deaths before "we have this beast locked up," putting the final death toll at nearly twenty-six thousand. She added that a vaccine was being developed as quickly as quality control would allow, and that she hoped it would be ready for the open market before the end of the year. In the meantime, she urged the public to continue using extreme caution and follow the guidelines posted on the Centers' website until the outbreak disappeared completely.

In Washington, Barack Obama was finishing up a phone call with Maziar Baraheri. Obama apologized for the accusations and the threats, asking for Baraheri's understanding. The Iranian president insisted there was no need for apologies, and he meant it. He suggested that perhaps it was finally time for an American–Iranian summit. Obama thought that was an excellent idea. Then Obama asked what had become of Shalizeh.

He couldn't help but smile when he heard the details.

When the Jensens were twenty miles out from Carlton Lakes, the chatter in their van was still steady and spirited. At ten miles, a little less so. By the time they saw the first road sign indicating the remaining distance—the name of the town on the left, a *3* on the right—it dwindled in brief stages until only the sound of the road remained. Even Scooter, whom they had collected from Elaine's house an hour earlier, seemed unusually subdued. Dennis and Andi's hands were linked together in her lap. His was warm and sweaty, and every now and then it twitched. She watched him from the corner of her eye but said nothing. She had been skeptical about his apprehensions at first. Now she would be lying if she said she didn't feel a few of her own.

They left I-287 at Exit 53 and took the jughandle that flowed into the first traffic light. There was a sub shop on the corner, facing a sixteen-pump Sunoco on the right. The former was still closed, with signs in each of the three big windows saying as much; the legend CLOSED UNTIL FURTHER NOTICE was printed in large letters on sheets of eight-and-a-half-by-eleven-inch paper. At first, the Sunoco appeared to also be abandoned. Then they saw someone moving inside the little convenience shop. Whether it was an employee or a looter they couldn't tell, and they had no intention of finding out. The neon OPEN sign was unlit.

A quarter mile down Andi gasped, her free hand going to her mouth. Dennis saw it at the same time but didn't display any reaction—the Reformed Church, with its sleek white exterior and towering, slender steeple, had been reduced to a charred ruin. Only the concrete foundation and the chimney in the rector's quarters remained intact; the rest was a jumble of smoking wreckage. Andi was unable to take her eyes off it as they drove by. They'd never been inside, but she had commented several times how beautiful she thought the building was.

A little farther on they saw the first signs of "legitimate" life—three men in boots, jeans, and plaid shirts, all wearing leather gloves and picking up glass from the shattered windows of the Passaic Valley Savings Bank. That's where they kept the bulk of their money.

"I wonder if someone tried to rob it," Andi said.

That piqued Chelsea's interest, who strained against the seat belt to elevate herself for a better look. "Cool!"

"No, not cool," her mother replied.

"Just *kidding*."

"With all the cameras and the big door on that vault," Dennis said quietly, "that'd be stupid." He paused before continuing with, "Then again, lately a lot of people haven't been, y'know. . . ."

He never took his eyes off the road, and Andi regretted saying anything. She was hoping to distract him. Now she realized he was in a state of mind where pretty much anything she said would be pulled in that direction. *Lately, a lot of people haven't been . . . doing things they'd normally do. . . .*

They curved to the right and came to another intersection. Two vehicles—a newer Volkswagen Beetle and an aging pickup truck—had jumped the curb and were now sitting on someone's front lawn. It appeared as though both had swerved to avoid each other, but the truck hit the Beetle on the passenger side. The latter was now tilted, the tires a few inches off the ground. The driver's doors were wide open, but there was no one around.

When the light turned green and they began moving again, Andi felt a pins-and-needles sensation from top to bottom. Their street was the first one on the right, about a hundred yards up. She stole one more glance at her husband, who had become visibly more ashen in the last minute. His hands were trembling steadily, as if there were an uneven electrical current flowing through him.

They took the turn, which was smooth and easy because their street cut away at a forty-five degree angle. They were now in what Dennis called the Hall of Elms—some time in the 1940s, town officials planted saplings along many of the secondary roads as part of a community beautification project. The saplings had since matured to full size, their broad canopies blotting out most of the sunlight and forming shadowy corridors. The intended effect was to be quaint and picturesque, but the illusion had been somewhat compromised when many of the hulking roots began pushing up the sidewalk pavers.

"Diana!" Chelsea exclaimed, pointing to one of the first houses on the right. It was a smallish but nicely maintained Victorian that sat on one of the street's few double lots. There was an in-ground pool in the back that, as far as Dennis and Andi could determine, Diana's parents used more for bragging rights than actual swimming.

"Where?" Andi said, turning abruptly.

"No," Chelsea replied. "That's her house! I wonder if she's home?"

They had two cars—the father's black Jaguar and the mother's green Range Rover—and only the Jag was parked in the driveway.

"I don't know, sweetheart. Maybe we'll try calling them later."

"Okay."

Andi was once again amazed by how easily Chelsea had shrugged off the whole experience. Just days earlier she was nose to nose with death, and now, with only the faintest traces of the infection remaining, she was acting as if it had never happened—just a minor bump on the road of life. Of course, they never told her how close they had all come to entering the Blessed Realm. But still, the naturally tempered resilience of her two children, and in fact of most children, was an endless source of fascination. Looking down at her hands and seeing the fading outlines of her own infection, she wondered if she would've reacted the same way when she was seven. Billy, two years younger, seemed even more indifferent. For him, it was as if none of it ever happened. Andi wondered if he'd even remember any of it in adulthood.

She was pulled out of these thoughts when

Dennis sighed heavily and said under his breath, "Okay, here we go. . . ."

They passed through a four-way intersection and crossed onto their slice of the street. There were ten houses in total, five on each side, and they knew everyone well. Dennis suddenly took on the hunted expression of a fugitive, eyes wide and darting about restlessly. A phone pole had been broken about ten feet from the ground and was now supported only by its wires. The front door of one house was still wide open, although there were no cars in sight. In fact, there were no signs of life at all—no adults making repairs or walking their pets, no neighborhood children on bicycles, not even a solitary police car on slow patrol. *It's still a ghost town,* Andi thought with tepid horror.

She held her breath as they approached their property. The tall hedgerow that delineated it from their next-door neighbors' to the east blocked the view of their front lawn—where Dennis's fear-glazed eyes were trained. From the passenger seat, Andi would get the first look by a split second. She zeroed in on the spot where Jack McLaughlin had fallen. . . .

He's not there.

It was true—the area where he had been lying when they sped away over two weeks ago was unoccupied by anyone or anything, just grass like the rest of the lawn. It badly needed cutting, but it was thick and it was green and it was *healthy. Oh my God . . .*

She turned to Dennis, who now looked more bewildered than anything else. As he brought the van to a gradual stop, he mouthed three words soundlessly: *Where is he?*

"Daddy, come on!" Chelsea urged.

"Yeah!" Billy joined in.

"Oh . . . sorry."

He went up the small incline and into the driveway. Getting out, he came around to look once more, as if his mind had tricked him into seeing what he really hoped to see. But no, Jack McLaughlin's body really wasn't there.

The cops already came and got him, his guilt taunted him. *Now they're waiting for you. They'll be here in a few minutes.*

A large ball of ice formed in the center of his stomach, and he found he had no desire to move.

"Daddy, the keys! The keys!"

"Den, give them to me and I'll open the door," Andi said.

"No, I've got it," he told her, his voice like something from a dream. His fingers seemed to find the right key on their own. He walked the three stone steps to the side door and worked the lock. When he pushed the door back, he paused.

Everything *looked* fine—but there was a smell as wretched as any he had ever known. It wasn't as pungent or vile as that of the fluids that leaked from the broken blisters in the hospital, but it was in the same family, a cousin, maybe.

Jack . . . oh God, no . . .

He somehow got inside after they drove away. Maybe he broke a window. *Maybe the glass cut him coming through, and he bled to death. Maybe that smell is the scent of his decaying body. Maybe he's slumped over your bed . . .*

Andi looked at Dennis as if she was thinking along similar lines.

"Oh, pee-yew! What's that?" Chelsea demanded, pinching her nose.

"I don't know," Dennis said. "Let me check it ou—"

"You want me to go?" Andi asked with no conviction.

"No, I got it." Whatever was in here, *he* wanted to be the one to find it . . . or fight it. Not his wife, and not his kids.

He walked into the kitchen; a bright bolt of sunlight slanted down through the window over the sink. He crossed into the living room and found nothing—and no one—there. Then he walked slowly up the stairs to find nothing in either of the kids' rooms, either. *Exactly as we left them . . .*, he thought with some surprise.

Back on the first floor, he kicked open the bedroom door like a cop; it whacked against the wall with a shudder. The bed lay unmade—but no one was on it. The two windows were still locked tight.

Through the dining room and into the den, there was still nothing. As he reached the back door, he discovered a clue to the mystery. *The smell isn't as strong here.* He unlocked the door and opened it to get some air circulating. Then he headed back to the kitchen . . . and found the source.

He pressed his foot gingerly on the pedal of the tall plastic garbage can, and the lid popped up. The bag inside was full, and sitting on top was a ripped-open package of decaying hamburger meat, covered with maggots. The fresh odor that rose into his nostrils made him light-headed. His hand went to his stomach, and for a moment he truly thought he was going to vomit.

"Dennis?" Andi called from behind the door and not more than fifteen feet away.

"I'm right here," he said conversationally. "I think we need to empty this garbage can."

She gasped. "Oh no, I forgot!"

"Yeah."

She stepped inside, the kids clinging.

"I'll take care of it," he said, pulling the bag up by its red strap-handles and tying them quickly.

"I emptied some stuff out of the fridge the day we left, but then I got sidetracked and—"

"It's no big deal," Dennis said as he walked past her with the bulging bag rotating slowly. "Just get some windows open in here. I'll start unloading the van."

"Okay."

For the next half hour, the Jensens worked in assembly-line mode, Dennis carrying bags and boxes to Andi in the doorway, and Andi giving them to Chelsea to be distributed in the appropriate rooms. Billy helped a little, too, in his own way.

Just as Dennis reached for the last suitcase—his own—someone said, "Well, look who's back."

He knew the voice, and his heart seized up like an engine. He spun around, certain his face was glowing with guilt, and found Janine Hartman, Carlton's self-appointed Minister of Gossip, standing there. *Judgment Day has come.*

She was a small woman, no more than five feet and perhaps an inch or two. She was slender, one could even say athletic, for someone in her mid-fifties. She kept her dark hair cropped short, severely so. But it was the eyes that caught your attention. Dennis and Andi had described them at various times as *sharp* and *gleaming* and *piercing*. They seemed to see everything, especially that which was not intended to be seen. Andi once said, "When I talk to her, I feel like she can see inside me."

She stalked the sidewalks like a specter, knocking on doors and peeking over fences. A visit from her was akin to a colon search. She knew who bought the house three blocks over, what married person was having an affair, when everyone left for and returned from work, how the town was going to pay for the upgrades to the high school's football field, and why the Italian place near the thrift store managed to stay in business even though it was never crowded. Every town had a Big Brother, and she held that claim in sleepy little Carlton Lakes. And as luck would have it, she lived just two doors down from Dennis and Andrea Jensen.

Dennis smiled but found it hard to maintain eye contact. "Hi, how are you, Janine?"

"I'm doing okay. Were you on vacation?"

It's over, Dennis thought. *Any hope we had of returning to our happy life is finished.* He imagined her clearly in his mind, going from house to house telling anyone who would listen that the Jensens had hit the road and left the rest of the town high and dry the moment things got tough. "Some neighbors," she'd say, sowing the seeds of resentment. That's what she did to people she didn't like. Then everything would quietly change—no one would wave to Dennis as he came down the street at the end of the day or stop and chat with Andi in the supermarket. No more free lollipops for the kids at the bank. When there was a local social event, a folded copy of the cheap-but-somehow-charming invitation hastily made on someone's computer wouldn't show up in the mailbox. No one would know the name of a good plumber or auto mechanic; no one would have a ladder Dennis could borrow or an extra egg so Andi could finish the brownies she'd already started. *We'd still live here, but we'd be in hell.*

"Vacation? Well, I guess you could say that." He swallowed hard before continuing. "We have a cabin in the Catskills, and we went there for a few weeks. Until this thing with the virus was over." He said this in a confessional tone, like someone in a witness box no longer able to deny the evidence set before him.

His next line was going to be something about feeling like they had no choice, what with the kids and all. An attempt at justification, maybe with the slightest note of sanctimony, just enough to make her think twice before going on the offensive.

Then she delivered a jolt to his system when she said casually, "I did the same thing. Except I went to my sister's house. She lives in New Hampshire."

He wasn't sure if he'd heard her correctly. "Your sister's house?"

"Yeah. She lives up in North Woodstock. You won't find it on many maps, but it's a great little place. I was thinking of going up to see her anyway, because it's really pretty up there." She smiled and sort of half flapped her arms. "So this was the perfect excuse."

Dennis stared dumbly at her, struggling to accept this miraculous turn of events. *She did the same thing. . . .*

"Wow," he said, unable to think of anything better. "How long have you been back?"

"I got in last night. I got a call from Terry Willis."

"Terry Willis?"

"He's a retired cop from town. He said a lot of people have started coming back."

"A lot of . . . you mean a lot left?"

Jeanine snorted a laugh. "Yeah, I think half the town left. Who'd be stupid enough to stay if they had someplace to go? I wouldn't. . . ."

She dismissed further exploration of this ridiculous topic by turning away to look up and down the street.

I guess that's right, Dennis thought, *I guess it really would have been stupid to stay. Two young children, a perfect place to hide out . . . who'd be stupid enough to stick around?*

She didn't know they had caught the infection, or that their dog had been responsible for the antidote that was now saving the world. The hospital staff had done a magnificent job of keeping their names from the media. And Dennis had no intention of telling her. That would've been *worse* than telling the media. If he were going to do that, he might as well call CNN directly.

"Have there been a lot of deaths here?" he asked. Half of him didn't want to go in this conversational direction; the other half knew it had to be done.

Jeanine sighed. "Yeah, quite a few. You know Karen Larsen, the manager at the ShopRite? Her and her two sons. And Brian Higgins, whose father owns the two liquor stores. He's dead."

She rattled off a dozen other names: some individuals, some entire families. Dennis knew maybe a quarter of them, and he felt some guilt about that. *All these years and we still don't know most of the people who live here. In the future, Andi and I are going to make a point of trying to—*

". . . was hit by a FedEx truck up on Harlan. Just walked right out in front of it. And then Sara Freedson, she had—"

"I'm sorry," Dennis said, "who?"

"Sara Freedson."

"No, before that."

"Jack McLaughlin. You know, the elderly man who does crossing-guard duties?"

"He was hit by a . . ."

"By a FedEx truck, right up there on Harlan Turnpike." She motioned in that direction. "A couple of weeks ago."

My God . . .

"You mean he wasn't . . . he was hit on the *road*?"

"Yeah." She sensed his confusion. "Why? Did

you know him well? I thought he just crossed you and the kids in the morning."

"No, right," Dennis said. "I didn't know him that well. I just . . . wow. That's terrible."

"It is."

"And Sara Freedson, you said?"

"Yeah, Sara was found in her home, up in her bedroom. . . ."

Jeanine reported the full details, but Dennis heard none of it. Then she cited a few others, wrapping up with the tasteless comment that the obituary columnist in the local paper deserved a raise. Finally, mercifully, she moved on, claiming she had to go over to Piedmont Avenue and see how old Mrs. Grady was doing.

Dennis lingered outside, watching her until she disappeared around the corner. When he got back in the house, standing in the empty kitchen, he covered his face with his hands and wept.

Andi heard him from the bedroom and came in, putting a hand on his back.

"Honey?"

He repeated the conversation. ". . . and of course it sucks what happened to him, but . . ." He looked in her eyes, already penitent for the rest of the thought.

"But you're glad it wasn't you who took his life."

He nodded and wrapped his arms around her, and she held him tight as the rest of the grief poured out. She felt not like a wife then but like a mother, something she had learned a while ago was at least part of being a wife in the first place. "*Thank God it wasn't me,*" he kept saying. "*Thank God . . .*"

They spent the next three hours getting the house back in order—putting away clothes and toiletries, storing their luggage, cleaning and straightening. It was Andi who realized first what they were trying to do—get back to their comfort zone. The philosophy they seemed to be following was, "If we can make everything *look* the way it did before, maybe it'll *be* the way it was before." When they were finished, however . . .

It's still not the same, Andi thought, standing in the living room. She could feel a wave of depression moving into her. *Something's missing. In fact, a lot of things are.* She looked through the big bay window at their neighbor's house across the street. Doors shut, shades drawn, no cars in the driveway, grass too high. *Are they all dead, too? Will we ever see them again?* And the most sobering thought of all: *Just how far from the "old normal" have we gone? Will it ever be anything close to what it was?* She felt tears threatening but fought them off; she'd cried enough in the last three weeks. If nothing else, this experience would put a little iron in her soul. She sensed that now. It was a fundamental change, although for better or worse she could not yet tell. There would be a lot of uncertainty for a while, and it would take some time to work through all of it. *How far from the old normal have we gone? . . .*

Determined to keep things as steady as possible for her own family, she went into the kitchen to start dinner. When she opened the fridge, however, she found it basically empty.

"I checked," Dennis said. "Nada."

"Then we'll just get something." She snatched the cordless phone off the wall and hit memory 5—Golden Garden, the Chinese food place.

"You think they'll even be open?"

"We'll see."

It rang six times, then seven, then eight . . . By ten, Andi felt the sting of tears again. *Damn.*

She went to put the phone back in its cradle, when she heard a garbled voice . . . or at least thought she did. *My imagination playing with me?*

"Hello?"

"Yes," someone said in heavily accented English. "Golden Garden, may I help you?"

Andi didn't say anything immediately; she permitted herself a moment to enjoy the sound of it. It was something familiar, something that was *still there.* Did the owners leave town and just recently return, too? She didn't know, and right now she didn't care. A magnificent warmth had just exploded in her belly and was now spreading elsewhere.

"Hello?" the man repeated. "Can I help you?"

"Sure. I'm sorry, hold on a second, please."

The tears streamed out now; she could no longer hold them back. As they drew glossy lines down her cheeks, she covered the mouthpiece and said to Dennis, "They're *there.*"

He smiled. "Well, let's get something, baby."

"Okay . . . what should we get?"

He considered it for a second. Then, with a mischievous gleam in his eye, he said, "How about our *usual*?"

She nodded and smiled back at this man she loved with all her heart.

"That sounds perfect."